Forgive Us Our Trespasses

by

Donald Silverman

authorHOUSE®

AuthorHouse™
1663 Liberty Drive, Suite 200
Bloomington, IN 47403
www.authorhouse.com
Phone: 1-800-839-8640

First published by AuthorHouse 7/23/2008

ISBN: 978-1-4343-6785-3 (sc)

Printed in the United States of America
Bloomington, Indiana

This book is printed on acid-free paper.

DEDICATION

This novel is dedicated to Donald Silverman without whose hours of writing and rewriting this novel would never have become a reality.

ACKNOWLEDGEMENTS

My thanks to my writing groups: Janet Segedy, Jackie Rossier, Mary Bearor, Diane Bryan, Mark Jacoby and David Shapiro. A special thanks to Judge Philip Hollman for helping me through the legal system and courtroom scenes.

Part One

Pip

CHAPTER ONE

"Hurry, Pip, you'll make us late for church," his mother called upstairs.

Philip Marshal was looking in the mirror. The year was 1950. He was thirteen years old, thin and short for his age. His friends called him Pip and although not everyone remembered how he got the nickname, he knew. It was short for pipsqueak. Almost no one called him Philip anymore.

His suit was not very clean and his tie was stained, but it would have to do. He looked about the room, strewn with his clothing, for his left shoe. He would have to tidy it before his father saw it and took the switch to him. He checked under the double decker bunk bed.

"Pip, come on, you can give Jesus one hour on the Sabbath," his mother hollered.

Give Jesus an hour on the Sabbath, he thought. He had to give Jesus his time everyday. They were always praying, at every meal, bedtime, "Give thanks to Jesus, thanks to Jesus." Everything was Jesus. And now they were making him go to a new Christian school.

Pip wondered why he couldn't embrace the Lord as his parents wanted, as others did. It wasn't that he didn't want to believe, but for some reason he just couldn't find it in his heart. He went to church, listened to the songs and prayers and envied those who so easily found the Lord.

Pip located his shoe and hurriedly put it on. He took a backward look at his room. The cross over his bed was at an angle. He slept on the top bunk and must have hit it in his sleep. He closed the door before scurrying downstairs.

"It's about time," his father said. "Doris, get his suit cleaned. It's an insult to Jesus."

"Yes, Walter," his mother responded. Her tone indicated she took full responsibility for the stains.

Pip came by his lack of height naturally as both parents were only about five and-a-half feet tall. Walter stayed thin but Doris's time in the kitchen, sampling her cooking had taken its toll.

"C'mon. You know how I feel about keeping the Lord waiting on His day," Walter commanded.

They got into the car, Pip in the back, crammed next to his father's brushes that took up most of the seat and all of the trunk.

Four days a week, his dad traveled from gas station to gas station, selling toilet cleaning brushes. Although he seldom lost a sale, it didn't provide a great income, or to hear him complain, much satisfaction.

"Careful of the brushes. Those morons won't buy if the box is damaged, and the Jews won't take them back," Walter said.

Philip had never met a Jew, but he knew about them. They were a heathen people who had killed the Savior. The minister shouted about them from the pulpit. The remainder of his education about the Jews came from his father who cursed the way they cheated him on his brushes. They were money-hungry and always charged him too much.

"They just went up on their prices. They never have enough," his father continued. "They'll get their punishment in the end. It's called eternal damnation, and they deserve it, as sure as I'm sitting here."

Pip was always fascinated by his father's description of Jews. He had heard about them for as long as he could remember, and he had accepted these views as gospel.

From his earliest memories, he knew that to oppose his father would lead to thrashings and until recently he had avoided upsetting his dad. His mother supported her husband as it said in the Bible that sparing the rod, spoiled the child. But lately, in spite of the beatings, Pip had become defiant.

"Why don't they believe in Jesus?" he asked.

"They're under the influence of the devil, son," Walter responded.

"Why doesn't Jesus save them, help them to believe?"

"Jesus doesn't do that, son. Ya gotta do it yourself."

"Could He if He wanted?"

"He don't want to. He wants Man to do it on his own."

Walter had begun the conversation as a patient teacher to a student, but Pip could tell his father was becoming irritated with him. The boy also knew he was safe from the switch while they drove to church. He enjoyed annoying his father during this safe time.

"Does He like sending the Jews to hell? I don't think that's very nice."

"Don't be blasphemous, Pip," his mother said. "You upset your father."

He appreciated his mother's concern for him, but knew how to handle his father, how far to push him.

Pip wanted to be a good son and didn't understand his rebellion. Maybe it was resentment for the time he was forced to devote to church and God. He knew he was never beaten for no reason or out of pure anger. It was the way he was taught to be a good person.

Next month he was going to start at the new Calvert Christian School. Everyone at church seemed excited at the founding of its own academy. No more teaching of evolution. It was an ambitious project that included all twelve grades.

Pip hated the thought of leaving his friends. He had looked forward to entering high school and had begged his parents to allow him to continue his public education, but to no avail.

"The kids at church are creepy," he argued.

"If we allowed you to go to public school, we could lose you to the devil," his father explained. "We're not going to risk the only child God has given us."

Pip made a face they couldn't see. Again his heart filled with unwanted defiance.

"If I ask Jesus to make me taller will He answer my prayer?"

"He'll answer if you're deserving," his mother replied.

"Am I deserving?"

"I don't know. Only He knows."

Pip shrugged his shoulders. You could never win when it came to Jesus.

ॐ

Pip waited for the bus. The public school was only four blocks from his home. The building was large and new. His current school didn't even have its own building. It was in the basement of the church, and only a hundred and fifty kids were enrolled, from first grade through high school. There were fifteen in his freshman class. Maybe it wouldn't be so bad.

Promptly at six forty five, the yellow school bus pulled up. On its side was painted The Calvert Christian School. His fellow riders appeared pleased. They were being led in song. "The Church is one foundation with Jesus Christ the Lord," they bellowed out. The windows were open and Pip knew it was the other passengers hope that every heathen within earshot would hear and perhaps be saved. Everyone seemed so sure, so glad to be one of God's chosen. Pip wished he also could believe, feel a part. There must be something wrong with him. Had he done something bad? Did the devil have a power over him he couldn't control? Why did these people seem so foolish to him?

The students came from surrounding towns and although the church was only five miles from Pip's home, the bus ride took over an hour. He sat next to a window staring out. No one spoke to him and he spoke to no one. By seven-thirty, the bus was filled, and fifteen minutes later they arrived at school. Teachers directed the students into the sanctuary.

"Take a seat," a voice kept saying.

Pip sat toward the back.

"Silence, please," the voice continued, and all were quiet. "I'm the administrator, Mr. Bruno. Let us pray."

Mr. Bruno bowed his head and folded his hands on the lectern. Pip was hit on the shoulder. He turned to see who had struck the blow. It was an adult, he presumed a teacher.

"Lower your head. Show respect for Jesus."

Pip did as he was commanded.

"Dear Lord," the administrator prayed. "Help us to work to our full potential. I know there is nothing we cannot master with the help of the One who gives us our strength. Your path is the path to knowledge, for You have taught us that the righteous are as bold as a lion. We ask your help in the name of Jesus. Amen.

"Now, we have rules. You'll be given a handbook outlining these rules. Read them well. Not knowing them will never be an acceptable excuse. We believe in loving encouragement and firm discipline. Do not be the recipient of the latter."

After the speech, the students were sent to their classrooms. Pip felt both excited and nervous. Maybe it would be okay.

Mr. Perkins was just an inch over five feet, painfully thin, and balding. His most outstanding physical characteristic was his huge Adam's apple. Pip had never seen one that size before and couldn't stop staring at it. Just as he was about to avert his eyes, Mr. Perkins looked directly at him. Pip felt his face flush and quickly turned away.

Mr. Perkins walked over to Pip and, without saying a word, extended his index finger, raised it over the boy's head, and jabbed it down on his scalp. The pain was unexpectedly sharp, and Pip had to control his anger. Mr. Perkins returned to the front of the class. There was total silence.

"It's rude to stare," he announced in a soft voice. "There are fifteen freshman at The Calvert Christian School," he continued. "This is your homeroom. You will be here in your seats, not talking, by seven forty-five.

"You will raise your hand if you wish to contribute to the class. You will never talk among yourselves in my room." He assigned desks by calling out each name, visually evaluating the student and then nodding to a seat.

"Philip Marshall?"

"Here."

"So you're Philip Marshall?"

"Call him Pip, everyone else does," a boy shot out.

Mr. Perkins turned in a flash toward the voice, his eyes bulging from their sockets, his face flushed with anger.

"Who sounded off out of turn?"

No one answered nor moved.

"Either whoever spoke admits to it, or we'll all spend Saturday walking in the school yard. Do you know what that means, Emily?" he said, looking down the roster.

"No," the girl answered in a whisper.

"It means you will all arrive at school at eight in the morning and you'll walk up and down the front walk until five in the afternoon. Does that sound like fun, Janet?"

"No."

"It was me, Mr. Perkins," a tall, lanky boy said.

All eyes turned toward the voice.

Again Mr. Perkins checked his roster. "Ronald Wheeler, is that right?"

"Yes, sir."

Ronald had attended junior high school with Pip. He was a boisterous child, always in trouble with the teachers but rather amusing, as far as Pip was concerned.

No one moved. The silence was deafening. Pip saw that fear had replaced the boy's customary smile.

"Mr. Wheeler, come here to me," Mr. Perkins said in a deceptively calm voice which Pip had already learned not to trust.

Slowly, Ronald stood and walked toward his fate. Pip was afraid for him. He felt partially responsible for what had happened.

Ronald arrived at the front of the room. Mr. Perkins glared at the boy, his silence challenging the lad.

"Put out your hand, palm up," Mr. Perkins finally said.

Ronald did as he was told. A twelve-inch wooden ruler came down on the boy's open palm at a speed that indicated Mr. Perkins was not a novice at meting out this particular punishment.

"Ow!" Ronald screamed, then fell silent. Pip could see tears at the corners of the boy's eyes, but no more sounds of pain or protestation came forth.

"Now I will tell you again, there's to be no talking in this room unless you raise your hand and I call on you. You may sit down, Mr. Wheeler."

Ronald walked to his seat. Mr. Perkins looked out at the class with a sardonic smile.

Pip knew this cruel man would have his way, that fear would rule. He faced his teacher, hands folded on his desk, trying not to stare at that incredible dancing Adam's apple.

"We will begin with a morning prayer. `These words which I command thee this day shall be in thine heart, and thou shall teach them diligently to thy children.' Lord give me the strength to teach and the children the power to learn. And forgive Mr. Wheeler his sin of dishonoring his teacher, by speaking in class. `Foolishness is bound in the heart of a child; but the rod of correction shall drive it far from him.' We ask this in Jesus' name, Amen. "

CHAPTER TWO

Walter's people went back generations. For all he knew they could have come over on the Mayflower. Both his grandfather and father were strict fundamentalist Christians who believed literally in both testaments. Their families had been patriarchal and so was Walter's. Eve came from the rib of Adam and was to be his companion, but not his equal, as it said of man and woman "And he shall rule over you." Walter knew no other way.

And so for many years Walter lived as his ancestors had, following the word of God until the devil insidiously captured his soul and he found himself breaking the Seventh Commandment; "You shall not commit adultery." Doris was also a true believer and would never doubt her husband's fidelity.

Pip was their only child and they adored the boy Jesus had given them. He was a wonderful gift, quick to learn, and Walter beamed with pride. But, as the boy reached adolescence, he inexplicably rebelled against his God. Walter agonized over this and sometimes believed it was the Lord's punishment for his infidelity.

∞

"I'll see you Thursday, Doris."

"Did you pack your raincoat? They say it might rain later."

Each Monday, Walter left for a four-day selling trip. He knew where every gas station was in all the surrounding states.

"I've been doing this for twelve years. I think I know what to take."

"Where will you be if I need you?"

"I'm not sure. I'll call tonight. You never know how it will go."

It used to be that Walter would leave Doris a detailed list telling her where he would spend each night, but that was before Helen. For some time now when he left Calvert, he temporarily abandoned Jesus and for good reason. Jesus did not save adulterers. At first it was pickups, but for the past year he was accompanied by Helen Anton.

His lips grazed Doris' cheek.

"See you Thursday," he mumbled again.

Walter drove to Helen's apartment. She had moved there from Ashton to be closer to him. He had made promises to her that he wanted to keep

9

but didn't know how. He had told her that when the time was right, he would divorce Doris. Unfortunately, the time never seemed right. Adultery was a terrible sin; divorce unacceptable. He preached Jesus in his home, but was a sinner on the road. It had happened slowly, insidiously.

It was his lousy job that had forced him into a life of hypocrisy. He had never drunk before he started his trips, and he had surely never had a fling, but being on the road was lonely and he was witness to the fact that loneliness was the tool of the devil.

When he first started traveling, his evenings would consist of a light supper, reading the paper, watching television in the lobby if it was a little classier hotel, and then bed.

After being on the road six months, he took to having a drink after dinner, and then a couple. The first time he picked up a woman in the bar, he was really the victim. The woman approached him.

"Hi, what'cha doing in this town? No one comes here."

"I sell brushes," Walter replied as he casually turned toward the voice.

She was about forty, short, with a puffy face covered with a thick coating of rouge and dark red lipstick which heavily encompassed not only her lips but also her surrounding skin. Her most startling assets were the biggest breasts Walter had ever seen. She wore a tight-fitting, low-cut dress that lifted and almost totally exposed them.

"Can I join you?" the woman asked.

Walter nodded, his eyes fixed on her bosom. He was aware of the weakness of the flesh of mortal man--but those breasts. His heart raced and his throat went dry. He quickly swallowed the remainder of his drink and ordered another scotch and soda.

"Can I get you something?" he asked hoarsely.

The woman lifted her glass to him, indicating she was fine.

"What do you mean, you sell brushes?" she asked.

"I travel to all the gas stations in four states. I use their john and then I tell them they won't keep their customers with toilets that pigs wouldn't use."

Walter knew he was being more talkative than was his custom. It must be the nervousness he was feeling. Show some control, he told himself. But those breasts were practically in his face.

"I show them my brush with its special contour handle that gets under the seat where all the, ah, splashing goes. They buy the brush. It takes me two years to cover the territory. Then I start all over."

The woman laughed as she put her arm effortlessly around Walter's neck.

"You sell brushes to clean shithouses?"

"Yah, I guess you could say that."

"I'll let you buy me that drink now," the woman said, holding up her empty glass.

That evening Walter became an adulterer. They went back to his room. He watched as she deftly and without modesty removed her dress and bra. Her breasts drooped to her midsection. She wasn't very attractive, but it didn't matter.

She sat next to him on the bed and gently moved him to a prone position. She unzipped his fly, took out his penis, and put it in her mouth.

"Oh, Jesus," he moaned, looking for the strength to turn away from this evil temptation, but he was lost. He had to have her.

"It tastes so good," she said. "Mary likes the taste."

Why did her name have to be Mary? Walter's penis became erect in her mouth. He stared at those huge breasts dangling from her chest, the nipples bouncing up and down as she moved.

"That's enough sucking for you. Now you have to take care of Mary."

She undressed him and guided him into her. He immediately had an orgasm, the climax wrenching him back to reality.

Standing, he looked at the woman with repugnance. He had not noticed how flabby she was or how large a rear end she had. He suddenly felt waves of contempt for her.

"You're a whore," he said, grabbing her by the arms and pulling her up.

"Get out of my room, you pig. Look what you made me do." He swung his fist at her, hitting her on the breast.

"You're crazy," she cried out. She grabbed her dress, threw it on, and ran from the room. In the doorway, she turned back to look at him.

"You're a real weirdo. You don't hit a woman on the tit after she eats you and lets you fuck her," she shouted, slamming the door.

Walter fell to his knees. Tears rolled down his face.

"I have sinned, sweet Jesus. My flesh was weak. I'll never stray again. I beg Your forgiveness."

He wiped his eyes with his forearm and stood. The room was dim, lit by forty-watt bulbs. He looked around. The furniture was cheap and old. He had never really noticed before. It was as if the experience had opened his eyes to the seaminess of the hotel rooms he could afford. His criteria were always the least expensive room in town. He wanted to provide as best he could for his family so he skimped on the road.

Walter went to the bathroom, urinated, and suddenly felt overwhelmingly dirty. He started the shower. The water was little more than a trickle and the hottest he could get it was lukewarm. It would have to do. For the next hour, he slowly and methodically washed his body. He never noticed the water becoming cold. He soaped his washcloth over and over, scrubbing his testicles and penis, washing the filth away. He dried himself vigorously until he was sure that no remnants of the slut remained.

He put on his pajamas and walked to the bed. He was appalled by the stains on the sheets, left over from his evil passion. Stripping the bed with one tug, he rolled the linen into a ball and threw it into a corner of the room. He looked down at the grey striped mattress with its stains of wear and was repelled by its impurity. The blanket seemed clean. He would use it for a sheet and cover himself with the spread. He put on his socks, not wanting his bare feet to touch the floor, returned to the bathroom and brushed his teeth. Overcome with exhaustion, Walter went back to the bed, turned out the light and closed his eyes. He was as purged of the whore as he could be.

"Forgive me, Jesus," he prayed over and over again until a fitful sleep overtook him. The Savior came to him. There was a sadness in His expression which silently conveyed His disappointment in Walter. And the slut was there, her buttocks wider, her breasts bigger than ever. In front of his very eyes, this evil woman became the Virgin Mary.

"Oh, my God, what have I done?" he moaned in his sleep.

He awoke with a start. It was six o'clock, an hour before he usually got up. His thoughts immediately focused on last evening. As he recalled the woman, his longings returned. What was the matter with him?

He got out of bed and headed for another shower. As he did, he noticed her bra on the rug. He picked it up and ran it through his fingers. As he recalled her breasts, he became disgusted with himself. He prayed that this would be the last time he would sin against his Jesus.

છ

At first, Walter didn't admit to himself that he was looking for women, but he did send out a signal that said "I'm available." Eventually, promiscuous sex became a part of almost every trip. He convinced himself he was possessed by the devil and it wasn't really his fault. It was as if there were two Walters. Only one of them was a God-fearing Christian, and that one never traveled the territory.

Each time after he took his pleasure, he became disgusted and angry with his partner. Although anxious to be rid of each slut, he held his temper and was courteous until she left. He would then fall to his knees and beg Jesus for help and strength in exorcising the devil that had possessed him.

CHAPTER THREE

"Could I speak to the owner?" Walter asked.

"He isn't here. Can I help you?" the woman replied.

"Who are you?"

"I'm the manager."

"A woman manager? What's America coming to?"

"Hey, it's 1951. Get with it, Mac. Women are working these days."

"I don't know how to tell you this," Walter said. "Your toilet is filthy."

He judged her to be in her late thirties. She was five- foot-five, lean, with a dark complexion. Her brown hair was gathered into a single braid that fell below her shoulders. She appeared strong and athletic, with wrinkles at the corners of her eyes and a smile that indicated how she got them. In spite of her navy Dickies, stained with oil, her equally filthy denim shirt, and dirty hands with grease under the nails, there was something sexy about her.

"Do I look like a maid?"

"I'm not telling you to clean the toilets, but someone had better. Your garage could be, pardon the expression, passing crabs on to your customers."

"What's it to you?"

"Listen, I usually don't deal with the ladies, but I might be able to help. I sell toilet brushes."

"What?"

"I sell brushes that are specially designed to clean toilets. Can I show you one?"

A horn honked, reminding the woman that she had forgotten the customer bell, which had gone off a few moments earlier.

"Hold your water," she shouted to the car. "I'll be right back, Mac. Don't go away."

He watched her as she bent over and spoke to the driver. Not bad. She walked to the pump, filled the tank, checked the oil, then went over and showed the dipstick to the driver. She reached for a can of oil and poured it into the engine, slammed down the hood, and washed the windows. The man handed her his money. She took a wad of bills from her pocket, made change and headed back to the station. Walter admired her self-assuredness.

"You sure know your business."

"That's what they pay me for. Now show me that brush."

Walter went to the car to get one.

"I usually demonstrate how they work, but I never showed a woman before."

"Hell, what's the problem? You're just going to show me how it works. You're not going to use the toilet. We'll go to the ladies' room. I'd rather you show me there."

Walter followed her. She opened the door with a key from her chain and stood aside, allowing him to enter. He took his brush from its box, applied the detergent, and started his pitch.

"The long handle allows you to clean the toilet without getting on your knees."

He took out his mirror and showed her how filthy it was under the rim of the bowl.

"Notice the shape of the handle. It permits you to get under there."

"Hey. This isn't a hospital. It's a garage."

Walter laughed. It was sure easier selling to a guy.

"Listen, lady, your customers like a clean bathroom. It's good for business."

"All right, you convinced me. How much are they?"

"Twelve ninety-five but for you ten ninety-five."

"Okay. We'll take one. My boss will probably kill me."

"I'll get you a new one. This is a demonstrator."

They walked to his car. He wiped the used brush dry with a rag and put it away.

"What's your name?" he asked.

"Helen."

"Hi, Helen, I'm Walter."

There was a silence as they walked back to the station. She took the money from the cash drawer. Walter drew a breath before asking, "Are you married?"

"Do you have to be married to buy a brush?"

"I'm sorry. It's none of my business."

"Was. He drove a ten wheeler. Last I saw him he was heading East with a twenty-year old as his co-pilot. Good riddance, I say."

"How about dinner with a lonely salesman?" He felt his heart beat quicken. The devil was again working his way into his soul. Walter was helpless against Satan.

She paused, taking a moment to look him over. He knew she was checking him out. He nervously played with an end of his waxed moustache, which extended smartly beyond either side of his upper lip. He wondered if he looked younger than his forty-one years. Walter was wearing gray flannel pants, white shirt with a red bow tie, complemented by a navy blazer. It was his uniform. Even though he sold only brushes to clean toilets, he believed that proper dress induced the garage owners to respect him and listen to his pitch. He hoped she wouldn't ask him about his marital situation. Smiling sheepishly, he anxiously awaited her decision.

"Sure, why not. If I interest you now, you'll love me clean," she laughed.

"I'm at the Eagle Hotel. Do you want to meet me there or should I pick you up?"

"Why don't I meet you at the Sunshine Cafe, seven-thirty. Know where it is?"

"Isn't it on Main?" Walter asked as he pocketed the money. "Seven-thirty. See you then."

෨

Walter spent the remainder of the day in eager anticipation as he visited seven more stations, selling six brushes. It was a good day's business.

He returned to his room and showered away the grime of a day on the road, cleaning toilets. He smiled at his reflection in the mirror as he combed his hair. It was no longer thick, but he was skilled at doing the most with it. Meticulously he fashioned his moustache. He always traveled with two outfits; the older one for work, the newer, for play. He finished his Windsor knot and was pleased with his image.

It was six-forty. He estimated the Sunshine Cafe was ten minutes from his hotel. One last chore before leaving. He picked up his shoes and took out his shoeshine bag, applying the black wax mixed with his spit on the toe of each. He buffed them to a glistening shine.

As he was about to go, Walter remembered that he hadn't called Doris. That could have been a crucial mistake. He always called her before he went prowling so she wouldn't interrupt him later. He sat back down on

16

the bed and picked up the phone on the side table. The hotel operator responded at once. He gave her his instructions for a collect call. Doris would accept the charge only if she had something to tell him. He liked the idea that he was outfoxing a big company like American Telephone.

"I'll accept," he heard Doris tell the operator.

This caught him by surprise. He looked at his watch. It was seven-ten. Damn, he should be leaving.

"What's the matter?" Walter asked with annoyance in his voice.

"It's Pip. He was insolent to his teacher. Mr. Perkins took the ruler to him, and Pip walked out of the school. Walked out of school, Walter."

"The devil is within him, Doris. I hate to say it, but I must take the rod to him."

"Oh, Walter, the devil is so powerful. From the day he was born we've tried to teach him about the goodness of Jesus. He's in his room, Walter. Will you speak to him, dear?"

Walter looked at his watch. It was seven-fifteen now. He was a punctual man and didn't want to be late for Helen.

"Put him on."

"Hello, Sir."

"Listen young man and listen good. Tomorrow you are to return to school. You are to apologize to Mr. Perkins. Also you must beg Jesus for His forgiveness. You have disappointed Him, Pip. Don't do it again. The devil is mighty powerful. Don't let him take over your soul. If the devil is still in you when I get home, I'll get him out."

His son was well aware how Walter intended to remove the devil, and the threat of a thrashing should be enough. Pip had been the recipient of his father's beatings before.

"But, Sir, Mr. Perkins..."

"I don't want no excuses, Pip. Good-bye."

Walter hung up the phone and jogged to his car. He kept checking his watch as he drove to the restaurant.

Running in, he surveyed the booths. No Helen. His heart sank. Well, he would eat here anyway. Damn Pip. He found a seat at the counter. As he took the menu he heard a voice.

"How come you were late?"

He turned. She looked like a different person. He never would have been bold enough to ask her out if he had seen her looking like this. She wore a simple shirtwaist, flower print dress that came down slightly below her knees. Her hair was long and straight with a part in the middle and matching barrettes on either side.

"I had a late call that took longer than it should have. Where were you?" Walter asked.

"I was in the ladies' room. I checked their toilet for you. They don't need your brush."

They both laughed. Walter stood as she took her seat across from him.

"All I know about you is your first name, and that you sell brushes."

"Just a traveling salesman. It's nothing great, but I do okay. It's a lonely job though."

"You seem to make friends pretty easily. You found me without much trouble. You probably have a girl in every city."

The waitress came over.

"We got ribs tonight, and they look real meaty."

"I'll have that," Helen responded.

Although Walter loved ribs, he was afraid of the mess. The sauce got all over, not to mention the annoying bits that got stuck between his teeth. Helen obviously didn't have his inhibitions.

"I'll have the ground steak, medium rare. And give me a Bud. How about you, Helen?"

"Sounds good."

"Want a pitcher?" the waitress asked.

He looked at Helen, who nodded her consent.

"Yes, thanks," Walter replied.

"I love ribs. They're so messy, but I can't resist."

Walter was enchanted by her easy manner. All Helen's predecessors had served only one purpose. Was this different? How could it be? He was married.

The food came.

"How about some extra napkins?" Helen asked the waitress as she poured a glass of beer for each of them.

Walter lifted his glass. "To us."

Helen took a long swallow before diving into dinner, pausing only to wipe her face and gulp beer after finishing each rib. "These are great."

Walter ate his food with far less gusto, more concerned with what the remainder of the evening would bring. He had never been with anyone as attractive as Helen. Was she as uninhibited in bed as she was at dinner?

"Coffee? Pie?" the waitress offered.

Helen ordered both. Walter decided to have coffee only. How did she stay so thin?

Helen took out a small compact and checked her makeup as Walter paid the bill. He noticed her examining her teeth before she applied lipstick.

Was Helen an agent of the devil, sent here to capture his eternal soul, once and for all? She was nothing like the sluts he had found in bars. He was confused, not sure how to proceed with her. If the devil had sent her, he was lost.

She looked at her watch. "It's almost ten. I have to be at the station at six in the morning. I'd better be going home." They walked to her car. "I had a very nice time, Walter. Call me the next time you're in the area. Maybe I'll need another brush."

She opened the door and started to get in. His mind raced. His plans called for him to be in Horizon tomorrow. He always meticulously planned his schedule and never deviated from it. Maybe it was time for an exception. Damn, he had to think fast. Taking her out again would pinch his budget. But he would worry about that later.

"I'll be in Ashton one more day. How about tomorrow night?"

"Why not? I'll pick you up. Seven thirty again?"

"Great," Walter responded. He bent over and gave her a kiss.

"Aren't you the one?" she responded at his awkward attempt to show his affection. She closed the door and drove off, leaving him to watch her car disappear down the road.

ॐ

Walter had fully covered Ashton yesterday. He filled the day trying to sell his brushes to bars and restaurants; but he sold only two all day and was beginning to regret his decision.

At four in the afternoon he returned to his room and took a nap, something he would never ordinarily do. He awoke startled and checked the time. It was six. Immediately he sat up. Tonight had better be special, he thought, as he reached for the phone and placed his collect call to Doris. She refused to accept the charges. At least everything was okay at home. He called her collect once more, her signal to accept.

"Everything okay?" she asked, her voice tight with anxiety.

"Yes, fine. I just wanted you to know I'm staying an extra night at Ashton. I'm still at the Eagle Hotel."

"How come?" she asked, knowing how unusual it was for him to deviate from his schedule.

The question induced guilt, which transformed to anger. "It's business, Doris. I misjudged the territory and couldn't cover it in one day."

"I'm sorry, Walter. I was only asking."

He passed the receiver to his other hand before continuing. "Did Pip apologize to Mr. Perkins?"

"I can't get him to talk, Walter. I think so."

"I'll deal with him when I get back. See you tomorrow."

He hung up, looked at his watch, and rushed to get ready.

Helen arrived promptly at seven-thirty. His heart accelerated as he opened the door. When he looked at her, he was glad of his decision to stay.

"Want to buy a girl dinner?" she asked.

"Sounds good to me."

They ate in the hotel dining room, then went to the lounge for a drink.

"Tell me all about yourself," Walter said, hoping to direct the conversation away from himself.

She confided little saying only that she married too quickly and was happy he was gone.

"I'm glad, too," Walter replied. "Any boyfriends?"

She paused as if considering the question, and took a sip of her drink. "I'm dating but nothing serious. Hey, I've been doing all the talking. What about you?"

Rather than replying, Walter went to the juke box, put in a quarter, chose five songs, and went back to their table. They were the only customers in the lounge.

"Wanna dance?" he asked.

Helen stood and took his outstretched hand. He held her close, wanting her to know of his desire. The song ended and he held her hand as they waited for the next record. As he took her again in his arms, she touched her lips to his in the most delicate of kisses, before they started to dance. He felt his arousal and knew she must, too.

As if able to read his thoughts, she whispered, "It feels good, Walter." She put her hand on his erection and held it there for a moment.

"Take me back to your room," she crooned into his ear.

Walter paid the check. You win, he thought, envisioning the devil, gleefully watching him succumb. I'll trade hell after death for this heaven on earth. I can't fight it.

Once back at his room, he took her in his arms. They kissed. She reached for the buckle on his pants. He removed her hand and quickly took off his clothes while she undressed. She was the most beautiful woman he had ever been intimate with. She got under the covers and looked at him, her eyes inviting him to join her.

He thought of his Lord and instinctively touched the gold crucifix around his neck.

"Thank you, Jesus," he mumbled. As the prayer tumbled from his lips he realized his blasphemy but was helpless to set it right.

After they made love, Walter reached for his cigarettes and lit two of them. Kissing Helen, he handed her one.

As the smoke curled upwards, each lay silent in their own thoughts. He knew this was different from all the other times. He didn't want her to go. He didn't feel dirty. He knew he had sinned against Jesus, done wrong, was an adulterer, but still he wanted her to stay.

She stood. He stared at her nakedness, not disgusted by it.

"You're beautiful," he mumbled.

"I have to be going."

"Stay with me for the night," he implored.

"I don't have anything with me. I can't go to work in a dress."

"Stay a while longer," he said, lifting the covers for her to return.

"I have to leave soon," she said as she responded to his invitation.

She felt so good in his arms. He squeezed her close. Could their nearness keep the devil from entering? How could this be wrong? He knew the answer.

"You're crushing me, Walter," she laughed.

"Sorry." He relaxed his arms and kissed her gently.

"Walter, I have to ask you. Do you do this in every city?"

"No. Never."

"One more question, Walter. Are you married?"

His stomach did a somersault, and his mouth went dry.

"No," he replied with as much calm as he could muster.

Just as he answered, the phone rang. Walter knew it could be only one person and he suddenly felt faint. Looking at the phone, he tried to shake his dizziness.

"Aren't you going to answer it?" Helen asked.

Walter thought he might pass out.

"No one knows I'm here. It must be a wrong number."

The phone stopped ringing.

"Walter," she said in a soft voice. "Walter, are you all right? You're so pale."

Again the phone began ringing, and Helen reached for it. "Don't answer it," Walter spit out, grabbing it from her. Maybe it was the front desk.

"Hello."

"Walter, Pip says he isn't going back to school. You must talk to him."

He listened to Doris, his mind and eyes on Helen.

"Doris, it's ten thirty. You woke me up. Can't this wait till I come... home?"

"I'm sorry, but he won't listen to me."

Helen started getting dressed.

"Put him on," he said.

"Hello, Sir."

"What's this about your not going to school?"

"Let me go to public school, please, Sir," Pip implored.

"I'm not going to give your soul to the devil on a silver platter," he said. "You'll go back to Calvert Christian." Maybe Walter was lost, but he loved his son and could still save his soul.

"I can't, Dad. Please understand."

As Walter talked to the boy, he continued to watch Helen helpless to stop her.

"You had better or else, young man." He had to terminate the conversation. "We'll talk about it when I get home. Good night, Pip, God Bless," he said with finality as he hung up the phone.

Helen was gone. He threw on his pants and undershirt and ran barefoot to the parking lot. As he arrived, he saw her car leaving.

"Damn," he mumbled as he walked quickly past the check-in back to his room glancing at the receptionist who never gave him any notice. A barefooted man in an undershirt was probably not an unusual sight in this fleabag.

Walter sat down at the well-used desk, folded his hands, and prayed as he always did after he sinned. In the past, however, he not only admitted to his transgression, but would also promise Jesus this would be the last time, that with the help of his Savior he would never commit adultery again.

"Jesus, Jesus, sweet Jesus," he began. He felt the hypocrisy of his cries but didn't know what else to do. "I'm a sinner. Please help save me, my sweet Lord. The devil has me in his grip, and he won't let go. I'm too weak against his power. I'm begging for help. I can't do it on my own." His body trembled.

He went to the bathroom, undressed and took a shower. He turned the water to its hottest level, as was his custom after sinning. He scrubbed until he could feel the scum of his ungodliness washing down the drain. It was cathartic.

Vigorously he toweled dry, then put on the flannel pajamas Pip had given him last Christmas. As he straightened the covers and got into bed, his thoughts turned to Helen. It was his first relationship that wasn't simply a weakness of the flesh. She was a person to him, not a faceless slut. He thought of Doris and of Pip, but his attention kept returning to Helen.

He slept fitfully.

"Come to Helen," he heard her call to him. The devil was standing at her side, dressed in fiery red. He had horns and a pitchfork in his hand. When he smiled, gleaming white fangs were exposed.

"Come to Helen," she repeated seductively.

Walter felt himself involuntarily pulled toward her. He heard a voice call to him. He turned. It was Pastor Warren.

"Walter, Walter, don't do it. You'll burn forever in hell. Don't give up eternal bliss."

Doris was at his side. She was wearing a house dress which did not hide the dowdiness of her rotund figure. He looked at Doris, then back at Helen.

"Come to Helen."

He started to run. Where was he going? He tried to accelerate his pace, but his legs were weighted and hardly moved. He awoke with a start and looked around. Helen, Doris, the devil, and Pastor Warren were gone, but not the tugging and pulling. He believed in Jesus as his Savior, yet he couldn't stop thinking about Helen and last night.

He had to get to work. His family counted on his earnings, which varied little. This week would be different. He felt trapped, like in his dream.

Walter gave most of his money to Doris, who paid the bills. She would wonder what happened. He had to come up with more money to cover himself, but doing this would mean leaving without seeing Helen once more. He couldn't let it end with her walking out. He rushed to get dressed.

As he drove into the station, he saw Helen at the pumps waiting on customers. He watched as she put the spray bottle into her back pocket and stretched across the windshield, wiping it with her cloth. He parked to one side of the lot, slowly got out of the car and walked over to her. He wasn't sure if she had seen him. She took no notice.

"Helen."

She turned toward his voice, looked him up and down.

"Walter, you're a liar. Get out of here."

"Helen, I'm sorry. Please talk to me for a moment. Let me explain. I don't want to leave this way," he said, nervously fidgeting with his mustache.

"Four fifteen," she told the customer. He took out a ten and Helen made change, handing him a complimentary glass. "You get one with every fill-up," she said.

The man took his change and the gift, rolled up the window and drove off. They were alone. Ignoring him, Helen turned and headed back toward the station.

"Please, Helen," he whined, following her. "Let me talk to you."

"Listen," she said, turning to face him. "I might not have minded as much, if you told me you were married. But you lied to me. How can I ever trust you? I liked you. I don't do this every night, you know. I'm not that kind of girl."

"I'm sorry. I was wrong. I lied. But I didn't know what to do. I'm sorry."

"Okay, I forgive you. Now, good-bye."

"Have dinner with me tonight?" he said, not knowing how he would spend the day.

"You're married."

"Please. Just dinner. Give me a chance to tell you about myself. The truth this time," he pleaded.

She looked at him and then laughed. "You're a scoundrel. Okay, Walter. Meet me at the Sunshine Cafe at seven-thirty. Now, good-bye."

Walter kissed her quickly on the lips. "Thank you."

He went to his car and drove off, not quite sure where he was going. The reality of his impulsiveness frightened him. He had bills to pay and had to sell some brushes. He pulled over to the side of the road and took out his map and list of stations. The closest virgin territory was about forty-five miles away. He would drive there and be back for seven-thirty. Doris expected him home that night. He would have to call her with some excuse. God, he didn't have a room. He would have to drive home tonight.

℘

"You look beautiful," Walter said as Helen approached his table. He had arrived at the Sunshine Cafe a half hour early and had used the rest room to groom

"What can I get you folks?" the waitress asked.

"We'll start out with a cold pitcher of Bud," Walter replied before turning his attention to Helen.

"Tell me about your wife," she said, not mincing words. Walter was startled by her directness.

"What's to tell?" he began slowly.

"How did you meet her? Does she know you cheat on her? Do you love her?"

He emptied his glass, poured a fresh one and ordered another pitcher before speaking. "This isn't easy, but you have a right to know."

He took her hand that was resting on the table but she took it away.

"We've been married almost eighteen years. She's a nice lady and I wouldn't care to hurt her. We've known each other since we were kids. Do I love her? I don't know. We're just...together. I don't give it any thought."

He twisted his mustache, his habit when he was nervous.

"And you have a boy?"

"How do you know?" Walter asked.

"Last night. The phone call from Doris. Remember?"

"I'm sorry. Yes, I have a son. He's a good boy, but I worry about him."

"That's what parents do."

They both ordered the ribs.

"Walter, don't lie to me again, please," she implored.

"I promise, Helen."

Now she took his hand. "You're a strange guy, Walter, but I do like you."

"And I've never felt this way about anyone," he said.

25

Walter was comfortable about eating ribs tonight. They talked non-stop until the waitress came over. "We're closing now."

Walter looked at his watch.

"It's ten-thirty," he exclaimed. He reached for his wallet. "I have to drive home tonight."

"Stay with me," Helen responded.

Walter hesitated a moment as he reviewed his options. He knew that was what he wanted to do, but how would he explain to Doris? It was too late to call. What excuse could he give?

Helen misinterpreted his silence. "Okay, go home, if you have to."

"No. I'll stay," he quickly replied. He didn't know what he'd tell Doris but was beyond caring.

Walter followed her to the apartment and parked next to her, walking over to open her car door. She got out and turned to him. They kissed.

He had an unflattering image of himself and couldn't believe that lovely Helen could care for him. He stood back, looked at her and smiled.

"What's so funny?" she asked.

"I was just thinking how lovely you are."

They walked the three flights to her apartment. When she opened her door, they were greeted by another flight of stairs.

"You have to be a mountain climber to live here," he said.

A cat was sitting on the first step waiting for her. She scooped the furry ball into her hands, kissed him, and lovingly carried him into the apartment.

"You've been a good boy, Rex."

"Rex?" Walter asked, panting.

"He's the king. If you ever had a cat, you'd know what I mean. Hey you're out of breath."

"That was a lot of stairs."

"Keeps me in shape and the rent's low."

They entered a spacious room with a high ceiling. The outside wall was brick. There was a crucifix with Christ on it on the opposite wall next to a velvet copy of "The Last Supper." She had never mentioned her religion, but Walter now knew she had to be Catholic as his church believed the Savior had risen and to put Him on the cross was sacrilegious.

She responded to his looking. "All good Catholic girls have a copy of The Last Supper."

"Some of us Protestants have copies, also," he said.

"Of course good Catholic girls don't do what I've done. Forgive me Lord, for I have sinned." She laughed at herself.

Walter witnessed how lightly she regarded her mortal sin. He could never be so free.

The kitchen area was tucked in one corner, shiny pots and pans hanging from hooks. The furnishings were sparse but well kept.

"Want a beer?"

"Sure," he replied as he sat down on the couch.

She walked to the kitchen area and took a couple of bottles from the refrigerator before joining him. Stretching out her legs and resting them on the coffee table in front of the sofa, she handed him his beer.

"Thanks," he said as he lifted his bottle. "A toast to us."

⋅⋅⋅

Sex with Helen didn't seem dirty to Walter. She guided their love-making. It was slow and caring. On the rare occasions he made love with Doris, it was both mechanical and fast. That was the way they both liked it, Doris to get it over with and Walter to have his orgasm as quickly as possible.

When Helen and Walter were finished, he didn't need to rush to the shower nor was he overcome with a desire to be rid of her. Rather, he gently held her in his arms as he fell asleep.

Jesus came to him. Behind his Savior stood Pastor Warren, Doris and Pip.

"I'm very disappointed in you," his Lord said, pointing a finger at him and shaking it.

"I'm sorry, Jesus. I try to stop, but I can't. It's the devil. I know it is."

"You can't blame everything on the devil," Pastor Warren scolded him.

"What else can it be?" Walter asked.

"I'm so ashamed," Doris said. "You are filth."

"And you want me to go to the Calvert Christian School. You hypocrite!" Pip shouted.

They were all pointing accusing fingers at him.

"Walter, are you okay?" Helen asked, shaking him back to consciousness. "You're jumping all over the bed."

He blinked a few times as he got his bearing. Helen was nude beside him. The dream was still vivid in his mind but he wasn't about to share it.

"It's nothing," he said as he looked at her small firm breasts, her thin, tan and available body. He leaned over and kissed her.

Again they made love and still no guilt, no need to shower. There was a twinge of pride at his sexual prowess. He fell asleep, again holding her in his arms. He had no more dreams that night.

∞

Walter awoke the next morning to the rich smell of brewing coffee and frying bacon. He jumped out of bed, threw on his pants and shirt and dashed into the bathroom. He groomed himself as best he could without his toiletries, which remained in his car. He put toothpaste on his finger and scrubbed his teeth. He combed his hair, twisted his moustache into place, until finally he shrugged his shoulders, resigned that it was the best he could do. He went into the kitchen.

Helen was wearing a red flannel robe which came to her ankles. She looked great. His life was going to become complicated.

"Sit down," Helen commanded. "How do you like your eggs?"

"Over and well done."

"Ugh. It sounds terrible." She served him his breakfast and kissed him on the lips.

"I have to get going. I start work at seven," she said.

He checked his watch. It was six-fifteen. She joined him at the table. They finished eating and each lit a cigarette.

"That was delicious," he said. "I usually just have coffee in the morning."

"They say the stomach is the way to a man's heart."

"It's not the only way," Walter replied.

"I noticed," Helen said as she brought the dishes to the sink.

They went to the bedroom. Walter couldn't believe how totally at ease he was with her. He watched as she put on her navy Dickies and chambray shirt.

"You start the day a lot cleaner than you end it."

She laughed. He took her hand in his and walked her out to her car.

"Helen, I don't know what to say. I'm like a kid again. I've never felt this way. I'll call you... if it's okay with you."

"It's okay with me."

They kissed. Walter was slow to let her go.

"I can't be late for work, darling."

The word "darling" warmed him.

As he watched her car turn the corner the other side of his life distastefully came into focus.

God, I never called Doris. What the hell am I supposed to tell her?

He found a pay phone, dreading the lie he knew he had to relate.

"Hello."

He heard the tension in his wife's voice. "Doris, the car broke down. I just started out for home, and the car conked out."

"Why didn't you call?" The relief in her voice told him she suspected nothing.

"I couldn't get to a phone. You know I would have if it were possible. I'll be home this afternoon. I'm going to try to sell a few brushes on the way. It hasn't been as good a trip as I had hoped."

Going against his God was getting easier all the time.

CHAPTER FOUR

"I'm exhausted," Walter told Doris, shortly after he arrived home.

"Why don't you go upstairs and rest, dear? You look beat. Supper will be ready soon."

"I think I will."

"It's Thursday, Bible class. Do you want to go?"

"Yes, I believe so. Let me clean up and rest first."

"Okay, dear. You do need a shave. Did you forget to shave this morning?"

He ignored the question. As he was about to leave the room, he recalled that his son had stayed home on Tuesday.

"How's Pip doing? Did he go to school?"

"He went today but he wants to talk to you when he gets home. I don't know what will become of him."

"I'll handle this. He'll go."

"Take it easy on him, Walter."

He saw the pleading in her eyes. She looked like a whipped dog when she pouted.

"Is his soul worth fighting for, Doris? I think it is. If you love him, you'll want me to come down hard on him."

∽

"Yes," Walter responded to the knock on his bedroom door.

"It's Pip. May I talk to you, Sir?"

"Come in, son."

As Pip was opening the door, Walter sat on the bed and reached for the Bible he kept on the bedside table. He quickly opened the book so that it would appear he had been reading it. He wondered if Pip would realize he wasn't wearing his glasses.

"The devil is fighting for your soul, Pip," Walter began. "You must fight back. Let us pray together."

He put his Bible aside, and bowed his head. Pip sat at the corner of the bed and did the same. Walter took his hand.

"Dear Lord Jesus. My son is lost in the wilderness. He looks for You, but says You are not there. Help him to find You, Jesus. Amen."

"Amen," Pip echoed. "Father, I beg you. Let me go to the public school. I can still be a good Christian."

"Why can't you give Calvert Christian more of a chance? It's only been two months."

"I hate it there. Please, Father, let me go to public school. I'll continue to go to church. I'll be a good Christian. Please."

"Finish your freshman year, and then we'll discuss it. You must give it a chance."

Suddenly, Pip's attitude changed. He took his hand away from his father. "I told you I hate it," he shouted. "I won't keep going, and you can't make me."

Walter jumped up from the bed, flushed with anger. He grabbed his son's shirt and pulled the boy toward him.

"'Children, obey your parents in all things, for this is well pleasing unto the Lord.' Colossians 3:20," he spat at him. "You will go to the Christian School. Do you understand me?"

"No, I won't."

Walter was confounded by his son's obstinacy. He pulled his belt from his pants, folded it in half and struck the boy twice across his backside. Tears filled Pip's eyes but he was silent.

"Go to your room," Walter commanded.

Pip did as he was told. As Walter watched his son leave the room, his anger turned to remorse. Why couldn't he have controlled his temper? His sins far outweighed Pip's disobedience. Walter had been so sure of himself, so sure of his beliefs before he had yielded to this weakness of the flesh. Was this God's method of punishing him?

He went to his son's room and found Pip sitting at his desk. He put his hand on the boy's shoulder.

"The road to salvation isn't an easy one," he said.

Pip stood, his face stained from tears. "Oh father, I'm sorry. I don't want to be a disappointment to you. I'll try."

"That's good, my son. You won't be sorry." Walter hugged his boy. He did love Pip. His own salvation was in doubt, but why should that preclude leading his son down the path of righteousness?

∞

On Fridays, Walter visited the factory to pay for the brushes he sold that past week and pick up new ones. He maintained a good relationship with his boss, although secretly he resented him for his sin of crucifying the Savior, not converting and most importantly, cheating him by over-charging him for the brushes.

"Walter, my prices have gone up. I pay more, you pay more, they pay more. That's the way it works."

"I can't charge more, Herb. They won't stand for it."

"They'll pay it. You're a salesman. Do your job."

Walter left the factory fuming. He knew God was punishing him for Helen. First Pip, now Herb. He arrived home in time for lunch, as he did every Friday. Few words ever passed between Doris and Walter. She served him a tuna fish sandwich on white bread with sweet pickles and a coke.

Walter was steamed at the prospect of having to pay higher prices for the brushes. Damn Jews. He looked up from his lunch and watched Doris as she performed her chores about the kitchen. She was oblivious to the turmoil he was suffering. Why couldn't she be Helen? Why couldn't he forget Helen and be satisfied with Doris?

Doris was washing the dishes. He noticed her backside. It seemed bigger than he had ever remembered it. Her hair was unkempt. She turned and came toward him. There was something different. Now he knew. She usually hummed a mindless tune as she cleaned. She wasn't humming. He stared at her stubby fingers as she methodically cleaned the table with a sponge. Was there no redeeming quality to this woman? Had she always been this unappealing?

Damn, he missed Helen. He felt like a kid in high school. There was a fluttering in his stomach, a terrible longing to be with her. It was so painful.

Doris sat down at the kitchen table. Something was wrong. Did she somehow know?

"I got a call from the school. Pip wasn't there today."

"What! Not in school? I can't believe it. Where is he? Why didn't you tell me sooner?"

"I wanted to. I've been so upset, I didn't know what to do. You look so worried these days, Walter. I didn't want to aggravate you further."

"You didn't want to aggravate me! Doris, I don't know what to do with that boy."

"Maybe you should let him go to the public school."

"You want to hand his soul to the devil on a silver platter? Is that it? Don't we owe it to Jesus to try harder? He must obey his parents, not defy them. To defy us is to forsake the Savior. No, Doris, he'll obey even if he has to suffer until he does."

"Walter, please." She was wringing her hands as she always did when stressed.

"Bow your head, Doris. Let us pray."

She did as her husband commanded.

"Dear Jesus, our son is lost in the wilderness. Help us to lead him back to Your path. Amen."

"Amen," she moaned.

"Doris, I have to plan my trips for the next few weeks. Send Pip to me as soon as he comes home."

Taking his beat-up briefcase with him, he went to the dining room, sat at the table and surveyed his map. He located Ashton and stared at the name of the town as if the word might conjure up Helen.

"Oh, Helen," he mumbled to the empty room.

He took a string and lightly drew a circle on the map with Ashton at the center. From the exterior of the circle to Ashton was about one hundred and twenty miles. He could do that distance in about two and a half hours. He was surprised that he could plan six separate trips within that circumference. If he was clever about it, he could end almost every day no more than an hour from her. How would she feel about that?

His thoughts were interrupted by the sound of the front door closing. He knew it was Pip. How could he justify his anger with the boy, knowing the lust that was within him? And yet his sinning seemed to intensify his concern for his son.

With his whole heart, Walter literally believed in the Bible. It was God's teaching. For certain, he was going against those teachings, and he could expect nothing less than eternal damnation But he could still save Pip.

He heard Doris speaking to the boy. A few moments later, Pip appeared in the doorway.

"You want to see me, Sir?"

"Why didn't you go to school today? Didn't you promise me?" he asked, as he nervously twisted his mustache.

"I couldn't."

"What do you mean, you couldn't?"

"I have a note for you. I was supposed to give it to you yesterday."

He handed his father a crumpled piece of paper.

"Where were you all day? Your mother was worried."

"I walked around. I just walked around all day."
Walter unfolded the paper.

Mr. and Mrs. Marshall:

Philip is a very disruptive influence in class. Before he
returns to school, I would appreciate a meeting with you.
I will be available tomorrow morning at seven-thirty.

Mr. Perkins

"Your teacher wanted to see us today. He will think we don't care,"
Walter said, putting the note down and looking up at his son. He had
struck the boy only yesterday and it had done no good. His temper was
ready to explode.

"What does Mr. Perkins mean 'disruptive?'"

"I refused to pray or sing hymns."

"You what?"

"They don't make any sense to me."

"They don't make any sense to you? The word of God doesn't make
sense to you? Does this make sense to you, heathen?"

Walter stood, unbuckled his belt and snapped it from around his
pants. He swung wildly at his son, hitting him across the face. In the past
Walter had hit Pip with a conscious use of his strength, simply doing as
God had commanded. But this time he was out of control.

Pip threw his hands up to protect himself. Walter saw the marks left
by the belt across the boy's cheek. He wanted to stop but swung again,
hitting the boy on the backside. Pip fell to the ground face down and
Walter swung again. He heard the child scream in agony as he jumped
to his feet and ran to the hallway. Walter pursued, catching up to him.
"We'll go to school with you Monday morning. We'll see Mr. Perkins and
promise him that this will never happen again. You'll spend the weekend
begging Jesus for His forgiveness. Your mother will bring your food to
you. You will accompany us to church on Sunday. Other than that you'll
not leave your room. Do you understand?" Walter raged, spittle forming
at the sides of his mouth.

Tears ran down Pip's face as he nodded his agreement, not able to
speak or catch his breath. Walter dragged the boy to his room and threw
him to the floor before storming out, slamming the door behind him.

Pip looked up at the Cross over his bed. He touched the crucifix with his hand, feeling the outline of the symbol of where Christ had died for everyone's sins.

"Jesus, if you are the Savior, why do you want my father to hit me? Give me a sign by letting me go to public school, I beg you."

He lay down on the bed, burying his face in his pillow. He sobbed uncontrollably, gasping for air, until, exhausted, he fell into a deep sleep.

℘

Walter returned to the dining room table. He was out of breath. As his temper abated he felt terrible for having beaten the boy while out of control. He looked down and saw Perkin's crumpled note next to the map. One represented his son's sin, the other his own. Walter took a deep breath. He had to speak to Helen.

"I have to go on an errand," he shouted into the kitchen. "Pip is to spend the weekend in his room praying. You'll bring him his meals."

Doris came into the dining room. She was wiping her hands with a dishtowel. Her eyes were red from crying.

"Weren't you a little hard on Pip?"

"He has to learn, and it's my job as head of the household to teach him."

"He's only a boy."

Walter had never heard Doris question him before and rarely did she weep. He wasn't capable of admitting that he had indeed over-reacted and her tears only angered him.

"Have you ever heard `spare the rod and spoil the child,' Doris?"

"It just seems..." her voice trailed off.

"I'll be back by dinner."

"Where are you going?"

"Out."

℘

Walter drove a few miles past his neighborhood to a small grocery store.

"Got a pay phone?" he asked the young boy at the counter.

"Over there," the lad said, pointing with his hand while keeping his eyes on his comic book.

"Could you give me change for a dollar?"

The boy looked up, picking at a blemish. He took the dollar, opened the register and handed him the coins.

Walter went to the pay phone. He took the paper with the two numbers from his pocket and called the one with the "H" after it. No answer. He dialed the second.

"Mulrooney's Service and Gas."

It was her voice.

"Deposit eighty-five cents," the operator commanded.

His hand shook, and the coins fell to the floor.

"Operator, I dropped my money," Walter shouted into the phone. "Please wait a moment."

"You're suppose to have your money ready, sir," the operator whined in a nasal voice.

Walter dropped the receiver and bent over to retrieve the coins as quickly as possible. He jumped up, hitting his head on the shelf that extended from the wall below the phone. He fell back down, recovered, stood up and grabbed the receiver.

"Hello. Did you say eighty-five cents?"

The line was dead.

"Witch," he cursed, as he carefully put the coins on the shelf before starting the process over.

"Mulrooney's Service and Gas."

This time he put the money into the pay phone.

"Helen?"

"Walter?"

"Oh, Helen. I can't stop thinking about you. I had to call."

"I've missed you, Walter. To be honest, I've missed you."

His spirits soared. Nothing mattered except to be with her.

"I'm scheduled to be in the area next week, again. Can I see you?"

"I didn't know there were so many gas stations in my part of the state," she laughed.

"I didn't either," he responded, joining in her merriment. "I have to see you."

"I want to be with you, too, Walter."

"How about the Sunshine Cafe at seven thirty, Monday?"

"How about my place? I'll cook you dinner."

"Oh, Helen, that sounds wonderful. I'll see you then."

He hung up the phone, looked at it for a moment, turned and headed back to his car, but didn't get in. He just wasn't ready to go home. Instead, he aimlessly walked for over an hour, thinking of Helen and Doris and Pip. His Lord and Savior must be so disappointed in him.

"I'm sorry, Jesus. I'm so sorry," he lamented as he slowly drove home. He had a terrible headache.

෨

"I try, but I can't believe. Oh, Ma, I wish I could."

It was Sunday morning. Doris was taking breakfast to her son who had not left his room since Friday, and hadn't uttered a word of complaint. He was lying on the lower bunk.

"I know you do." She bent over and kissed the boy. "We leave for church in two hours," she continued. "Be ready to go. I hung a clean shirt in your closet and took most of the stains out of your suit. Try not to get it dirty. You know how your father is about appearance. Now, I have some dishes to do." She turned to leave.

"I'm too old for father to hit me anymore. He'd better stop because I won't stand for it."

Doris turned back and looked at her son. His face was pale, his eyes sunken. He was a strange lad, so hard to manage. He was right, but wasn't it her duty to support her husband's decisions?

"Your father loves you and worries for your salvation."

"He didn't hit me out of love. He beat me out of anger. Is that the way of Jesus?"

Doris watched his lips quiver as he spoke. She didn't know how to respond so she simply kissed him again and left the room.

෨

Walter looked at his watch as the three of them walked into the Calvert Christian School. It was a few minutes before seven-thirty.

"I should be on the road, young man, providing for you and your mom. It's difficult enough without you making it harder with your behavior."

Pip didn't respond. There was a vacant look on his face. It seemed he no longer heard or cared. There were bags under his young eyes, and he was breathing through his slightly opened mouth. Walter regretted his words.

They walked to Pip's classroom. The door, which was closed, had a glass panel in the upper half, and Walter could see Mr. Perkins sitting at his desk. He recognized the book his son's teacher was reading. It was the Bible. He wondered if the man was as pure as he appeared, or if he was more like himself. Mr. Perkins looked up as they entered. His Adams apple seemed to dance a jig.

As was the custom of the church, the teacher embraced each of them. "I'm glad you're here. Please be seated." He gestured to the students' desks. Mr. Perkins sat in his chair facing them.

"We begin each day with a prayer, the Pledge of Allegiance to our country, and a promise of loyalty to the Bible and the Christian flag. I noticed that Pip would stand but his lips wouldn't move. I asked him why he wasn't participating."

"What was his answer?" Walter asked.

"He would give no satisfactory answer. He would shrug his shoulders or say he didn't know. For a while he participated again, but then he stopped. Once more I confronted him, even took the ruler to him. He simply refused. I couldn't believe it. I told him to leave the school and not return until I met with you. I don't want to lose Pip to the devil. I love the boy. But I must consider the other students. If he's under the power of Satan he could influence them, and their souls are also important."

"Pip's sorry. He'll not do it again," Doris said weakly.

"He has spent the weekend in prayer. We hope he has seen the way. What do you have to say, boy?" Walter asked.

The three of them looked at him. There was no response.

"Well, boy, say something," his father urged.

"I feel funny when I say those things. They sound stupid to me. How do you know that Jesus is the Savior?" Pip's voice was barely audible.

"How do we know?" Walter shouted before gaining control and continuing in a calmer voice. "You know how we know. It's in the scriptures, the holy book. Pip, you must give Christ a chance."

"I try, but it doesn't happen."

"Try harder," Doris said. "Please."

"I have spoken to the Administrator, and he told me Pip must change his attitude if he wishes to come back," Mr. Perkins said.

"He will," his mother answered.

"Pip?" Mr. Perkins responded.

"I'll try."

"That's not good enough, Pip. You must promise," Walter said.

"No, Mr. Marshall," Mr. Perkins interrupted. "That will be good enough for now. If he'll really try, Jesus will take care of the rest. May we pray?"

He bowed his head. "Jesus, help Pip to find You. He's having more trouble than the other students. We know if he truly calls on You, no evil power can match the strength of your grace and compassion. Thank you, Lord. Amen."

Walter and Doris echoed their Amens, and the three of them looked at Pip.

"Amen," he acknowledged.

They all stood and each hugged the other.

"I'm sure it's a closed issue," Mr. Perkins said.

CHAPTER FIVE

During the next five weeks, Walter's life was a roller coaster ride. As he drove off each Monday, he would scrutinize his double life, analyze his options, and make a promise that he would extricate himself from this sinful relationship. One last week and that would be it forever. Jesus would forgive him, and he would never stray again. Just this one last week.

By Tuesday, Walter wondered how he could ever survive without Helen. On Wednesday he became depressed knowing this was his last night with her for the week. On the sixth week, he realized he no longer could travel in that area, as there was no where left to go. Walter had to continue to earn a living.

He had put hundreds of additional miles on his car these past few weeks, but it had been worth it. He had never known as much happiness. Could such joy be evil? For the first time in his life, he began to doubt the Word. But he also knew that when Satan took hold of you, he had the power to cause you to vacillate in your belief in Christ.

Walter reviewed his alternatives as he drove out of Calvert on that sixth Monday since he had met Helen. He knew she shared his feelings. They had spoken of love. He contemplated divorce. Didn't he had a right to this happiness, a blissfulness he had never experienced before Helen?

But divorce was sinful. The only reason the church allowed it was if your spouse was an adulterer. Unfortunately, in his case it was Doris who could divorce him and still remain a part of the Church. He wasn't ready to give Helen up, and he didn't want to leave the Church. The two alternatives were so damn incompatible. He had prayed, but his prayers went unanswered.

Walter traveled his route, made his stops, sold his brushes by rote. Without concentrating, he still made most of the sales. His mind never left his predicament until finally he arrived at Helen's apartment. It was eight-thirty in the evening, and he was exhausted from the additional driving. Dragging himself up the three flights of stairs, he took out the key she had given him, unlocked the door and, greeted by the smell of steaks cooking, he stared at the final flight. As he reached the top step, Helen was there with a cold beer in each hand. He took the drink, touched his glass to hers and took a deep swallow.

"Slow down," she said gaily.

He took her in his arms and held her tightly.

"You're breaking my ribs. What's the matter?"

"The matter is I love you and I'm not supposed to. It's a transgression. I'm an adulterer and there's nothing I can do about it because I care for you too much. Why should that be a sin?"

Helen led him to the couch.

"Walter, I'm sorry, but I don't share your view of God. We're human and people make mistakes and take happiness when they can without thinking it's a sin. I see a good man, a man I care for, but you must choose between me and your family. And if your God says you can't have me, I guess you must choose between your God and me."

"I'm not a good man. I've sinned against God." He fell onto the couch, covering his face with his hands.

"Only if you believe you have."

"I can't lose you, Helen. What am I to do?"

"Only you can choose. I've already decided I want you, in spite of the teachings of my church. Now you must decide how much you want me."

"According to my religion, if I divorce Doris I must leave the church."

"I can't help you choose. I can only hope."

After dinner, Walter led Helen to the bedroom. When their love-making was ended, she lay in his arms. He lit two cigarettes, passed one to her and watched the smoke rise and take on its free form. He was content, at peace, when he was with her. His anger, his pent up frustration was gone. Helen stubbed out her cigarette and climbed on top of him. Her sinewy body gave off a warmth and security. He felt her small, firm breasts against him. She looked down, smiling, and with her pinkie, slowly traced the outline of his moustache.

"You have told me about a Walter I don't know. I'm only aware of a good sweet man and yet I only know him when he's an adulterer," she said in a soft voice.

"Helen, move to Calvert. Travel with me. I can't be without you and I need time to work everything out."

"You want to have your cake and eat it, too. Is that fair to me?"

He kissed her breasts as she continued.

"Walter, you can't be serious. How can I afford to support myself without working? You can't pay for two families. It doesn't make sense."

"Please. If you lived in Calvert, you could work weekends and travel with me during the week. It won't be forever. A year at the most. Give me a chance to figure out how to do it. Please think it over. With you at my side I could sell twice as many brushes." Walter was shocked at his own suggestion. Was he crazy, committing himself? He didn't care. He would work it out.

For the next two nights, they talked of their plans. When Walter left Thursday morning it was settled. Helen would move to Calvert. They would try it out. She walked him to his car.

"I won't be your mistress forever, Walter."

"Give me a year."

They kissed. She watched until he turned the corner and she could see him no more.

CHAPTER SIX

She must be insane, she thought, as she sat, stretched out on her couch, slowly, methodically stroking Rex. The cat was purring with a contentment that was eluding Helen. What was it about this lean, dapper, little man that attracted her to him? She had been with other men who would have more appeal to most women. But not to Helen.

And she believed she knew why! Her childhood was filled with frightful memories of a father who deserted her, a stepfather who abused her mother and eventually took his pleasure with Helen. She had just turned thirteen when Hank came to her room. At first, he spoke to her as an adult would a child, asking about school and friends. She had been lying on her bed reading and became uncomfortable as he sat next to her.

As she answered him, she started to get off the bed but her stepfather took her arm and pulled her back down with a gentle but firm hand.

"Let me rub your back," he suggested.

"No. That's all right," came her nervous reply.

"Why don't you like me?"

She wanted to tell him that she despised him for the way he treated her mother but she was too frightened. "Please," she said.

But it was too late. With an overwhelming strength he took her. It was quick but forever left its ugly scar.

"If you tell anyone I'll kill you," he told her after he was done. She believed him.

Helen felt helpless and alone and she receded inside herself. She couldn't tell her mother, who was powerless against Hank. A month later he took her again and once more threatened her. She vowed this would be the last time.

"If I tell, you'll kill me?" she asked.

"You'd better believe it, Missy."

She went to her bureau and took out a kitchen knife she had stored away. "And if you ever touch me again, I'll kill you. Believe me. You'll go to sleep one night and never wake up."

"Bitch," he replied. "I'm done with you anyway, you scrawny slut."

He never did approach her again. But Helen knew how he relished being cruel to her mother in front of her. As much as her mother was afraid of him she was more fearful of being without a man. Helen swore she would never allow any man to treat her that way, but she didn't keep her promise.

Helen escaped by marrying a "Hank Junior" when she was sixteen. Rock was a truck driver twelve years her senior. He had his own home which was more a shack than a house.

She had dreamed of extraordinary consensual sex but it wasn't to be. Fact was she came to abhor it and would perform the act as seldom as she could. She knew Rock expected it when he returned from a run and doing it was preferable to fighting and being abused. The marriage lasted only a few years before Rock found another woman and left as quickly as he had arrived.

After the break up of the marriage, she enrolled in modeling school. The agency connected with the school got her jobs at bachelor parties and stags. They claimed it was where you had to start. She enjoyed the work for a while, finding a certain satisfaction and safety in taunting men with her body. But when she saw it wasn't leading anywhere or paying the rent, she got a job pumping gas. She hoped that would tide her over until her career took off, but it worked the other way around.

She became proficient as a mechanic and bookkeeper. Her boss was generous and rewarded her by giving her his job running the station, allowing him to open another a few miles away.

Helen wasn't one for lots of friends, but would occasionally date. No one ever suited her. She knew she was attractive, but the men wanted what she wasn't ready to give and she feared the pressure. That was until Walter.

Helen continued to stroke Rex. Why was Walter different? He was like a child full of wonder at her beauty. He worried about his son and believed in his God. He was never aggressive with her or demanding. Instead he appreciated her. He loved her in a way that was foreign to her and this brought out a craving she had never known or believed possible. At last, she enjoyed being with a man in bed.

Helen hadn't lied to Walter, but she certainly hadn't told him everything either. Now he wanted her to move to Calvert and become his... call it what it was Helen, become his mistress. Could he ever leave his wife? What would be the consequences to his son? She had her own happiness to worry about.

Yes, Walter was different from her other boyfriends. Not as good looking but it wasn't looks that mattered to Helen. No one had ever loved or needed her so completely and that was important to her. In fact it was everything.

℘

Three weeks later Helen moved to Calvert. Walter found a small apartment for her and they fixed it up together.

Helen accepted the fact that she would not be with Walter Friday through Sunday. He picked her up each Monday and together they worked the territory. They were a wonderful team, and sales increased to almost double. Each Thursday evening, he would drop her off at her apartment and return to Doris and Pip.

She had no trouble finding a weekend job pumping gas and servicing cars. The owner was reluctant at first.

"You a woman mechanic, too?"

"Uh huh."

"I don't know. You say you want to work weekends?"

"Yes."

"Maybe you've been sent from heaven."

"You might be right."

"A woman mechanic who wants to work weekends." He shook his head. "What the hell, I'll give you a try."

45

CHAPTER SEVEN

Four months had passed since the conference with Mr. Perkins, and there hadn't been any trouble. The boy had learned his lesson. The Scriptures were right and the beatings had helped his son to find Christ. Walter was so busy with Helen he hardly noticed how quiet and withdrawn Pip had become.

The family attended church each Sunday. Walter no longer asked Jesus to forgive him. He knew there was no redemption without the promise of righteousness, and he wouldn't be giving up his adulterous ways. His hope was to save his son. That would have to be enough.

୫ଠ

The doorbell sounded as Walter was about to go out to pick up his new brushes. It was Friday morning. Pip was at school, and Doris was cleaning. Strange time for someone to be calling.

"I'll get it," he hollered.

"Walter Marshall?"

A policeman stood at the door. His voice was crisp and official sounding. What would an officer want with him? He thought of Helen. Was he being arrested for adultery? No, that was ridiculous.

"Yes."

"I'm Sergeant Conolly of the Calvert police. I'm sorry to tell you this, sir, but your son has climbed to the roof of the Calvert Christian Church and is threatening to jump."

"What?"

Doris joined her husband, wiping her hands. "Is everything all right?"

"You'd better get over there right away. I can take you or you can follow me."

"Yes, of course. We'll follow you."

Walter took Doris by the arm and led her to the car as he explained.

They drove behind the squad car, siren blaring, lights flashing. "Sweet Jesus, help me, help my boy," Walter mumbled as he drove.

When they arrived at the school, Walter saw a crowd gaping upward. He looked to the roof, not believing what he saw.

"Oh, no, no," he gasped. Immediately he made a deal with Jesus. Save my boy he prayed, and I'll repent.

Pip's arm was around the steeple, his feet on the roof. His body formed an arc, which swayed precariously in the air. He was shouting something. Walter broke through the crowd and hollered up to him. The people quieted.

"Pip, Pip, what are you doing up there? Please come down."

"I want to jump. I want to join Jesus in eternal bliss."

"Suicide's a sin. You'll be denied heaven if you jump," Pastor Warren hollered. "Come down, Pip, and Jesus will surely forgive you."

"Tell me Jesus might not exist, Pastor, and I'll come down."

"But He does exist, son," the Minister shouted back.

"Can't you be wrong? Can't the Jews be right or the Buddhists, or some other religion? How do you know Jesus is the Savior?" Pip shot back.

"I know, Pip, and if you come down I'll try extra hard to help you find him."

"Tell me he doesn't exist, Pastor, or I'll jump. Just tell me he might not exist."

"I can't do that."

Walter grabbed the Pastor by the arm. "For God's sake, it will keep him from jumping. Tell him Christ might not exist."

Pastor Warren seemed to consider this momentarily, then nodded. "Christ may not exist, Pip," he called up to the boy on the roof.

"Now I want everyone in the school to tell me Christ might not exist, and I'll come down. If they don't, I'll jump. I mean it."

Walter again spoke to the Pastor. "Have them do it." Each told Pip Christ possibly wasn't the Savior until a thin girl, the last to take a turn, looked up at him. Pip recognized Kristen Allen. There was some sort of awful story about her.

"Please, Pip, don't make me say it. I just recently found Jesus and it would hurt me too much to betray my Savior. Please."

Pip stared at the girl, silently at first. He considered letting go, flying to his death but he couldn't do it to this sweet girl. He envied her, her faith. If only he could believe as she did how good things would be. And if he couldn't embrace Jesus, why couldn't he at least fake it.

"It's okay, Kristen. You don't have to say it," he finally replied.

Then the officer in charge spoke. "You made a deal, son. We did our part. Now it's your turn. We're sending someone to help you down?"

Walter watched as an officer appeared on the roof with rope around his shoulder. He tied the line to his waist and then around Pip.

Jesus would never save the son of an evil sinner. The Lord didn't have time for those who didn't follow Him in deed. Walter knew it was his fault Pip was lost, and he now felt immense guilt as he feared for his son's life.

"Don't look down," he heard the officer say.

"Please be careful," Walter whispered to himself.

He watched the policeman take Pip's arm and gently help him from the steeple, then lead him to the trap-like door that was built to give workmen access to the roof.

Once on the ground, the officer in charge led Pip to a squad car as Doris and Walter ran to their boy.

"Where are you taking him?" she asked.

"To the state hospital for observation. You can come with him or meet us there."

"The nut house?" Walter asked.

"I'm afraid so. It's the law with an attempted suicide."

"Doris, you go with them, I'll get the car and meet you."

ဢ

Pip stayed at the hospital for a month. Doris and Walter were allowed to visit him in the evenings. Despite his anxiety over his son Walter continued his sales trips as he had to earn a living. Helen always went with him.

Walter suffered great remorse because he couldn't keep his promise to Jesus that he'd repent if his boy was rescued and he could never ask the Lord to trust him again.

ဢ

Pip wasn't allowed to leave his unit without permission. Each evening he and Doris would sit either in the common room or his bedroom. Sometimes they would walk the corridor. At first he talked more about the other patients than himself. Pip showed great compassion for them. He'd tell his mother of their sicknesses caused by an ill-fated love or alcohol or no apparent reason at all. It wasn't until half way through the third week that Pip spoke about his own problems.

"What I did was crazy," he told his mother. "I realize that. I just couldn't help myself."

"I know," Doris responded, not really knowing at all.

"I didn't want to be a disappointment to you or Dad. I was so confused. Don't you think I want to believe, be like all the others? I try. I want you to be proud of me." His lips quivered but he didn't cry.

"You're not a disappointment, not to me."

"It's just that I don't understand. So many religions. What makes ours the right one?" he went on.

Doris took his hand but didn't know how to answer.

"My doctor is Jewish. Did you know that? And he's very nice. I asked him about religion."

"What did he say?'

"He told me we each had to decide what was right for ourselves."

Doris nodded, wondering how Walter would handle this if he were here. Her husband was a fine man only doing as he did out of love for Pip and fear for the damnation of his son's soul. She, too, was a believer. But Pip was a good boy and maybe that was enough for God. No. That was blasphemous.

"I'll pray for you, son," she promised.

ଛ

Walter watched nervously as the doctor looked through some papers. It was the first time he'd ever seen a psychiatrist and he wondered if the doctor could read his thoughts.

"I've spent some time with Pip, and I think he'll be fine," the doctor told them.

"When can he go home?" Doris asked.

"Tomorrow. He wants to go to public school, and I think that would be best."

"He has no choice. His school called and told us they didn't want Pip to return. He's too disruptive. They said it wouldn't be fair to the other kids if he were to stay," Walter replied.

The doctor scanned some papers on his desk and then slowly looked up. His glasses rested on the tip of his nose, and he peered over them at Pip's parents.

"When we examined the boy, we saw bruises. Do you know how he got them?"

"We believe in the word of God, and when Pip doesn't live by that word, we're afraid for his eternal soul. I've had to discipline him. Can you understand that?"

"I don't wish to interfere with your beliefs. I just urge you to be gentle. The boy's been through a rough time. He's confused. He's a good lad. Give him a chance."

"We will," Doris responded, with a determination that surprised her husband.

℘

Pip entered Calvert High School half way through his freshman year. Jesus received His hour on Sunday. The rest of the boy's time was spent working on non-parochial activities.

As if his sadness had inhibited his stature, Pip enjoyed a burst of growth. He showed a new ambition, and his grades reflected his work. He joined the wrestling team and attacked his athletics with the same new fervor as his courses.

His weekdays consisted of school, practice and study. After supper each evening, he would go to his room, undress down to his shorts, lie on top of the upper bunk surrounded by books and papers, and work until sleep overtook him. When he could study no longer, he would reach over and turn off his light, and not stir until the next morning when he would jump out of bed, eager to get going.

Doris noticed a change not only in Pip, but in her husband. He appeared relaxed, more at peace with himself. Most surprising was his attitude toward his work. When he left each Monday, he never complained.

Walter accepted Pip's dismissal from the Calvert Christian School with astonishing calmness. He even attended his son's wrestling matches when he was home.

Doris wasn't sure what had caused this change in her husband, but whatever it was, she was grateful for it.

℘

Sitting between Doris and Walter each Sunday, Pip participated in the church service, singing with gusto, partaking in the responsive readings and looking attentively at the minister during the sermon. Nothing had changed in his heart, but he did it for his parents.

After services, a few months after entering Calvert High, a young woman approached him.

"How have you been doing, Pip?"

The girl nervously played with her hands. It was Kristen, the one who couldn't forsake her God.

"I'm fine," he replied.

"I was watching you at services. I knew if you gave Jesus a chance you would find him. I'm so glad."

"Thank you," Pip replied.

"Well, bye."

CHAPTER EIGHT

"I'll see you Thursday. You have my schedule."

Walter bent over and brushed Doris's cheek with his lips. She looked up at him, taking a moment from her dusting to acknowledge his leaving.

His life was becoming routine, and he was comfortable with the arrangement. He drove to Helen's apartment and honked the horn twice before she came to the door, waved and disappeared back into the apartment. She hadn't mentioned marriage since Pip had been in the hospital eight weeks ago, and that was fine with him. He watched as she reappeared, locked her door, and walked toward him, a small overnight bag in her hand.

She got into the car, leaned over and planted a kiss on his lips.

"Hi, honey," she said.

"How are you doing?" He put the car in gear and headed for the highway.

"Great, now that I'm with you." She smiled, then became serious. "Walter, honey, we have to talk."

He knew what was coming. It had been too good to last.

"It hasn't been easy for you these past weeks, the scare that Pip gave you and all. I don't want to sound selfish but..."

"I know. I'm not being fair."

"You did promise to make an honest woman out of me."

There was a silence. Helen looked at Walter.

"What are you thinking?" she finally asked.

He was again dwelling on his religious beliefs. Since he had met her he certainly was less dogmatic. He'd been so sure, so damn sure. But now? He didn't know. He wanted to tell Helen he needed more time, time to straighten out his relationship with his son, if it wasn't already too late. And yet he didn't want to hurt this woman whom he loved more than he thought possible.

"There was a time when I believed that anyone who lived like I am was heading straight to hell in a hand basket."

"You mean an adulterer. Can't you say the word?"

He paused, gathering his thoughts. "I no longer believe my feelings for you are bad. I'm confused. All this happiness can't be a sin."

Helen took his hand. "That's sweet, Walter. But still someone has to be hurt. If you want me, you must leave Doris."

"Give me another month, two at the outside. Let me just be sure Pip can handle it."

ℰℭ

"Nice fight, Son."

Pip was surprised that the football coach was at his match or even knew who he was.

"Coach Harvey said I should come watch you. He thought you had natural ability and with some proper coaching could learn to play football. How do you feel about that idea?"

Norm Shepherd stood six foot, two inches. He was not only tall, he was big and totally bald, which added to his tough, formidable appearance. His oversized hairless head sat on a bull neck.

"I've never played football."

"You're an athlete, boy. Your coach tells me you're not afraid of hard work. He tells me you're a winner. Come out for spring practice. I'll teach you to play football. I like your quickness and tenacity. In the meantime, keep lifting weights and eat lots of potatoes. I need a little more meat on those bones."

"I'll try, Coach. Thanks. Thanks a lot."

Coach Shepherd slapped Pip on the back and turned to leave. As the boy watched him walk down the hall, a huge grin spread slowly across his face.

ℰℭ

"Three Bs, two Cs. I'm proud of you, son," Walter said.

It was Thursday night. He was sitting at the kitchen table as Pip was setting it, and Doris was making supper. Walter could feel their relationship growing stronger. "You know what I like even more, Pip? I like the comments. They all say that even though you started in the middle of the year, you're doing real well."

"There's more, sir. The football coach asked me to try out for the team. What do you think?"

"Football, huh? I think it's great. Coach went up to you?"

"Yes. Says I'm an athlete."

"Football," Doris interjected. "I don't want you playing football. It's dangerous. No. Stick to your wrestling. That's risky enough."

"Builds character, Doris. It's good for him."

"I don't know," she responded, shaking her head.

Walter fidgeted with the fork. "It's hard to say this, boy," Walter said. "I was wrong. You're much better off at Calvert High. I can see that now. Salvation comes from the Lord, and I can only guide you. You have to find Him for yourself."

"I'll try."

Walter put his arm around his son as Doris served the casserole.

"Get it while it's hot," she said.

ℜ

"I love watching you wrestle," the girl whispered to him. "You destroyed that guy."

Pip looked over at Mary Lou Osgood sitting at the desk next to him. It wasn't that he hadn't noticed her before. She sat beside him in math class every day. He had a crush on her that seemed to paralyze him. Each day he could only manage a nod to her or mumble a hello. Every time he thought he had built up enough courage to say something more, his mouth went dry.

She was thin, maybe skinny, with small, new breasts, and waist-length brown, thoroughly combed out hair. Her tortoise framed glasses seemed to add to her image of self- assuredness. The only time she was without her glasses was when she was cheer-leading. She performed with an enthusiasm that left the impression any success the basketball team had was due to her.

"Thank you," he replied. "Do you go to many matches?"

"When I can. I'll be there this afternoon."

"I'll try extra hard."

The teacher began his lecture, but Pip heard little of the lesson. He was thinking about Mary Lou, his eyes focused on her ankle socks with their delicately embroidered edge.

ℜ

Knowing Mary Lou was in the little gallery of spectators added to Pip's intensity. He had been nervous all day. What if his opponent was better than he was? Pip had lost one match and that happened in only his second outing.

Once he was on the mat his concentration was entirely on his opponent. He knew it was the only way to be victorious. He pinned his adversary in less than ninety seconds.

As he sat down in the gallery to watch the other matches and cheer the team on, he looked for Mary Lou. She was sitting with another girl and waved at him as their eyes met. When he boldly approached her, the other girl stood to leave, saying, "I'll call you tonight."

Mary Lou nodded to her friend before turning her attention to Pip. "Good going, Tiger."

"Thanks," he replied, trying to work up the courage to add to the conversation. Why was he tongue-tied when it came to her?

"How about walking me home?" she asked.

"Sure, great. Let me shower and change. I'll be with you in a moment, okay?"

"Okay, tiger."

As he ran off to the locker room he wondered where she lived. What did he care? He was going to walk her home. He heard the spectators cheering his teammates. Suddenly, he remembered the wrestling match. My God, he wasn't supposed to leave until it was over. He'd forgotten all about it. The hell with it. Opportunity may only knock once.

℘

"I'm going to pick up my brushes and then do some errands. I'll be home by supper."

Doris stopped folding the laundry long enough to nod good-bye.

It was Friday. Walter spent the morning at his house doing his paper work. He would visit Helen at the gas station after he picked up his week's supply of brushes. It had become his custom to fill his tank with gas on Fridays. It gave him a few stolen moments before the long weekend without her. He also wanted to make Pip's match.

"Fill 'er up. And check the oil. I like to watch your rear end when you're under the hood."

"Walter, you're terrible. I'll be off in fifteen minutes. Can you bring me home? My car wouldn't start today so I took a cab."

"You're a mechanic. Can't you fix your own car?"

"I didn't have time. I'll fix it tonight. Nothing else to do."

Her sarcastic tone wasn't lost on him. "Sure. I'll read my paper while I wait." Walter checked his watch. No way to make the match. It was more like twenty minutes but he didn't mind. He half read the paper, half watched Helen. She was so independent, so sure of herself. He was a lucky man. He had to speak to Doris, he promised himself again. It would be painful but it had to be done.

"Ready," Helen said as she got into the car.

They drove to her apartment in silence, holding hands.

"Goodnight, Walter. I'll see you Monday. Be a good boy."

I'll walk you to the door," he said impulsively, wanting his time with her to last.

ℰ

"Where do you live?" Pip asked.

"South end. I live with my mom in an apartment. We used to live in a big house but that was before the divorce."

"Your parents are divorced?"

"Last year. It was real lousy."

"I don't think my parents would ever get divorced. It's against their religion... our religion."

He thought how his father would be pleased that he had included himself.

"Do you live near here?" Mary Lou asked.

"The opposite direction."

"I'm sorry."

"Oh, I don't mind. I'll run home after I leave you."

"With all those books?"

"I don't mind."

She put her arm through his, and his heart skipped a few beats.

"How do you like Calvert High?" she asked.

"Very much."

"Is it true what I heard?"

Pip became nervous.

"What did you hear?"

"That you threatened to jump off the roof of your school if the teacher didn't say Christ wasn't God?"

"Yeah. Something like that. I was pretty screwed up."

"I'm sorry. Did I embarrass you? That was stupid of me."

"It's okay."

"That's where I live," Mary Lou said, pointing to a brick apartment building across the street.

They walked up the stairs to the front door, which opened into a vestibule. Mailboxes for the tenants covered the left side. The right wall and floor were white marble, yellowed by time.

"I have to check for mail," Mary Lou said as she opened her box with a little key. It was empty. "I never get mail. Would you write to me?"

Pip laughed as Mary Lou took out the key that would bring them past the foyer into the apartment building. She piled her books on his already full arms and opened the door.

"Well, thanks for walking me home."

At the door to the first apartment a man was kissing a woman.

Pip stopped short unable to believe his eyes.

"Dad," the boy gasped.

Dropping the books, he put his arm over his eyes as if that would make it all go away then turned and started to run.

"Oh, no. Oh, no, it can't be," the man blurted out. "Oh God, no."

છ

Pip ran into the night. Sweat poured down his face in spite of the cool winter air. He felt no fatigue as he raced toward his home. Tears rolled down his face, and he hollered over and over into the empty streets, "You hypocrite. You fucking hypocrite."

A car slowed down and drove beside him. The honking of the horn brought him out of his thoughts. It was his father. Walter rolled down the window and shouted to his son.

"Pip, Pip, please get into the car. Let me talk to you."

The boy stopped running and glared at this stranger. "I don't want to hear anything you have to say."

"Please, Philip. Please get inside the car."

Pip opened the door and got in. He buried his face in his hands and bent over so that his knees almost touched them. He shook off the arm his father tried to put around him.

"Don't touch me."

"Pip, I can only be honest with you and somehow hope that will be enough. It may hurt, but I don't know what else to do."

"You have a whore. You're an adulterer. You told me I was a sinner. What the hell does that make you?"

"A hypocrite, a sinner, an adulterer. I can't blame you. Please, son, if you ever had any love for me, give me a chance to have my say."

"What about Mom? Did you forget about your Christian wife?"

Walter started to cry, at first softly and then with more force. Pip had never seen his father weep.

"No, I haven't forgotten your Mom. I don't want to hurt her. That's why I've been sneaking around like a thief. I told myself that I was possessed by the devil, that it wasn't my fault. Before this happened, I believed all that I taught you. Life was simple. I knew what was right."

"Who is she?"

"She's a good woman. I want to marry her."

Pip couldn't comprehend what his father was saying. In a matter of minutes his world had collapsed. He wiped the tears from his face with the back of his hand and tried to catch his breath before replying. "No, you can't. What about mother? You can't do that to her. It'll hurt her so much. You said you loved me. Do it for me. Please, Father. You're all she's got. Please, I beg you."

Walter began to hyperventilate. "I love Helen. She's my life, my whole happiness. Don't do this to me. Please."

Pip looked up. "Don't do this to you? You bastard," he spat out. "What about the things you've done to me? I hate you and your whore. You're a fucking adulterer. You think only of yourself."

Pip opened the door and jumped out of the car. "I wish you were dead." He slammed the door and ran into the night.

෨

Doris was setting the table when Walter got home.

"Is Pip here?" he asked.

"Thank God, you're home. Something's going on with him. He's in his room. He ran into the house, not even a hello." Walter sat down at the kitchen table, not knowing what to say. He took out his handkerchief and mopped his brow.

"Is something wrong?" Doris asked. "You look funny."

"No," he replied automatically. "Well, yes. Yes, something is wrong. Sit down, Doris."

She did as she was told.

"Doris, I'm sorry, I'm sorry for what I'm going to tell you."

"Walter, what is it?"

He saw the fear in her eyes. "It's not your fault, Doris. It's mine. I'm leaving. I want a divorce. I'm sorry." His calmness surprised him. There was a feeling of relief as the words tumbled out.

"No. No, you can't. Why? When? When are you leaving?" she asked.

"Tonight, Doris. I think that will be best." He played with one end of his mustache, feeling the stiff wax between his fingers.

"What about the boy, Walter? What about PIp? "

"He knows. I'll say good-bye before I leave."

Doris wailed as she ran to her husband, grabbing him by his shirt. "No, Walter, don't leave. You can't. What will we do? What will become of us?"

He knew this was the time to make the separation. He didn't want to hurt Doris but there was no choice.

Pushing her aside, he walked toward the stairwell. Doris called after him. "Walter."

"Yes?"

"I hate you, Walter. You will burn in hell."

"I know."

Walter moved out that evening.

CHAPTER NINE

Walter tried to re-establish a relationship with his son, but the boy would have none of it.

A month after he left his family, he telephoned. "Pip, have dinner with me."

"No."

"I'm moving to Ashton. I don't want to lose touch. Let me see you before I leave, please."

"Rot in hell," Pip replied.

There was a pause. Pip knew his words would have resulted in a beating only a few months ago. Now he was beyond his father's temper.

"I'm sorry, Son."

"If you're sorry, why did you leave? `As you sow, so shall you reap." He relished assailing Walter with a quotation from his precious Bible.

"If you ever decide to forgive me, I'll be there for you. I don't know what else I can do."

Pip's only response was to hang up the phone.

⁊

It was a cool early spring afternoon. Pip wondered if he was making a mistake. He surveyed his teammates. Although he had grown, put on weight, at five ten and one hundred and forty-five pounds, he was still one of the smallest boys on the practice field. There were a couple of other guys from the wrestling squad, both in a heavier weight class. Everyone else was a new face.

He stood around feeling out of place, not talking to anyone, until the coach blew the whistle and waved to the team to gather round.

"Good afternoon, men. Today will be our first and last easy workout. After we finish with calisthenics, you are to report to the equipment room for your gear. Practice will be from three-thirty to five-thirty for the next five weeks. When spring practice ends, I expect you to keep in shape, so that when you report to me on August fifteenth you will be ready and raring to go. From then until we win the championship in November, you'll be mine.

"That doesn't mean you don't study. I expect hard work on the field and high grades in the classroom. If you have problems, I'm available to help you. Now, can we go all the way?"

"Yes!" came the response in unison.

"Are we winners?"

"Yes!" they shouted.

"Okay, let's get started. Five laps around the field and then some calisthenics."

The boys started running. Pip joined the pack. Soon he was in the lead, and as they finished he was half a lap ahead of his nearest team-mate.

There was a broad grin on Coach Shepherd's face as he looked up from his stop-watch, then back down to double check Pip's time.

ℰ

"I'm home," Pip hollered as he came through the door.

"Wash your hands and come in for supper," Doris responded.

"Whose house did you clean today?"

"Mrs. Powers. It's only her and her husband. She's very nice, and it's an easy place to keep tidy."

Doris had been cleaning for folks since Walter left. A lady from the church asked her if she would be interested in doing a little housework. Doris wasn't sure and talked it over with Pip. She had come to lean on the boy since the divorce, his encouragement helping her to face each new day. Pip thought it would be a great idea. They needed the money; she could make her own hours. Soon after Doris started, it seemed everyone wanted to hire her. She was able to increase her prices and chose her employers carefully.

"I'm starved," Pip said as he filled the water glasses. "What's for supper?"

"Pork pie. How was school?"

"Good. I had football practice today."

"That's right, too. How was it?"

"I don't know yet."

"It's a dangerous sport, Pip. I wish you'd think it over."

He saw the worried look on her face.

"I think I could be good."

"What if you get hurt?"

"Don't worry. I'll be careful."

"Sometimes I wish your father were here to help bring you up."

"Don't say that. Don't ever say that. You're doing a wonderful job." Pip knew his mother still missed Walter. This made him angry, though not toward her.

"I just worry..."

Her words trailed off as Pip put his arm around her. "Well, don't. You're doing... we're doing fine."

ॐ

"It'll take more than one bar of soap to get the dirt off you," Bob Burns said.

The left guard whose locker was next to Pip's was the biggest boy on the team. He was an excellent football player and colleges were falling over themselves trying to recruit him. Pip was fascinated by all the attention schools were giving this big, left guard.

"Listen, Bob, if you would make a larger hole for me, I wouldn't get tackled in that mud bowl they call a field."

Bob laughed. "You listen, little buddy, if you weren't so slow you wouldn't always be getting caught."

"Thanks, pal."

"I think Coach Shepherd's going to start you. You've impressed him."

"Oh, I don't think so. Alvin's a senior and started last year," Pip replied, hoping Bob could be right.

He looked at his filthy uniform crumpled on the floor. His bones ached. What a sport. He picked up his bar of soap and headed for the shower.

"Hey, Pip, I heard that you were in the nuthouse. Is that true?"

Pip spun toward the voice. It was Alvin Lewy, the senior halfback. He knew Alvin didn't like his starting berth being threatened by a new inexperienced kid. Pip had enjoyed the competition. It got his juices going and brought out the best in him. Apparently, it didn't do the same for Alvin.

"You heard me. You ain't deaf too, are you? I wanted to know how you liked being in the nuthouse!"

Although Pip had suspected that some students knew, he had never spoken about it with anyone but Mary Lou. He felt the blood rush to his head.

"What difference is it to you?" he responded, continuing toward the shower.

"We don't want no nuts on our team," Alvin responded, yanking Pip toward him. "Don't walk away from me when I'm talking to you, nut." Saliva flew out of the boy's mouth as he spoke. Pip wiped the spit from his face. Teammates attracted by the altercation started gathering around the two adversaries.

"Take your hands off me."

Alvin was half a head taller than Pip.

"Who's going to make me, you little fruitcake?"

Overwhelmed with anger and without considering his actions, Pip punched his antagonist with a left to the stomach. As the boy folded in half, Pip swung again, so hard his body left the ground. He landed a right to the jaw. Alvin fell like a stone on the cement floor, out cold.

"Wow, little guy, not bad," Bob Burns said.

Alvin began to come around. He looked up at the crowd of nude and partially clad teammates and then at Pip. "You son-of-a-bitch," he cursed. "I'll get you for this." There wasn't much enthusiasm in his threat.

"Next time don't make fun of a crazy person," Pip said. "You never know what he might do."

ॐ

"We've worked hard for today. It's the first game and I know you're nervous. Use that energy to our advantage. Play tough every minute you're on the field. Use your body and your mind every moment. Concentrate. Remember Riverdale is as nervous as you are. Now get out there and win."

Coach Shepherd believed the boys were ready. Although you could never tell for sure in this business, his team might be extraordinary and he knew why.

As the players ran to the field, he called to Pip. "How do you feel, Son?"

"Nervous, Coach."

"You're fast, and you're strong. You have the ability. Today we'll find out if you have the instinct and the courage I think you have."

"Thanks, Coach."

The stands were full. Mary Lou was at the sideline in her cheerleader's uniform. Their eyes met and she waved her megaphone at him. He smiled in return before surveying the stands, looking for his mother. He couldn't find her. Chills ran through him as the band played "The Star Spangled Banner." As the national anthem came to an end, and the crowd roared its encouragement, Pip's legs started to run in place, as though he was reving up the engine of his body. He couldn't stand still as he watched the coin toss. Calvert to receive.

On the first play from scrimmage, the quarterback handed the ball to Pip who picked up twelve yards behind Bob. The crowd roared.

"Not bad, little guy." The big guard smiled at him back in the huddle.

Before the game was over, Pip would carry the ball seventeen times for one hundred and thirty six yards, leading Calvert to a twenty-six to thirteen victory over Riverdale. He thought he had done well. The hugs and accolades of his teammates and fans confirmed it.

સ

It was the fall of Pip's junior year.

"You're not just an athlete," Coach Shepherd told him. "It's important that you get the best education you can. Football is a means, not an end. Understand?"

"Yes, Sir."

"You do well in history and civics and better in English than math or science," he said, putting his hand on Pip's shoulder. "What do you want to study?"

"I'm not sure. I think I would like to be a lawyer."

"You'd be a good lawyer, Pip, but it's not easy, four years of undergraduate and three years of law school."

"I can do it, if I have the chance."

"Well, let's see what I can do to help."

સ

After the last game of Pip's junior year, the coach accompanied by another man, went to the locker room. They watched the boys celebrate another championship season. After the team had exhausted itself with screams of joy, the coach went over to his star.

"I want you to meet someone, Pip."

"Yes, Coach."

"This is Pete Brindisi."

64

"Nice game, Son."

"Thank you, Sir."

"Pete is a scout at the University of Michigan. He came down to watch you today. I didn't want to tell you until after the game."

"I'd like you to visit Michigan as my guest. I've asked Coach Shepherd to come with you. I want you to see our program."

❧

"They can't promise you law school, Son," Coach Shepherd told Pip on the plane trip home from Michigan. "But they have one of the best in the country. The coach gave me his word that if you give him the grades, he'll go to bat for you. They've offered you a full scholarship, room, board, and tuition."

"That's incredible, Coach. How can I ever repay you?"

"Don't you understand, boy? You already have. You're my legacy. A coach can only hope to discover one Pip Marshall. Just do me proud, Son."

❧

By the end of his senior season, Pip held a pocketful of records, and his team had won the state championship for the third straight year. Doris never missed a home game. Walter was frequently in the stands but Pip never knew.

CHAPTER TEN

"Dan, this is Lew Plaisted, Michigan coach."

"Hey, Lew, good to hear your voice. Congratulations. That was quite a season."

"Thanks. Listen Dan, I have a client for you that's going to make your day. How would you like to represent Philip Marshall?"

Dan Lamb, one of the foremost sports attorneys in the country was tough but fair, able to evaluate a situation and know when to agree and when to fight for more. He had the respect of both owners and his player-clients. He chose his clients carefully. Dan, along with the rest of the country, had followed Pip's career.

Pip Marshall had led Michigan to two undefeated seasons, a Rose Bowl victory, and two undisputed national championship. He compiled numerous records along the way, and was a candidate for the Heisman Trophy.

"He'll play anywhere you tell him," Lew said. "He knows he can trust you. But part of the deal must be that he'll be free each spring semester to attend law school at Michigan with no claims on him by the team. He's very serious about getting his law degree."

"He's married, isn't he?" Dan asked.

"To his high school sweetheart. She also plans to go to law school. They're both single-minded achievers. I want you to meet them."

෨

Dan took an immediate liking to Mary Lou and Philip Marshall. Pip was different from most of his clients. Dan sensed that football really wasn't an end but rather the means.

"I want to build a nest egg while I'm in law school."

"I understand and I'll get you what you want. Now tell me your secret. How did you carry the ball as many times as you did without fumbling?"

Pip held up his hands, fingers spread wide apart. "Glue!"

෨

Jake French knew next season could well be his last. You didn't keep your job in the National Football League if you didn't produce. Management had forgiven him this past year of three wins and thirteen losses. It was the coach's first season in the pro's and he certainly hadn't inherited much talent. The year before he took over, the team had won only two games, and his bosses had told him the first season could be a rebuilding one.

While most of the other teams in the National Football League were playing to sell out crowds, his club couldn't fill the stadium no matter who they played. The bottom line was making money and that required a winning team.

In this year's draft, there was no question who would go first. There was only one college athlete capable of turning a franchise around, and that was Pip Marshall. Jake had the first pick in the draft, but The Boston Patriots of the American Football League were competing with him for Marshall, and there was talk that money would not stand in the way of Boston getting him. He'd heard that eight hundred thousand dollars wouldn't be out of the question. His owners would never match that. Dan Lamb, who hailed from New England, and was known to have a solid relationship with Boston management was representing Marshall. Why couldn't there have been two Marshalls this year?

Jake had met with his scouts and assistant coaches. They couldn't agree upon anyone but Marshall for their first pick. But it was too dangerous. If he drafted Marshall and couldn't sign him, he would miss any chance of turning things around. Better to play it safe and choose a player he knew he could sign.

Wearily, he sat at his desk reviewing the stat sheets on the other potential candidates. He'd been at it for three hours, knowing the final decision had to be his. Placing the papers on his desk, he put his arms up over his head and stretched, letting out a loud groan.

"Shit," he said to the empty room. "What the hell am I going to do?"

He smiled as he realized he was talking to himself. As if to torture himself further, he picked up the stat sheet on Marshall. His eyes fell on the words, "Calvert High School." Why did that sound familiar? He went to his file cabinet, opened the drawer on active player personnel and browsed through each folder until he found what he was looking for. Maybe he could get Pip Marshall after all. It was an outside chance, not one hundred percent kosher, but he had no choice.

૬૭

Mary Lou was surprised when her husband announced that his old team mate Bob Burns had invited them to "The Rooster Tail" in Detroit, for dinner.

"Wow, pretty classy. I didn't think linemen did so well. What's he doing in Ann Arbor?" she asked.

"He was vague on the phone. Just said he had to be here on business and asked to take us out."

"I'll pass up an evening of studying for "The Rooster Tail" anytime," Mary Lou said. "What's he like? I never really knew him in high school."

"A good guy. You'll enjoy him," he replied.

℘

The maitre d' took them to their table which overlooked the water. Yachts were tied up at the slips. Others were moored in the harbor.

"That's the way to live," said Bob, peering through the window.

"Not for struggling students," Mary Lou responded.

"It's not so great," Pip said. "Alumni have taken me out. They kept slapping me on the back and saying, isn't this the life. I was afraid I would heave up my lunch."

"Your husband never had much class," Bob responded.

She laughed. "You're telling me."

Pip hadn't seen Bob Burns in seven years. He had followed his career as a guard for the Pacers, a man who got the job done, was consistent, but never made all-pro.

They studied the menu. Whenever Pip was entertained by scouts or alumni, entering this other world of genteel affluence he became the victim of culture shock. The prices always astounded him. The cost of a single meal could buy food for Mary Lou and himself for a week.

"Something to drink?" the wine steward asked.

"Champagne, Dom Perignon," Bob ordered.

"Very good, Sir."

"First class," Pip responded.

"Why not? The Pacers can afford it."

"Are they paying for the meal?" Mary Lou asked, suddenly on guard.

Bob changed the subject. "In high school, I thought you ran all those yards because of the holes I opened up for you. I guess it wasn't just me. You're some kind of football player."

"Actually it was you. But Michigan also had a few guards who were almost as big and tough."

"Aw, you're just saying that," he replied.

The wine steward brought the champagne, removing the cork with a flourish.

"It does tickle your nose," Mary Lou proclaimed as she took her first taste. "Hey, it's not bad. Maybe we should get a few bottles for the apartment. It would be a nice treat after a long night at the books."

Bob ordered another bottle with dinner. When the waiter asked them about dessert, he ordered three chocolate soufflés. Pip was too mellow from the Dom Perignon to protest.

"The champagne's getting to me. I have to go to the little girls' room," Mary Lou excused herself.

"She's great. You're lucky," Bob said as they both watched her walk off.

The two friends drank their coffee.

"You asked what brought me to Michigan. I said it was business. The business is you, Pip."

"Me?"

"I know I was good in high school, not bad at Auburn, but in the pro's I'm nothing special. I gave it my best shot but my career could be over. The coach has as much as told me so. At twenty-six, you're old in this league. New young bucks are forever breathing up your ass. Listen, Pip, I'm not a bull-shitter so I'm going to tell you straight out. Coach guaranteed me the starting position for next season if I can get you to sign."

"Bob, I've been negotiating with Boston. I prefer the American Football League. It's not as prestigious, but it will serve my purposes better."

"I hate asking you this, little guy," Bob said, taking his napkin in his huge paw and wiping the beads of sweat from his forehead. "But playing is an addiction. The crowds, the cheering, even the recognition for a big dumb Irish second-rate lineman is hard to give up. I would sell my soul for one more season... I guess maybe I have. Oh, fuck, I know I got no right to ask you."

Pip looked at his friend. He was twenty-six but looked years older, and the best part of his life was probably behind him. Seeing Bob reaffirmed his own decision to have professional football work for him. When he turned twenty-six, he was going to make damn sure his life would be beginning, not ending.

The waiter refilled their coffee cups.

"I don't know what to say, how to answer you," Pip began slowly. "I want to help you. It just isn't entirely up to me. I'll have to talk it over with Mary Lou...and my agent. I'll get back to you."

"I understand," Bob said. "At least we had a damn good meal on the Pacers."

"Listen," Pip responded. "We don't care where we live. The prospect of playing in a snowstorm in December is reason enough to look elsewhere. If we can do it, we will."

&

Just when the Boston fans were about to celebrate the beginning of a new era, Dan Lamb announced the signing of Pip Marshall by the Pacers. It was the only subject on sport talk-shows for days. Boston had offered a four-year contract at seven hundred and twenty-five thousand a year, but Marshall accepted six hundred and ninety from the Pacers, saying the prestige of playing in the National Football League was worth the difference.

&

Pip turned the franchise around. Jake French was hailed as a candidate for coach of the year. He knew he deserved it but not for his outstanding coaching.

Marshall piled up the yardage, and Jake's deal with Burns proved not to be as bad as the coach had feared. The big lineman cost the club forty grand but, surprisingly, he was earning his keep this year. Burns loved opening up holes for his old school-mate.

Occasionally, Bob would be interviewed. The fans never tired of hearing him tell of how small Marshall had been in high school. Advertising agencies discovered Marshall and Burns made a great duo in commercials as well as on the field.

The Pacers took a six and two record into their home game against the Giants. Eighty thousand screaming fans greeted their heroes. There was a sign draped along the third tier railing that must have been fifty feet long.

YOU CAN'T BEAT OUR MARSHALL PLAN

When Pip was introduced, the crowd went wild. He ran onto the field and slapped the hands of his teammates. Bob was waiting for him, his big mitt open and ready to be smacked by the friend who had done so much to change his life.

Burns only had to wait for the third down from scrimmage for the quarterback to call his play.

"Forty-three left on two. Halfback dive left."

He felt the adrenaline build and pump, build and pump. He had to make a hole for his man and, damn it, it would be there. All he had to do was move that two hundred and fifty pound hulk out of the way for a split second, and Pip would be through. He got down on his stance, not looking at his intended victim. It was a game of poker, cat and mouse. Mustn't give the play away.

"Hut one, hut two."

Bob now focused his attention on the tank he had to move aside. Planting his legs into the ground and with all his strength, he tried to push the lineman to the right. His body shot up as he aimed his shoulder pad at the man's gut. As he felt the involuntary movement of the giant, he intuitively knew Pip had crashed through. The opposing lineman tried vainly to reach over Bob, making a wild grab at the ball carrier. He missed but the force knocked Bob on his backside. Hearing a cracking noise as he landed he instantly knew he was hurt.

"Shit," he mumbled as the agony shot through him. He got to his feet. Pip had run for forty yards down to the Giants' thirty.

Bob hobbled back to the huddle. On the next play Pip scored and Burns had a chance to go to the sidelines and assess his injuries. The excitement from the fans pumped him to play through his pain. When the final gun went off announcing the Pacers victory, Bob struggled to the locker room.

For the next few days, he whirl pooled and worked with the trainer but the pain wouldn't go away. He procrastinated, not wanting to see the team doctor, afraid to confirm what he really already knew.

Serious preparation for next Sunday's game began on Wednesday. All the pain and suffering from the past battle was supposed to have been worked out in the first two days of easy drills. Slowly, he dressed for practice, hoping for a miracle that he knew wouldn't be coming. He could barely walk to the field as Pip came up behind him, whacking him on the butt.

"Come on, boy. Move your ass. We have work to do."

"I don't think I can, little buddy. It hurts too much." The smile vanished from Pip's face, as his friend continued.

"I can hardly walk."

"What's the matter?"

"It's my back, my legs. Something pulled. God, I don't know."

They were heading down a tunnel under the stands that led from the locker room onto the field. They saw a couple of reporters at the other end and stopped walking.

"What did the doc say?" Pip asked.

"I haven't gone yet. I was hoping I wouldn't have to but I can't practice. Shit."

"Go to the doctor, asshole. I'll tell the coach. See you at lunch."

෯

What's so important you had to call me away from practice?" Jake asked.

"You've a hurt player," Chip responded.

Chip Lowe was owned by Jake French and both knew it. He'd been a good orthopedic surgeon who had been felled by a malpractice suit. The jury had found negligence where he knew there had been none and awarded the defendant five-hundred-thousand dollars. He legally could have continued to practice but the system had destroyed his confidence, broken his spirit.

He applied and was hired by a small college as its athletic physician. Jake French had been the football coach. Chip didn't especially like Jake but each time the coach moved up the ladder, he took Chip with him. Now they were in the big time together, and Dr. Lowe knew the rules had changed. Winning had always been important but nothing compared to the pressure of the pros.

"Burns?" the coach asked.

"He has a herniated lumbar disc."

"English, Chip. Speak to me in English."

"He shouldn't play again this year. He should have surgery."

"What are the other alternatives?"

"There really aren't any."

Jake knew if he pushed Chip there would be a way that Burns could play. Not that the guard was so good. He had back ups who were as talented. It was the combination that worked. Burns knew when to open the hole, Marshall knew when it would be open. The timing between them was uncanny.

"Come on, Chip. This is old Jake here. I need him Sunday. What can we give him to take away the pain?"

Chip looked at the coach. He knew he would do Jake's bidding.

"I could give him a medrol dose pac."

"English, Chip."

"It's a steroid medicine that will cut down the inflammation and take away the pain, but he'll still have a herniated lumbar disc."

"Give him the medicine. I need him. We're talking potential championship here."

"He could end up a cripple. One wrong hit. At least, give Bob a choice," Chip said.

"Give him the medicine. Case closed."

∞

The score was fourteen to fourteen. It was the third down of the third quarter. Bob had been ferocious all game. The doc had truly worked a miracle. The team needed four yards for a first down.

"Forty-three left on three," the quarterback called.

Pip would be coming through his hole. He crouched down in his stance, facing his adversary, and listened to the cadence. "Hut one, hut two..." He was going to move this son-of-a-bitch to the left for a split moment as Pip passed by his right.

"Hut three..."

Bob's feet dug firmly into the ground. He mustered all the strength he could as his calves and thighs propelled him upward into his target. There was the familiar sound of his shoulder pads crashing into his opponent. The weight of the blow to his upper torso was immediately transferred to his lower back. He ignored the strange pop he heard and felt at the same time. His adversary involuntarily moved to the right. He knew Pip was past him from the shift of direction by the opposing lineman. Bob fell to the ground, knowing his job was done. This time there was no getting up.

Chip Lowe ran onto the field and spoke to him for only a moment before calling for the stretcher. Bob was carried to the ever-waiting ambulance. Within six minutes, the game resumed, the attention of the fans again riveted on the all-important contest. The Pacers lost twenty-eight to fourteen.

∞

"I've just come from the hospital," Pip announced to the team doctor.

He had gone to the small medical office, deep in the bowels of the stadium. Chip Lowe looked up.

"He may never walk again. I spoke to the doctor at the hospital. I told him about last week. You son-of-a-bitch, you masked his pain. He should have been operated on, not given that shit. You never gave him a chance."

"Oh, God, Pip, it wasn't my idea. I swear. I begged the coach..."

"Was there a gun to your head, you son-of-a-bitch? Was there?"

"What was I suppose to do?"

"You were supposed to tell the poor bastard he needed an operation. You were supposed to, at least, tell him his options."

Lowe started to sweat profusely as he put his head into his hands.

"I'm such a fuck-up," was all he muttered.

"Why? Why the hell did you do it?"

"I didn't want to. I begged Jake not to. I swear it on my mother's life."

"You'd sell your mother for a buck. I want the x-rays you took of Bob last week."

"I didn't take x-rays."

Pip grabbed Lowe by his shirt-front and pulled the doctor toward him so that their faces were but inches apart.

"Listen, you son-of-a bitch, Bob told me you took x-rays. I want them. I want them now." He stood over the doctor who was cowering in his chair, his hands shaking. The fucking liar...

"I'm not a fool. I destroyed them."

Pip walked over to a stack of x-rays lying carelessly in a pile. The task was easier than he expected. Bob's were on top, marked with his name and date.

"I suggest you pack your things and get out of here. If you ever practice medicine again, I'll have Bob file a malpractice suit that will make your past problems seem like a walk in the park. The only reason we aren't going after you now is you don't have a pot to piss in. When we sue the Pacers and that slime ball, French, we'll expect your cooperation."

ಬಿ

"Bob may never walk again," Pip said. He'd promised himself he would control the venom he had for this man.

"Football's a risky business."

Pip wondered if Lowe had spoken to the coach. French was acting too self-assured to know anything.

"It shouldn't be as risky as it was for Bob," he responded, unzipping his briefcase.

"Doc gave Burns a clean bill of health for the game. It's not my responsibility to determine the condition of my players."

"He'll testify differently," Pip said as he passed the x-rays and a piece of paper over to the coach.

"You've spoken to Doc? What the hell is this?"

"It's the x-rays. Notice the date and Bob's name on the left-hand corner. And the letter is from Bob's doctor. It's a diagnosis based on these pictures. You crippled my friend."

Pip watched Jake. The coach remained calm. The bastard really didn't think he had done anything wrong.

"Hey, Man, that's the way the game's played in the N F L. You understand. Half the coaches would have done what I did. Jesus, Man, this is the big time. People get hurt."

Jake stood and walked around his desk. He put his arm around his halfback, as if they were pals, and he had something confidential to tell him. Pip was seething but restrained himself as the coach continued.

"We'll take care of Burns. The Pacers take care of their own. Now get yourself together. We still have a championship to win."

"You'll take care of Burns because you have no choice. You'll go to the owners. Tell them about the x-rays and the letter from the hospital. I want six hundred thousand for Bob."

"Are you crazy?"

"My season with the Pacers is over," Pip continued, ignoring the interruption. "You can put out any story you want. Say I was hurt, nothing serious because next year you'll trade me to the team of my choice, and you'll want to get as much for me as you can. And I expect you to pay me for this season. If not, these x-rays and I will go to court. Oh, by the way, don't try to reach Doc. We've already taken his deposition."

"The owners will never go for it. Please, Pip, be reasonable."

"I think I am. You have forty-eight hours to give me your decision before I blow this thing into the biggest sports scandal this country's ever seen."

∽

The Pacers offered Burns a hundred thousand dollars.

"I'm set for life, Pip. A hundred grand," the big lineman declared.
"They'll pay more."

"Don't fuck up the deal, little buddy."

"I won't," he promised.

The Pacers agreed to four hundred thousand and Pip knew he was going to be a damn good lawyer.

SO

Jake French was fired before the season ended. Pip played the next five seasons for the Riders. He graduated from Michigan Law School and hung up his cleats in spite of the thousands of letters he received from fans begging him not to quit.

"No one leaves at the height of his career," his coach urged. "I'll get you more money. You'll be the highest paid player in the history of the league."

"Sorry. I made myself a promise."

Part Two
Susan

CHAPTER ELEVEN

As a child, Susan Russo never really liked herself. She was a skinny runt, with teeth too big for her mouth and large brown puppy-dog eyes that sadly surveyed her world.

She lived in an oversized old Victorian house in a quiet neighborhood in Providence, Rhode Island. There were twelve rooms for three people to ramble about. Susan had trouble understanding why they lived in such a large house or why it seemed so important to her mother. Her father owned a luggage store and spent all his time working. Her mother, Theresa, came to accept the fact that Louis' time would be consumed by his business, seven days a week. In exchange, Louis provided them with a comfortable life.

Theresa helped her husband whenever he asked. Over the years, his dependency on her increased, so by the time Susan was in high school, they both worked full time.

Theresa enjoyed selling more than caring for the house or her daughter. They substituted their lack of attention by providing the child with what they considered to be the better things in life. One of the advantages they insisted upon was that she attend St. Joseph's Academy, an exclusive Catholic school in Providence.

Susan wasn't sure if she was too proletariat or her classmates too upper crust, but she always felt out of place.

"No one likes me," she would cry to her mother. "I have no friends."

"Why do you have no friends? Do the other kids have friends?"

"Okay, it's my fault."

"I'm not saying it's your fault, dear, but you could try harder."

"I do try."

"Try harder."

୫୨

When Susan was sixteen, she tried too hard. His name was Henry, his hair was long and his face was pimply. He lived next door and she had known him all her life. He was four years her senior. They had never really been friends, he had just always been the boy next door, until the night circumstances brought them together.

Her parents gave a party. They had planned the affair for weeks, hiring a band, a bartender, and a caterer. They rarely entertained.

"We owe so many invitations," Theresa lamented.

"Who cares?" Louis responded.

"One party. We'll take care of everybody. Please, Louie."

He usually had his way, but this time she was insistent.

It was a hot Saturday night in July. Susan helped greet the guests.

"Can I have some punch?" she asked her mother.

"There's alcohol in it," Theresa replied impatiently. "Okay, have one."

Susan emptied her glass in a moment, not tasting the liquor, only seeking relief for her parched mouth. She took a refill which she nursed and then, out of boredom, took a third. The sweetness of the punch obscured the alcohol. She felt tipsy but happy as she left the backyard and started walking down the road. She got no farther than the house next door.

"Hey, Susan," Henry called to her. He was sitting on the steps of the front porch.

"Hi, Henry. What are you doing?"

"Listening to the party. Sure is noisy."

"It's your parents making all the racket," Susan replied lightheartedly.

"Probably is. Want to sit?" he said tapping the step with his hand.

"Sure, why not."

"I leave next week," Henry said, taking the corner of his shirt and wiping the sweat from his face. "God, it's hot."

"Where are you going?"

"Army. Two years."

"Wow. I didn't know that."

"I didn't have much choice. I flunked out of the University of Rhode Island and got drafted."

Susan was silent, not knowing how to respond.

"Want to come into the house? It's air conditioned," he asked after a minute.

"Sure."

Susan realized it was the first time she had ever been in Henry's house. The blast of cold air felt refreshing. He led her downstairs to the family room.

"Want a beer?"

"Why not?"

He went upstairs. She gazed around and saw a juke box in the corner. She walked over and examined the song titles.

"Like it?" he asked, startling her.

"Does it work?"

"Sure does," he replied, opening the bottles with a blade from his pocket knife and handing her one.

Susan had never had a beer. She took a sip. Bitter but cold. She took a long swallow.

Henry reached behind the juke box, turning it on.

"Want to hear anything special?"

"I don't care."

"Press what you want. You can make three selections."

She studied the panel and made her choices watching as the jukebox responded and put a record on the turntable. The arm came over and rested on the recording. Johnny Mathis started to croon.

"Want to dance?"

"Sure, why not."

Her head was spinning. Is this what it felt like to be drunk? she wondered.

He held her close and then moved back, looking down at her. "You're very pretty."

"I am?" She laughed.

He bent over and put his lips on hers, attempting to part them with his tongue. Henry was the first boy to ever kiss her.

She had read about french kissing. He was trying to french her. Well, what the hell. His hands found her breasts. Susan knew she didn't want this and pushed them away.

"No, Henry, don't."

A moment later they again found their way back to her bosom.

It was hot. The air conditioner no longer felt cooling and sweat dripped from her face. The song ended. Henry got a couple more beers and led her back to the couch. What was happening? She couldn't stand the boy. Why wasn't she resisting more? She should leave now, return home, go to sleep. Her head was spinning. She was exhausted.

Susan took a deep swallow. It felt so refreshingly cold. It would be nice to be loved. Her blouse was opened and her bra unhooked. His hands went from her breasts to her undergarment.

"No, Henry."

But it was off. Now he was on top of her. What was happening? No, no, she shouldn't be allowing this. It was wrong. He entered her and she immediately sobered but not fast enough.

"Oh, oh, I'm coming. Oh, God."

"What did you do?" she screamed, not believing what had happened. She was afraid. "What did you do?"

"What do you think I did?" There was a stupid grin on his face.

"Oh, my God. I could get pregnant. Oh, God, I don't believe this."

His smile was gone now. "I don't think you can get pregnant from one time."

"Why not?"

"It usually takes a few tries."

She wanted to believe him. How much experience did he have? She suspected this was his first time, also. What other girl would be stupid enough to sleep with Henry? She looked around. There were beer bottles on the floor. The couch was rumpled and peeking out between two pillows was the lacy edge of her pink undergarment. If only she had worn slacks rather than a blouse and skirt. Something as simple as that, and she would still be a virgin. Susan grabbed her panties and put them on in one motion. She scrutinized the boy. He would forever be her first. How foolish she had been.

She left without another word. The band music mixed with the sound of laughter as she walked toward her house. As she approached the sanctuary of the bathroom, a friend of her mother's was coming out of it.

"Hi, Susan. Some party."

She nodded rushing past her. Looking in the mirror, she broke into tears.

"Why? Why?" she asked her reflection.

She stripped and took a hot shower hoping the water could wash away the sin.

∞

One afternoon late in September Susan was in her room reading when there was a knock on the door.

"Can I come in?" her mother called before entering.

Susan quickly hid the book she was reading under the pillow as she looked up.

"What's the matter?" Theresa asked, not wasting time on small talk.

"Nothing."

"Susan, something's troubling you." She sat on the bed next to her daughter.

Susan had told no one and yet thought of nothing else.

St. Joseph's Academy had won its first two football games. School spirit was high. Life seemed so perfect for everyone but her. She knew she had to share her burden with somebody. Susan looked at her mother's troubled face, knowing she was about to devastate her. Would her mother be loving, comforting? Maybe.

Susan bit her lip before speaking. "I think I'm pregnant."

"What? What do you mean?"

She burst into tears. "Oh, Mother, I'm not bad. I'm not. I only did it once. I'm so sorry. Please don't hate me. I only did it once. I know I shouldn't have, but I can't take it back now."

Her mother stood and headed for the door. Was she walking out? Susan became frightened. No, she was closing it. Theresa turned toward her daughter, crimson-faced. "How could you do this to me? How? Who's the father?"

The questions hit Susan like a physical blow. She'd hoped for compassion and was receiving recrimination. She was ashamed to answer. Silently, she looked at her mother.

"You were brought up to know better. It's a sin. You're a Catholic. What are we supposed to do? Damn, how could you do this to me?"

"How could I do this to you? How could I do this to you?" Susan jumped from the bed. She reached under her pillow and grabbed the book she had hidden, throwing it against the wall. The plaster cracked from the force of the blow. She swept her arm across her bureau, sending everything on top of it flying, then looked down at her broken jewelry box, the assorted earrings, her favorite necklace, her hair brush, and childhood panda bear lying face down, all strewn on the floor.

"I didn't do anything to you? I did it to me. Why are you hurting me more? I'm already hurting. Can't you help me? I did it once. I was wrong. And it wasn't even my fault," she screamed. "How many times do I have to say it? God damn it, I was wrong. Now help me. For God's sake, please help me. I don't know what to do."

"It's a little late to be sorry. And watch your language, young lady."

"Are you deaf? I want to die, that's how sorry I am."

Theresa led her daughter back to the bed where they sat. She took her daughter's hand.

"How could this happen?" Theresa said with a new calmness. "Who was the boy? I have to know."

"I should have stopped him. I just couldn't."

"Couldn't stop him? Oh God, you were raped, weren't you?"

"No, I wasn't raped. It happened the night of your party."

"Oh, my God. Was the father one of my guests? I must know."

"It was that jerk, Henry, from next door."

"Henry?"

Susan scrutinized her mother before continuing. She just didn't want to talk about how it happened. "I want an abortion. I don't think I could have the baby. Please find a doctor who will do it."

Theresa grabbed her daughter by the shoulders. "What do you know about abortions? Is that what you talk about with your friends?"

"What friends?" Susan picked up the book she had hurled against the wall and handed it to her mother.

"<u>Abortion, A Woman's Choice.</u> This is trash. Where did you get it?"

"From the library."

"I can't believe they have such filth at the library. Abortion is wrong. You can't kill your baby."

"It's not a baby. Not yet. It's too small. It's my body. I want an abortion. Please, help me. At least read the book."

"Never. I can help you but not to have an abortion. Don't you understand? That's a human life you're carrying."

"No. The book says a baby should be conceived in love. This is wrong."

"You were wrong, but it would be a worse sin to kill the infant."

Susan stared at her mother who was looking forlornly at the panda lying face down on the rug.

"You're but a child," Theresa said, almost to herself.

"Please. I don't want to stay pregnant," Susan implored. "I can't. Everyone will know. I'll be so humiliated." She gasped for air.

"You could go away."

"Where?"

"I don't know. Let me talk it over with your father."

"Oh, please, don't tell Daddy."

&

"Louis, we have to talk."

"Not now, Theresa. I'm paying the bills. If you don't pay by the tenth, they don't ship."

"Louis, for God's sake, this is important. It's about your daughter. Take a minute off. They'll still ship."

Louis was at his desk in his study, a small room at the far end of the house. He closed the checkbook, placed it on top of the pile of bills and slowly looked up at his wife.

"What is it now?" he asked.

"Louis, I don't bother you that often. This is important."

"What's such a big deal, it can't wait?"

She might have broken it to him slowly but, he was such an impatient man. "Susan's pregnant."

"Holy Jesus, no. You can't be serious. She's only a baby!"

"Wake up, Louis, she's sixteen."

"That's no time to lose her cherry. For God's sake, Theresa, you're her mother. You're not supposed to let it happen."

"You're a stupid man, Louis. I didn't let it happen."

"Don't call me stupid, Theresa. Who's the son-of-a-bitch that did this to my girl?" He banged his fist on his desk.

"Louis, calm down will you. What are you going to do, kill the guy?"

"I just might, the son-of-a-bitch."

Theresa was still standing. There was only one chair in this office and Louis was in it.

"Listen Louis, we have to concentrate on what to do about Susan."

"Agh, the shame. Everyone will think our daughter's a whore." He hit his forehead with the palm of his hand. "The shame."

"Not if they don't find out."

"You can't hide her belly, Theresa."

"Why not?"

"You mean send her away?"

"It's the only answer."

"Where would you send her?"

"I was thinking about my mother. I'll call her in the morning."

"Your mother. That might be best. It's better if no one knows. Yes. It's such a shameful thing."

"Do you want to see your daughter?"

"You're her mother. I have work to do."

Theresa turned to leave.

"Who was the father?" he called after her.

"Henry, that twerp from next door."

"Jesus, I should strangle the son-of-a-bitch."

"He's never to know, Louis. Never."

∽

Theresa noticed the red around Susan's eyes as she left for school.

"We'll talk when you get home. I'll have some answers," she said, kissing her daughter. "It'll be all right."

Theresa lit her first cigarette. Smoking was her one vice. She poured a cup of coffee, sat down at the kitchen table, inhaled deeply, exhaled and watched the smoke fill the room. She thought about her predicament. How could Susan have done this? She phoned her mother.

∽

Sophia Marino had been a widow for thirty-one years. Tony had loved her enough to last a lifetime, and she never wanted to replace him. She kept a picture of the two of them on her bureau. She would smile and cross herself each time she looked at the fading photograph in the silver frame. He had been an obese man more then six feet tall whose size belied his gentleness. She was a wisp of a woman, barely breaking five feet.

Her boys were ten and twelve when he died; Theresa, nine. The family depended on Tony. The suddenness of his death left them devastated.

The man loved to eat. On his last day, he finished off two pounds of pasta, loaded with homemade sauce ladened with sausage and spices.

"Excuse me," he said with that twinkle in his eye, as he put his napkin to his mouth to disguise a burp.

The young ones giggled.

"Children," Sophia admonished.

Tony stood, slapping the boys affectionately on the top of their heads and kissing Theresa before picking up the newspaper.

"Time for my constitutional."

It was his ritual. He usually took twenty minutes. When half an hour had passed, Sophia knocked on the bathroom door.

"Tony, Tony are you okay?"

When there was no reply she turned the knob. It was locked. She shouted for the boys, and all three children came running.

"Anthony, break it down."

The youngster threw himself against the door, and the eye and hook easily gave way. Tony was dead on the bathroom floor, his pants around his ankles. No one ever spoke about how he left this world.

Her husband had never talked business. Sophia knew he had something to do with exporting but that was all. Much to her surprise she learned he had over a half-million dollars in life insurance.

She was careful with her money and was able to raise the children in comfort. The boys went to college; Theresa married a university man. Sophia's job done, she busied herself with the church. Her only vices were bingo and penny poker.

∞

Sophia sat by the window in the front room in Huntington, Long Island, thumbing a magazine and looking out. When the car pulled into the driveway, she did not jump up, but rather observed Theresa and Susan as they got out of the car. Each took a suitcase.

Susan's smile was missing and Sophia noticed the girl's resigned shuffle as they approached the front door. She took a deep breath and went to greet them.

"Welcome. Let me look at you, Susan. You're getting so tall. Give me a kiss. Where's Louie, Theresa?"

"Had to work, Ma."

"He always has to work. And how's my little girl?" Sophia asked her granddaughter.

"Good, Nonnie."

"Mmm, what's that smell?" Theresa asked. "Nonnie's such a great cook. You'll eat well, Susan."

"How long will you be staying?" Sophia asked her daughter.

"A couple of days. I'll help Susan get settled and interview the tutors. I want to meet her doctor."

"C'mon. I'll show you your room," Sophia said to her granddaughter.

It was a large house. The ceilings were high and the rooms spacious. It was an old building but homey and comfortable. The overstuffed furniture were covered with lace doilies.

Susan's room was big and bright with a large bed, a roll top desk, upright chair and oak bureau.

"I emptied the drawers for you," Sophia said. "Such junk. I threw it all away. I think some of the things belonged to your mother when she was in high school."

"Thank you."

"I hope you'll be comfortable here. I want you to feel at home. I hope I can make it easier for you."

Susan sighed as she put her suitcase on the bed. "Thank you, Nonnie."

℘

Susan's tutors were teachers from the local high school. One taught her English, history, and French, the other, math, and biology. One arrived at three-thirty, the other at seven. Susan spent her days studying. She longed for friends her age but knew this was impossible. However, her grandmother helped fill the vacuum with her gentle companionship.

It was the week before Christmas.

"Come, supper is ready," Sophia said as soon as the teacher had left.

Susan quickly set the table, as she knew they had to finish dinner before the second tutor arrived. Her grandmother said grace before they ate.

"You're starting to show."

"I know. I think I've felt the baby. I still can't believe I'm pregnant."

"It happens."

"Only once. I did it only once. Do you believe me, Nonnie?"

"Yes, of course."

"It's true, but I don't think my mother believes it. That's the worst part. I wanted an abortion. Did you know that?"

Sophia moved uncomfortably in her chair.

"Abortion is wrong, child. It's against God."

"It's my body. I should have the right to decide."

"You're a Catholic. Life begins at conception."

"I get so confused. I'm glad I'm a Catholic. I think it's a wonderful religion, but I don't think life begins at once. Nonnie, it was so dirty, so wrong. I wouldn't tell this to anyone else."

"Even so, it's an infant. You're giving life to a child, and we can't decide when life begins."

Sophia took her granddaughter's hand and kissed it. "You'll have the baby. It'll be adopted by a couple who can't have a child, and they'll love it."

"I guess so. You've been so good to me. I'm lucky to have you."

"We're both lucky."

℅

It was the first day of spring. Susan felt the warmth filtering through the windows and could concentrate on her studies no longer. She went to the refrigerator. Being more nervous than hungry, she closed the door without taking anything. She turned as Sophia entered the kitchen.

"How are you feeling, today?" Sophia looked at Susan's stomach as she asked.

"Fine, Nonnie. The baby won't let me alone."

"He's a kicker. Let me feel," she responded, putting her hand on her granddaughter's belly.

"Oh, God," Susan screamed as her grandmother's hand touched her stomach.

Sophia pulled away, thinking she had caused the shriek.

"Oh, God," the girl repeated, putting her hand to her belly, "I think I'm having a contraction."

Sophia led Susan to her bed where the contractions continued. She called the doctor.

On the way to the hospital Susan spoke. Her tone was urgent.

"Will they let me see my baby?"

"I don't know if they allow that."

"I want to see my child. Please make sure they let me see my baby. It's important."

"They have rules. I'm not sure. I wish we had asked when we signed the papers."

"It didn't seem important then. Oh," she screamed. "Oh, it hurts so much. Please hurry."

I am, honey," Sophia replied, removing her right hand from the steering wheel to squeeze her granddaughter's arm. "I am."

They wheeled Susan into the labor room. Sophia waited outside. In six hours and forty-five minutes it was over. The doctor came out.

"It's a boy," he told her, pulling the gloves from his hands and wiping the beads of sweat from his forehead. "Susan is fine."

"Can I see the baby?"

"It's irregular to allow any member of the natural family to see the child if it's being put up for adoption," he replied.

"It's my great-grandchild. Please."

"Come with me." He led her down the long hallway.

"Stay here," he said. He put on his mask and went into the nursery. Nurses were gathered around the infant, washing and dressing him. They brought him to the window.

Sophia looked down at the baby.

"My bambino. My sweet bambino. I pray for you all the best."

The doctor came to her side. "He's a healthy baby."

She looked hard into the doctor's eyes. "I promised my granddaughter she could see her baby."

He shook his head. "It's against the rules, strictly forbidden."

"Please. It's so important to her." She paused before adding, "and to me."

so

"I tried, my pet," Sophia said.

"Oh, Nonnie. I so wanted to see my baby once. I carried him for nine months. His parents will have a lifetime with him. I only wanted a minute."

"Maybe it's for the best. They should know," she replied, not really believing her words. "I tried."

There was a knock on the door. A nurse was standing there with a small bundle in her hands.

"The doctor told me to bring you your baby. He said he would take responsibility. Most unusual."

She handed the infant to Susan who took the child with outstretched arms and brought him to her bosom. She looked down at her baby, tenderly touched each of his ten fingers and began to weep as she kissed him on the lips. Her tears fell on the cheeks of her child and she wiped them away.

"I love him so much, Nonnie. I love him so much. No one will ever love him more. I don't want to give him up."

"You must love him enough to let him go," she said through her own tears.

so

That evening Sofia called her daughter from the hospital room.

"Everything's fine," she told Theresa. "She's right here."

Her grandmother handed Susan the phone.

"Now you can get on with your life," Theresa said. "Everything's set at St. Joseph's."

Susan wanted to tell Theresa of the baby but knew her mother didn't wish to acknowledge its existence. "What have you been telling everyone?"

"That you've been caring for Grandma and will be home soon."

"I'm going to miss Nonnie," she said. "I want to stay here. I'll return to school in September." She looked at Sophia. "Is that okay with you, Nonnie?"

"I would love it, but it's up to your parents."

Susan returned to the phone. "Mother, I want to stay. Nonnie says it's okay."

"It's too much for her," Theresa responded.

"It'll be easier than when I was pregnant."

"Maybe it would be best," Theresa said. "You can start fresh in September."

"It will look better," Susan responded.

"Yes, maybe it will," her mother agreed, hearing her daughter's sarcasm but choosing not to respond to it. "You'll come home for the summer? I'll arrange for you to take your tests then."

CHAPTER TWELVE

Susan did well her senior year. Theresa had wanted her daughter to attend a Catholic college but the girl had other ideas.

"I've had enough parochial education. I've spent enough time on my knees."

"Show some respect," her mother admonished.

When Susan entered Boston University, she promised herself life would be different. She would force herself to get past her shyness. She knew the ugly duckling had become a swan. Her teeth fit her face, her coal black hair accentuated her fair complexion and fell down to her shoulders in naturally curled ringlets. She noticed how the boys looked at her.

Theresa drove Susan to the University. Louis had to work. "Your daughter's starting college. You could take the time off to help her get settled," Susan heard her mother say. She imagined her father's face turning crimson.

"Who the hell's earning the money to send her to that damn school? Do you know what it costs?"

"It's a good thing your father had to work," Theresa said as they drove off. "There wouldn't be any room for him."

Susan felt a churning in her stomach as they approached Boston. It was a strange mixture of emotions: fear, excitement, insecurity and determination. They arrived at the university and were met by an upper class student who had been trained to deal with nervous incoming freshman.

"What school are you in?" Neal asked as he unloaded the car, carefully putting Susan's belongings into a laundry cart.

"Liberal Arts," she replied, adding nothing extra to the conversation. Neal continued to be friendly. Susan wanted to respond but was too nervous. Three loads later, the car was empty.

"Thank you for your help," Theresa told him.

"You're welcome, Ma'am. If I can be of any help to you, Susan, you can call." He took out a pen, pulled an envelope out of the wastebasket and jotted down his number.

"Thank you," Susan said.

After Neal was gone, Susan watched her mother check out the room. One bed was made, one closet filled, one desk taken. There was a note on the unmade bed.

Dear Susan,

If you want to change beds or desks, it's okay with me. I can't wait to meet you.

Patti

"Sounds like a nice girl," Theresa said as she started going through the roommate's closet.

"What are you doing?"

"Checking her out, sweetheart. Nice labels. She's a small girl. Size three. Come, I'll take you out to lunch."

"Should I leave a note?"

"That would be nice."

"I don't know what to say."

"Then forget it. Come on. I have to get back. You know your father."

They found a coffee shop. Susan barely touched her tuna melt. Each time she picked up the sandwich her hand shook.

"What's the matter?" Theresa asked.

"I'm scared," Susan replied, her voice cracking, tears filling her eyes. She looked around the restaurant filled with young people. They were all laughing and carrying on. It seemed to come naturally to everyone else. Why did she feel so different? Her mother held her hand.

"I haven't seen you like this since I took you to your first day of kindergarten."

"I'll be okay, Mother. I'm scared but I'll be okay. I'm going to do it no matter how frightened I am."

She wiped her eyes and blew her nose. She <u>was</u> going to fit in.

They went back to her room. Patti still hadn't returned.

"I have to go," Theresa said. "I'll call tonight."

Susan left the door to her room open as she put her things away. She saw other students pass through the hall. Who among them would become her friends?

When she was finished unpacking, she surveyed her small, fully filled, closet.

"Hello."

She turned. As she looked at the trio standing there, she smiled, almost laughed. Her mother was right. It had to be her roommate and parents. The tallest among them was the father, at maybe 5'2".

"Susie? I'm Patti."

CHAPTER THIRTEEN

In May, Theresa helped her daughter move home. Susan had fulfilled her promise to herself, worked hard, made good friends and even had a beau. She had become a confident young woman.

"Bye, Patti. I'll see you in September. You'd better write," Susan said.

"I will," her roommate replied, putting her arms around Susan, and hugging her with a force that took the girl's breath away.

Susan walked to the car, where Billy Eckstrom was packing the last of her things into the trunk. He turned to face her.

"You'll come visit me? The Cape is the place to be. You promised," he said.

"I'll make it. Don't worry. After I get a job. I'll let you know when."

Shyly, he kissed her good-bye. Susan had not been able to show Billy the affection he wanted. She knew it was because of the mental scars she carried from her pregnancy. They were difficult to overcome. Billy had given her every reason to trust him, but she couldn't accept his goodness. Not yet.

℘

Susan found employment working for an answering service. The pay was good and she could work as long as she wished, often over sixty hours a week. It was a perfect summer job.

"Time-and-a-half on the weekends and over forty hours. I'm rich," she told her mother. "I'll have lots of spending money this year."

By August, Susan was becoming anxious to return to school. Her mother was getting on her nerves and she had only a few acquaintances, with no close friends.

Susan worked the second shift on the last day, ending work at ten in the evening. The sky was clear with an unusual chill for August. She bicycled home slowly. It had been a boring summer, highlighted by the July fourth weekend with Billy. The Cape had been crowded beyond her endurance.

Billy and his parents fawned over her. He gave her his room and took the living room couch for himself. He never rushed her. They kissed and held each other. He seemed to sense that was all she wanted and respected her wishes. "I'm a good Catholic girl," she had told him.

As Susan approached her house, she was surprised to see it in darkness. Had they lost their electricity? She entered and was about to announce her arrival with a loud Hello when she was startled by the sound of someone quietly crying. She followed the sound to the family room, that was lit only from the light of the street lamp filtering through the windows.

"Mother, what's the matter?" Susan asked, sitting on the arm of Theresa's chair, taking her hand.

"It's Nonnie."

"What's happened?" she responded, assuming the worst.

"She has cancer. It's very bad. The doctors give her six months at the most."

"Oh, Mother, that's so awful." She felt the tears filling her own eyes. "Poor Nonnie."

They sat in silence. Her wonderful, loving Nonnie was going to die.

౿

Theresa and Susan drove to Long Island to spend the weekend with Sophia. It was back-to-school season and Louie couldn't leave the business at such a busy time.

As they drove into Sophia's driveway, Susan recalled her time here three years ago. Then she had been frightened for herself, now it was for her grandmother. The poor woman was living alone, facing this final ordeal by herself. She shouldn't be separated from her loved ones. It wasn't right.

"Nonnie," Susan cried, throwing her arms around her, "How are you?" What a foolish question!

Sophia smiled, as if reading her granddaughter's mind. "I'm fine, darling. I'm really fine. Come, bring your things to your room and then we'll visit. I have cookies and tea for us, just like we used to do."

The sterling silver set was on the dining room table when Theresa and Susan returned from the bedroom. Sophia poured the tea into the cups and passed the cookies. Susan looked at her grandmother, noticing how much the woman had aged these past three years. Why had she not had time to visit her over the summer?

"Nonnie," she heard herself saying, "I'm not going back to school. I'm moving in with you."

"What are you talking about?" Theresa shouted. "You're going back to school. Your father's paid the tuition. Are you crazy?"

Susan went to her grandmother, ignoring her mother's outburst. She put her arm around her.

"You were there for me and I'm going to be here for you. I love you, Nonnie, and I'm going to take care of you." She turned to her mother. "I'll get a leave of absence. Nothing will change my mind."

Sophia looked up at her granddaughter. "No, my child. You must continue with your life. You can't take time out to wait for an old lady to die. Please!"

"No. My life will wait. You won't. I'm staying and that's final."

"I agree with Nonnie, Susan. It's a wonderful gesture but you must return to school."

"It's not a gesture, Mother," Susan shot back. "I'm getting a leave of absence and staying. Father will get his precious money back."

When Sophia knew she couldn't persuade her granddaughter, she began to weep, and took her hand.

"My bambina."

❦

Sophia died in November, with Susan at her bedside. The girl never regretted her decision. It had been a special time, a closeness that Susan knew she would never experience again.

❦

"I think I'm going to join <u>Speak Easy</u>," Susan said.

"You'd be a natural," Patti responded.

"Do you think I'd qualify?"

"Of course you would. It's right up your alley."

Speak Easy was an organization of peer counselors. Any student with a problem, real or imaginary, could call or visit the club for free help. The volunteer student staff was familiar with all the community resources and would refer the student to the proper agency. Common problems included school work, depression, relationships, or roommates.

Susan submitted her application and was invited to be interviewed by an officer.

She walked from her dormitory to the Speak Easy quarters at the Student Union. The wintry air turned her breath to steam as she crossed Commonwealth Avenue. Students were scurrying in every direction.

She entered the building. The warmth felt good as she shivered a temporary good-bye to the cold and walked into the office. A student sat behind a desk, reading. Speak Easy's low priority in the university system was evident by the shabbiness of the furniture. The light green paint on the cement walls was chipping away and conflicted with the worn olive green linoleum.

"Excuse me. Is Mark Reingold here?"

"Hey, Mark, your appointment's arrived."

A young man came from the back to greet her. He was about her height, with thick glasses which he removed as he walked toward her. He rubbed an eye with the palm of his hand. His hair was thick and wavy but mussed.

"You must be Susan Russo. Welcome." Mark led her to a desk in the rear of the office and offered her a seat. He told Susan what would be expected of her. "You're a psych major," he continued, looking at her application. "That's good, but you must remember you're not a therapist yet. You can't treat our clients. We handle what we can, but it's important to know when you're out of your league and refer the student to the proper agency."

"I understand."

"This is a list of organizations both on campus and off. Become familiar with it. If you have any doubts at all as to how to handle a case, you must seek help. That's why we're here."

Mark gave Susan some hypothetical situations and asked her how she would handle them. Two hours later, the interview concluded.

"Congratulations. You're a peer counselor."

"Thanks. I won't disappoint you," she said as she started to put on her coat.

"Now, how about a cup of coffee at the Union?"

"Sure."

They stood in the cafeteria line.

"I'm getting an espresso," Mark said.

"Sounds good. I'll have the same."

"How much?" she asked after they found a table.

"It's on me."

She learned Mark was a senior and had been accepted to medical school. He was from Braxton, a suburb of Boston, and lived at home.

"It's a lot cheaper," he said. "I couldn't afford the room and board. My father's a Rabbi - not a big paying job."

"A Rabbi?" Susan replied. "You're Jewish."

"Most sons of Rabbis are." He laughed. "I notice you're a first semester sophomore. Did you start early or late."

"Neither," she replied. "I took a semester off to be with my grandmother. She died in November."

Conversation came easily, and they talked for over an hour.

"Can I walk you to your dorm?" he asked.

"If you like freezing."

"I have to go out anyway."

They bundled up. The wind greeted them with a howl and they crouched to diminish its blow. Mark took her arm and led her through the elements to the warm safety of her dormitory. Once inside the foyer, he turned to face her.

"Good luck at Speak Easy. I know you'll be great."

"Thanks," she replied.

He put his arms around her, kissed her cheek, turned and was gone.

That evening, as she sat in bed, a book propped against her thighs, her mind kept wandering, refusing to concentrate on her studies. What was it that allowed her to relax with Mark as she couldn't with Bill? There was something about Mark that made her feel safe. He wasn't sexy, not as good looking as Billy... Why can't I get him off my mind, she wondered.

‰

The following week Susan began at Speak Easy. She arrived at seven in the evening. For the first half hour she watched the silent phone before finally opening a book. As studies captured her attention, she became oblivious to the surroundings and the sound of the ring startled her. Checking her watch, she logged the time, nine thirty, took a deep breath and answered the phone. She felt a rush of excitement.

"Speak Easy. How can I help you?"

"I've an awful problem," a squeaky male voice replied.

"I know we can help. What is it?"

"Can I come over to talk to you?"

"Sure. You know where we are?"

"Yes."

"Will you be okay 'till you get here? What's the matter?"

"I'm horny as hell and need someone to suck my dick."

Susan slammed down the phone. Although Mark had warned her about such calls, she wasn't ready. She could feel the blood rush to her head.

"You son-of-a bitch," she yelled at the receiver. Her shift ended at ten. There were no other calls that evening.

෨

The next afternoon, Susan returned to Speak Easy.

"How did it go?" Mark asked. Save any lives?"

"I helped a pervert."

"You shouldn't have been left alone the first time. That was thoughtless. Can I make it up to you by taking you to the movies Saturday?"

Susan was caught off guard. She usually did something with Billy on Saturday evenings.

"I'm sorry. I'm busy."

"Okay."

Susan detected and shared Mark's disappointment. Billy never made anything definite. It was just assumed... Hell, maybe she could... "I'll shift my plans for Saturday. Yes, I would like to go out with you."

"Great! You sure changed your mind fast. Is it something I did? A new technique I'm not aware of?"

Susan laughed. "I just figure you owe me."

෨

They took a bus to see a foreign film in Cambridge. The movie ended at ten o'clock. It was a crisp clear February evening and although the temperature was about freezing, the lack of wind made the air comfortable.

"Want to walk home?" Mark asked.

"That's a long walk."

"A few miles. Good for you."

"Sure. Why not?"

He put his arm through hers and led her toward Boston.

"Who is Susan Russo?" he asked.

"Just a girl trying to grow up," she replied, surprised at her answer. "You know much more about me than I know about you. You interviewed me, remember? Tell me what it's like having a Rabbi for a father."

"You get to celebrate a lot of holidays and you have to be nice to a lot of people you may not especially like."

"Hey, Buddy, got any change?"

They both turned. A short man with stooped shoulders and long unkempt facial hair was approaching them. His clothes were torn and an old quilted vest, more black than its original tan, was all that protected him from the cold. His shoes were so worn that his bare toes showed through.

Susan stepped back from the man. Mark reached into his pocket and handed him his coins.

"God bless," the beggar said before he disappeared into the night.

"You're just paying for his booze," Susan said.

"I hope not," Mark replied.

They walked through the park in silence, eventually passing a woman sleeping on a bench.

"See her over there?" he said pointing.

Susan nodded.

"That's wrong. Not in America. There are people in my father's congregation who are wealthy. It's okay to have money. They earned it. But they should give enough back to society so no one goes without food or shelter."

Susan looked at him. She remembered being in New York as a child when a bum asked her parents for a hand-out. They had turned their backs on the man and told their daughter people should not beg, but rather work for what they need. Mark was a strange boy.

They arrived at her dormitory.

"How will you get home?" she asked, remembering for the first time that he lived in the suburbs.

"Streetcar. I had a good time tonight."

"I did, too."

He hesitated and Susan knew he was trying to decide whether to kiss her or not. She wasn't sure how she felt about it. They were different from each other, and she didn't want to lead him on. Their lips almost touched. He pulled back.

"Goodnight," he said and turned to leave.

As she watched him walk away, she regretted they hadn't kissed.

∞

Susan and Mark had been dating for three years and this wasn't Mark's first sleepless night over their differences. He sat at his desk doodling. He could never love anyone as he loved her. They would be engaged now if it wasn't for "the problem."

"My father's a Rabbi. He will be so hurt."

"I'm not religious," Susan replied. "But my family. How can I do it to them?"

Mark looked down at his pad surprised at what he had written. "God should live in the heart and not in the church."

ॐ

Rabbi Arthur Reingold was a wisp of a man. His crew cut had turned white while he was in Rabbinical school. He enjoyed blaming his premature graying on the rigors of his education.

He had been an outstanding student who believed strongly in the Jewish teachings of peace and justice. He prayed to a God he never fully understood and whose very existence he often privately questioned. And yet his pulpit and the Rabbinate were more meaningful to him than he could ever have anticipated. He loved his congregation and worked diligently to help them be good people, satisfied with themselves.

Rabbi Reingold was the leader of a small reform congregation in Braxton, a suburb of Boston. It had been his only pulpit. He arrived with the belief that this would be a stepping stone on his way to a large temple. However, when the time came, when other synagogues reached out, he chose to stay. He'd made good friends, his family was content and he was satisfied this was mission enough. Often, Rabbi Reingold would peruse the job descriptions that crossed his desk and wonder. Was he too complacent? Did he lack ambition? No, he was needed here.

At conferences Arthur would listen to his fellow Rabbis tell of the politics of their large congregations. They would speak of hidden agendas and back stabbings. The higher wages and prestige were not worth it to him. Too much tuchus kissing for his liking. It wasn't his way. Let the other Rabbis measure their success by the size of their flock and the money they received.

Mark was a disciple of his father's preaching. Together they had picketed against the war in Vietnam and joined Martin Luther King in his <u>March</u> <u>on</u> <u>Washington.</u> Now he found himself in conflict with a tenet Rabbi Reingold held dear. He could remember his father telling him about the folly of intermarriage.

"Six million Jews died in Nazi Germany. If we intermarry, Judaism could vanish from the earth. We are an endangered species."

"What if I fall in love with someone who isn't Jewish?" Mark had asked.

"You don't let it happen. There are enough problems in marriage. Don't compound them by taking a wife who isn't Jewish."

How could he tell his father, the Rabbi, he was living with a Catholic girl and planned to marry her?

Susan was a senior; he was in his second year of medical school. There wasn't a parent between them who knew they lived together. Susan still lived with Patti, Mark with Patti's boyfriend, Ike. It wasn't a total lie. The four of them did share a two bedroom apartment.

"We have to tell them," Susan said.

"Do you think we could get married and not mention it to anyone?"

They laughed and he kissed her.

"Oh, Susan, I want to marry you. We must visit our parents."

"Yours first."

"No. Yours."

❧

Rose Reingold's husband and son were her life. She wanted nothing more. Her son was going to be a doctor. What else could a mother ask?

She thought of his mysterious call. He was coming for dinner, not an unusual thing but he told them he had something important to discuss.

She started cooking Thursday night, and was up early Sunday putting the final touches to the dining room table. She found herself humming as she prepared the matzah ball soup.

❧

"Dinner was delicious, Mother. I needed some of your home cooking," Mark said after a quiet dinner.

"Thank you, darling." Rose replied.

Mark knew it was time to break his parents' hearts. How he had feared this moment.

"I have some news."

"Yes. What's this big mystery," Arthur responded.

"I'm engaged to a wonderful girl."

"That's marvelous," Rose replied. "Where is she? Why didn't you bring her home with you so we could meet her. You ashamed of your old parents?"

"I'm afraid she's not Jewish."

"Not Jewish," his father replied. "Impossible. You wouldn't do that."

"Father, Mother, this is so hard. I love you both. You know I do. But it has happened. I'm so sorry."

"It's a passing thing," Arthur said.

"It's a permanent thing. I'm sorry."

Arthur had counseled others on dealing with this problem. Don't lose your child, had been his advice. Know what you can't change and accept it. But this was different. It was his only son and Arthur was a rabbi. This was wrong and Mark knew better. Had he no respect for his parents?

"Mark, can I see you in my study?"

"Of course, Father."

Arthur closed the door and turned to face his boy. "You're going to marry a shikse? I can't believe you plan to marry a shikse. No warning. Just 'how do you do? I plan to marry a shikse.' And your poor mother. You probably just signed her death warrant."

"I didn't know how else to tell you. I couldn't do it on the phone, could I? Maybe I should have brought her with me. Once you meet her, see how wonderful she is for yourself, you'll understand."

"How serious are you? It's not too late..."

"Dad, I love her. I'm going to marry her."

"He loves her. He's going to marry her. Simple. No problem. Will you be able to attend your mother's funeral before the wedding?"

"Father, I'm sorry, but I won't be changing my mind. I've heard you tell others that it's not the end of the world. Practice what you preach."

"There are other fish in the sea. Jewish fish. Marriage is difficult enough without religious differences."

"Seems I've heard that before. Listen, Rabbi," Mark had always called his father Rabbi whenever he was upset with him. "Susan is everything you would want for me if she were Jewish. I can't do anything about her religion and I won't give her up. I don't want to cause you to suffer, but I love her more than I thought possible."

Arthur sat down at his desk and put his head into his hands. He had lost. His religion was his life. It was supposed to be passed down from generation to generation. If it wasn't, it would die. Over five thousand years of Jewish people would come to an end. And yet he could think of no way to stop his own son. "Susan will convert. The children, they will be brought up Jewish." It was both a statement and a question.

"We haven't gotten that far. Let me talk to Susan. I'll tell her how important it is to you."

"Let me live to see my grandson's bar mitzvah."

CHAPTER FOURTEEN

"Speak Easy. How can I help you?" Susan asked.

She was the Vice-President of the organization. Although officers usually didn't work the phones, she still took her turn.

"I need to talk with someone. I'm in trouble," a female voice responded.

"If you can tell me the problem, maybe I can help or get you someone who can."

"Will this be confidential? No one else can know."

"Yes."

"How do I know I can trust you?"

That was impossible to answer." Come over and meet with me. Don't tell me your problem until you feel comfortable."

"Oh, God I can't."

The line went dead. Susan looked at the receiver in her hand, then put it back to her ear. "Hello, hello," she tried, knowing the girl had hung up.

Susan attempted to study but couldn't get the urgency or fear in the girl's voice out of her mind. She jumped when the phone rang again twenty minutes later. It was the same voice.

"I don't know where to turn, what to do," the girl said.

"Where are you?"

"Warren Towers."

The call came from a dormitory across the street.

"I'll go to you. I can be there in two minutes."

"No, you can't come here. I'll come to you. When?"

"Now. My name is Susan."

"I don't know..."

"Meet me. You don't have to do more than that if you don't want. Please."

Fifteen minutes later Susan introduced herself to Marie Langlois. Everything about her was thin, her bones, her sparrow- like nose, her long sinewy fingers. She reminded Susan of herself as a little girl. She led her to a private room and offered her a seat before going behind the desk. She tried to make Marie feel comfortable with small talk.

"What year are you in?"

"Freshman."

"I'm a senior. I graduate in June." More silence before she continued. "What's your major?"

Marie surveyed Susan before speaking. "I'm frightened."

"Tell me what's bothering you," Susan urged in a soft even tone.

"I'm pregnant."

Susan's entire being was flooded by memories of her own experience. "Do you want to talk about it?"

The girl played nervously with her ring.

"I'm Catholic. I was raised to believe that abortion's a sin."

"Do you want the baby?"

"No. I think I want an abortion. I don't want my parents to know how I've messed up my life. I'm so mixed up."

It was like looking into a mirror. Susan could feel Marie's pain.

"An abortion? That's a difficult decision." She reached for her manual of services. "There's a clinic that's very good in helping women in your situation reach a decision. Can I call for you, just to talk to them?"

Marie nodded.

Susan pointed to a phone at a desk just outside the office. "Why don't you listen in?" She dialed the number. After the first ring, she nodded for Marie to pick up.

"Bay State Family Planning Center!"

"Yes, hello. Is Tess Green there?"

"This is Tess."

"Hi, Tess, This is Susan Russo over at Speak Easy."

"Hi, Susan. How have you been?"

The woman's voice was soft but confident. Susan looked out at Marie who stood motionless, listening intently.

"Tess, there's a girl on the other line with us. Her name is Marie. She's pregnant. Would you be so kind as to describe the services of your agency?"

"Hello, Marie."

"Hello," came a barely audible response.

"Marie, I would like to meet with you. This is very difficult to do on the phone. There's no obligation. I could just explain your options and help you reach your own decision."

"What do you do?" Marie ventured in a whisper.

"We're a family planning clinic. We're equipped to perform abortions if that's what you decide. Before we carry out the procedure, however, we discuss all the alternatives."

Marie appeared a bit more relaxed. Susan knew the realization that she could be in charge of her own life was making a small difference.

"Thanks, Tess," Susan responded. "I'll talk it over with Marie and we'll call you back."

She placed the receiver on the cradle and watched the girl return to the office.

"What do you think I should do?" the girl asked.

"I can't answer that. You must decide for yourself."

"It would kill my parents. They would tell me to marry the boy. They would be impressed with him. A good Catholic, they would say. A college boy. But I don't love him."

"Does he know?"

"Yes. And he says he'll marry me. But he acts like he's doing me a favor. No thanks. I don't need favors like that.

Susan nodded.

"Tess seemed very nice."

"She is. Do you want me to make an appointment for you?"

"Okay," she replied after a pause.

"Would you like me to go with you?"

"Yes," she answered, her face lighting up. It was the first time she had smiled.

୫

Susan and Marie took a cab to the Bay State Family Planning Center. They were dropped off in front of an old brick apartment building that looked the same as all the other dwellings on the street.

"This is it," Susan said, putting her arm through Marie's. They pressed the bell and were let in by a buzz that unlocked the door.

The empty waiting room was small but clean and recently refurbished. A woman appeared almost instantly.

"Hello, Tess," Susan said, extending her hand. "This is Marie."

The counselor turned to the pregnant girl. "Would you feel more comfortable if Susan joined us?"

"Yes. Yes, I would."

"Come," Tess said as she led the two women into a spacious office.

"We're an abortion clinic," Tess began, looking at them over her cluttered desk. "It doesn't mean all our clients choose ultimately to have an abortion. I'm an options counselor and before we consent to perform the abortion, I must determine it's what you want, that it's your own free choice. I want to be sure no one including me, is talking you into something you don't really want."

Marie appeared to relax. Tess is good, Susan thought.

"How old are you?" she continued.

"Eighteen."

"If you decide on an abortion, you don't need parental consent."

Susan watched Tess and Marie talk for the next hour and-a- half. The therapist skillfully elicited her client's attitudes. As the session came to an end, Marie understood her choices and her own feelings.

"Yes. I know I want to have an abortion," she concluded. "It's the best way for me."

"I think I can recommend that. Will next Tuesday be okay?"

"So soon... Yes, that will be fine."

"I'll come with you," Susan said.

"Would you like to see the clinic? It's two floors up," Tess asked.

"Yes."

She took them to the third floor. In contrast to the nearly deserted admitting office, medical staff scurried around.

"It's so... clean," Marie offered.

"It is," Tess responded, "and the procedure is safe and quick. Our doctors are wonderful. You won't be kept waiting. After it's over, I'll spend some time with you."

"You've been wonderful. I just wish I wasn't so... so scared."

They took the elevator back down.

"How many options counselors do you have?" Susan asked.

"Two. We're understaffed, but finding funds is difficult. We've spent a fortune on the third floor but it was worth it."

"Tuesday," Marie said almost to herself. "I'll be so glad when it's over. I'll have my life back."

CHAPTER FIFTEEN

Susan simply had no idea how her parents would deal with Mark. It would please them that she was marrying a doctor, but a Jewish doctor? Although Susan knew nothing would prevent her from spending her life with Mark, her parents' approval was important to her.

The young couple drove to Providence in Mark's father's beat-up Chevrolet. It was a ten-year-old car with over one hundred and thirty thousand miles on it. Rabbi Reingold had given Mark a five gallon jug of water, mixed with anti-freeze and had told him there was a leak in the radiator and to add the liquid as needed. The steam pouring out of the hood increased Susan's anxiety.

Mark seemed to take everything in stride. They pulled over to the side of the road and he poured some of the bluish fluid into the steaming motor.

"I'm so nervous," she said, standing next to him.

Mark slammed down the hood. "Let's hope this heap can make it to Providence so I can meet your parents. Everything will be fine."

Susan wasn't sure if she wanted the car to make it or not as she directed him to her house. Mark whistled as they pulled into the driveway. "You live in a mansion."

"It's big, isn't it? I don't know why they need it. It's only the two of them. Maybe so they can hide from each other."

As Susan rang the bell, Theresa flung open the door. She kissed her daughter.

"And this must be your young man."

"Mother, I want you to meet Mark Reingold."

"A pleasure to meet you," Mark said, extending his hand.

"Come, children. Your father is waiting for you in the living room."

Susan introduced Mark to her father, who invited them to sit.

"You have a lovely home," Mark said.

"Thank you," Theresa replied. "Susan has told us so little about you. It's like a secret. What do you do, Mark?"

"I'm in medical school."

"Medical school? Did you hear that, Louie? Mark is in medical school."

Louie grunted, then asked, "Where are you from?"

"Braxton. It's near Boston." Mark answered.

Susan knew that wasn't what her father wanted to know. She watched as he tried to figure out how to politely ask the question that would give him the information he sought.

"You look Italian but Reingold isn't an Italian name."

"No, I'm not Italian," Mark responded. "Susan tells me you're a merchant."

"I have a luggage store."

"Sounds interesting."

"I don't know how interesting it is. It's hard work, but it's a living. What kind of a doctor are you going to be?"

"Just a family doctor. I think I'd like to practice in a small town."

There was a lull in the conversation before Susan spoke. "We have some news, Daddy. Mark and I want to get married."

Theresa jumped to her feet and hugged her daughter.

"Oh, honey. I was hoping... This is wonderful."

"It's okay that he isn't Italian?"

"He's even better, he's a doctor. We'll have a big church wedding."

"There's a problem with that. Mark's father wants to marry us."

"What is he, a justice of the peace or something?" Theresa asked.

"Obviously, Theresa, he can't be a priest." Louie laughed at his attempt at humor.

"He's a rabbi!" Susan responded, then held her breath.

"A what?" her mother stammered.

"A rabbi?" Louis questioned. "Is he Jewish?"

"Father, Mark is in the room. Why are you speaking like he isn't?"

"I like Jews," Louis responded. "I have Jewish customers. They're very nice. They like good luggage and don't mind paying. It's not that I don't like Jews."

"They make good customers," Susan responded, "but not great husbands for Italian Catholic girls?"

"Your father didn't say that. But...," Theresa said.

"But it's better if people marry their own kind," Louis finished. "I deal with Jewish salesmen. They're very nice, most of them are honest. But to marry? There are children to consider. How do you bring up the children?"

"With love and understanding," Susan replied.

"And Catholicism," Theresa added. "They must be brought up in the Church. How do you feel about that, Mark?"

"This is going fast," he replied. "Do I have to decide now?"

"It's important," Louis said.

"Maybe you can talk to Mark's father and we'll do whatever the two of you decide," Susan said.

"Now that's a deal," her father responded. "We'll probably decide you shouldn't get married."

"You probably would agree on that," Mark replied. "But Susan and I love each other. We plan to marry. We hoped for your blessing."

"Try to understand, we're Catholic," Theresa responded. "I want my grandchildren baptized. If they can't be baptized into the church, how can I give you my blessing? You must promise."

"We'll do what we can not to displease you," Susan answered.

Later, after the children left, Theresa turned to Louie. "I should have guessed he wasn't Italian. He's too skinny."

∞

Susan and Mark drove back to Boston.

"How are we going to make everyone happy?" she asked.

"I don't know. I guess we'll promise them anything and give them what we can. The car is heating up." He pulled over and took out the jug of anti-freeze.

Susan watched as he poured it into the radiator. She loved him dearly.

∞

That fall, Susan and Mark were married in a rented hall in Providence, with a priest and Rabbi Reingold sharing the honor of performing the ceremony. Rose looked at her husband as he stood facing the young couple. He was trying to be brave but his heritage was so important to him. This new generation just didn't understand.

Mark broke the glass and the right side of the hall said "Mazel Tov." He kissed the bride. Rose watched as her son led his wife down the aisle. It's a new world, she thought and I'm not going to lose my son. He's more important than my religion.

∞

Mark had to choose a hospital for his internship. The college had provided him with a list of places looking for interns.

"It's our chance to escape," Susan said. "We can go to some place far off and be real adults. We can join a Temple or a Church or a Mosque. We can have children and bring them up any way we want. To baptize or circumcise, that's the question!"

"I'll make a deal with you. If they're girls we won't circumcise them, if they're boys we will," he said with a laugh before turning serious. "But we don't have to run away to do what we want."

"Maybe you don't, Mark, but I'll always feel the pressure. If we move away, we can lie about everything."

℘

They reviewed the list together. He wanted a small hospital; she wanted it to be either west of the Mississippi or south of the Mason Dixon line.

Applications, interviews, visits, final decision. They would move to Calvert, South Carolina. It was a rural town with a small yet modern hospital. Mark was impressed with the administrator and staff. It was little things like the shuttle service for seniors and the day care for children of outpatients that convinced him.

They rented a U-Haul truck, loaded their possessions and waved good-bye to New England and their parents.

It was June 25, 1974.

℘

"Interning is hard work, long hours and lousy pay," Mark complained.

"Get used to it. It isn't much different than family practice," Dr. Goldstein told him.

Dennis Goldstein was his supervisor and mentor at Calvert Hospital. He and his wife Lucille had invited Susan and Mark to their summer getaway on Horizon Lake. It was a nearly deserted body of water, not very large. Their cabin was on the eastern side of the lake. Their view was of the water and an uninhabited gently rolling hill, as the western side was inaccessible by car. The four of them were in Dennis' boat, fishing for bass.

"We've been here two hours," Mark said, looking at his watch. "Aren't we suppose to catch fish or at least have a bite?"

"It would ruin the serenity," Lucille responded.

"It is peaceful," Susan said.

"How do you like Calvert?" Lucille asked. "It took me five years to get used to it and another five years to fall in love with it."

"It's a far cry from Brooklyn," Dennis added.

"We like it so far," Susan replied. "The only complaint I have is Dennis works Mark too hard. I never see him."

"I work him so I can take it easy," Dennis responded. "Every doctor needs a slave."

"I got one!" Lucille said.

"A slave?" Dennis asked.

"No, a fish," she responded as she skillfully reeled in her line.

"Careful," Dennis said. "Don't lose it, it looks like a keeper."

"Is it a bass?" Mark asked.

"I don't know. Quick, the net," Lucille yelled.

"God, it's ugly," Susan said as Dennis netted a two-pound catfish. "Look, it has whiskers."

Adeptly, Lucille removed the hook before displaying her catch. She then gently put it back in the lake watching it shake before swimming off. "Not bad for a little girl from the Bronx."

They settled back to their fishing.

That evening, they sat sipping gin and tonic, watching the sun go down.

"Dennis, start the grill, I'll make the salad," Lucille said. "The steaks are in the fridge."

"I was hoping for catfish," Mark said, feigning disappointment.

They went about the chore of preparing dinner. It was dark now, and a chill had replaced the hot Carolina sun.

"How do you like your job?" Lucille asked Susan.

"I would like it better if we weren't always picketed and threatened. The anti-abortionists are a very active and vociferous group."

Susan worked as an options counselor at the only abortion clinic in the area. Never having forgotten Tess Green and the way she had handled Marie Langlois, she hoped she was as helpful to her clients.

"Especially here in Calvert," Dennis said. "Many are fanatical in their belief that life begins at conception."

"That's their right," Mark responded.

"I decided a long time ago that abortion is wrong for me. But every woman should have the right to choose," Susan said.

"I agree but if you believe that life begins at conception, then you're protecting innocent lives by fighting abortion," Lucille replied.

"But a woman should be able to decide the fate of her own body," Susan reasoned. "And she has a right to privacy. It's no one else's business. A fetus is totally dependent on the woman and if she doesn't want it there, that's her choice."

"Hey, let's not talk shop," Mark said. "We're here to get away from it. Look at those stars. I'd say tomorrow will be perfect. The fish are in big trouble. We know they must be hungry. They weren't eating today."

Part Three

Kristen

CHAPTER SIXTEEN

"Sally's fine," Dr. Allen told the girl's mother. "She may have a reaction to the shot, but it's better than getting sick."

He patted his little patient on the head and smiled.

"Have you jumped off any chairs lately?" the doctor asked.

"You remember?" the mother responded, helping her daughter recall the accident. "That was over a year ago now. No, I think Sally learned her lesson, didn't you?"

The girl smiled her reply.

"No scar from the stitches," the doctor said, checking the side of her head. "I'm a pretty good tailor, if I say so myself."

Dr. Allen handed Sally a lollipop and watched them for a moment, as they walked down the hall. He closed the door, sat at his desk, and breathed deeply as he reached into the drawer and took out a pint bottle of gin. The liquor ran down his throat, into his stomach, warming each part as it passed.

"Ahh," he said to the empty office, "That's good."

He patted his lips with his handkerchief, took out a peppermint lifesaver, and pressed the intercom.

"Send in the next patient, would you, Julie?"

೮೧

Kristen and two of her friends had gone to see the movie, <u>Days of Wine and Roses.</u> While the film moved her friends, it terrified Kristen. Her parents were drunks.

Her father was a doctor. He should know better. The movie was about a couple, Mr. and Mrs. Clay, and their downward spiral into alcoholism. The Clays' had a daughter. God, it was like watching a film about Kristen's own family. As the movie ended, Joe Clay had beaten his illness through Alcoholics Anonymous but his wife was powerless to do the same.

Kristen came home excited with hope. She'd never spoken to her parents about their drinking before, but this movie gave her the courage. She wasn't alone. There were others, lots of others, in the same boat.

There was no help until the drunk admitted he was sick. That had been the difference between Mr. and Mrs. Clay. Kristen would convince her parents.

That evening, she told them about the movie.

Her mother responded with a blank stare.

"Maybe you should look into Alcoholics Anonymous," Kristen suggested.

"Us?" Her father laughed. "I'll admit we have a drink once in a while, honey, but we're not lushes. It relaxes us after a hard day, but that's all."

He kissed his daughter. She recoiled from his offensive breath.

&

George had returned to Calvert after his graduation from medical school, sixteen years ago. He bought old Doc Brown's practice and dedicated himself to giving his patients the best care he knew how. Even now he tried his best but the alcohol was getting in the way.

Lucy and George Allen always had a drink when he came home from work. In the beginning, a martini before dinner was a treat. Now, it was one more in an attempt to satisfy their unending need.

She handed him his drink and took one for herself, placing a shaker of refills on the coffee table in front of them. They sat on the couch.

"Where's Kristen?"

"In her room, doing homework."

Fourteen-year-old Kristen was their only child.

They talked their small talk, but their objective was the alcohol. The day had been routine for both of them. Lucy had spent the morning straightening up the house with the help of a tall Bloody Mary. At lunch with a friend, she only nibbled at her sandwich but drank two glasses of wine. The soap operas, accompanied by vermouth, took care of her afternoon.

George looked at his wife. Her hair was disheveled. There were bags under her eyes he knew shouldn't be there in a woman of thirty-six. And she was thin, painfully thin. Yet he was glad he was married to her. They sustained each other in their habit, never condemning, always supportive. They had met when he was in his first year of medical school. Lucy had been a secretary at the hospital. She was tall, big breasted, a knockout.

Medical school was a financial struggle. His loan and scholarship covered his tuition, but it wasn't enough to provide his living expenses. After they were married, Lucy took over the finances. She worked seven days a week at two jobs. They had both agreed it was worth it.

At thirty-eight his sexual urges were gone and she, also, didn't seem to have any needs. He nibbled on some crackers and cheese before refilling his glass.

"Hungry?" Lucy asked.

"Not very."

"There's some cold cuts in the fridge. I can fix you a sandwich."

"No," he answered, yawning and staring at the now emptied pitcher.

"Should I make some more?" he asked his wife but Lucy had fallen asleep. He could feel his eyes grow heavy. He didn't want his daughter to find them both passed out again, but he just didn't have the energy to do anything about it.

80

Kristen came downstairs knowing what would greet her. She looked at her parents sleeping on the couch. They were good people but she could never depend on them. Why did they drink? Her anger was mixed with resignation. How many times had her mother forgotten to pack her lunch? How many times had Kristen waited to be picked up after a dance, watching her friends drive off one after the other until she was alone, her parents too intoxicated to remember? Her eyes filled with tears as she looked at these two drunks who had given her life. She'd long ago stopped inviting friends over to her house because she was afraid they would discover her secret.

Without knowing why, Kristen sometimes blamed herself for her parents' alcoholism. She left them asleep on the couch and went to the kitchen to make herself dinner. After Kristen had eaten and cleaned up, she went to her room to study and listen to records. A few hours later, she went back to the living room.

"Dad, wake up," she said, shaking him.

He struggled to open his bloodshot eyes. "What?"

Her nostrils filled with his alcoholic breath. "You fell asleep on the couch," she said, as if it were not a daily occurrence.

Lucy opened her eyes. "I must have dozed off," she said. "Have you eaten, honey?"

It was a strange question. Kristen could not remember the last time her mother had prepared anything for her. "Yes."

"How was school today?" her father asked, his speech slurred.

"Okay," she replied, knowing there was no point in sharing any of her problems with them.

"What time is it?" George asked.

"Ten-fifteen."

"I've a long day tomorrow. I'm going to bed," he responded.

"I'll go with you," Lucy agreed. "Honey, will you clean up down here?"

Kristen nodded. She picked up the shaker, glasses, cheese and crackers and headed for the kitchen. What's the use, she thought. I'm not going to change them. She cleaned up and went off to bed where she lay awake thinking. She longed for a brother or sister to share her lonely life.

After seeing <u>Days of Wine and Roses</u> she had hoped her parents would admit to their problem and join Alcoholics Anonymous. It seemed so simple. But they claimed they weren't drunks. What were the chances of both her parents getting over this illness? Not much.

She fell into a restless sleep which included a recurring nightmare. In it she was looking for her parents. They had been lost a long time. She asked the neighbors if they had seen them. The answer was always No.

Drunks lined the sidewalks. They all looked like her folks but each time she got close, she realized she was mistaken. At last, she was sure she saw them. They were huddled together shivering. She tried to run to her parents but her legs were heavy, and she couldn't seem to reach them. At last, with great effort, she made it. They looked up at her. Her father was unshaven; her mother emaciated, her head almost a skull.

"I'm sorry," her mother pleaded.

"I'm sorry," her father echoed.

She looked around for their drinks, but there was nothing. She got close to smell their breath, but could smell nothing.

"Please forgive us," her mother asked.

Suddenly, spotlights illuminated the area. She looked out toward the radiance and realized the three of them were on the high school stage, the auditorium filled with her classmates. Her friends would see her parents. They would know that her mother and father were drunks. No, no, that couldn't be. She looked around the stage. There was a large white sheet, sitting on a table. She ran to it. Thank God, her legs were working now. She grabbed the sheet and threw it over her parents. Maybe no one had noticed.

"Help, help, we can't breathe," they shouted.

Kristen didn't care. She just didn't want anyone to see them. Suddenly the sheet went limp. She pulled it away and no one was there. She looked around for them but they were gone. All her classmates were wildly applauding. Kristen turned toward them and bowed.

She became frightened then and woke to daylight. She looked around her bedroom, and heard her father in the bathroom getting ready for work. He passed wind, as he did every morning. She wondered if he knew or cared that she was within earshot. She could hear her mother snoring in her room down the hall. Kristen got out of bed. It was six forty-five, a new day. Time to get ready for school. She knew this day would be the same as all her yesterdays.

ॐ

"George, I'm going to be blunt with you. Do you have a drinking problem?" his doctor asked.

The question confirmed George's suspicions. He had noticed his loss of appetite, which had never been much to begin with. When Kristen mentioned he was getting a pot-belly, he knew it wasn't from over-eating. It was a symptom. He'd started to vomit, almost daily, and noticed traces of blood. He had postponed the inevitable second opinion to his own until his eyes turned a sickly yellow. There was no point in kidding himself any longer.

"Yes. It's the first time I've admitted it."

"You have cirrhosis of the liver, and if you don't get help, it'll kill you. You must stop drinking."

"I can't, Stu. I just can't."

"It's a death sentence if you don't. Get help, George. Join A.A."

"Stu, you have no idea. I'm constantly depressed. I can't get a hard-on. I'm always vomiting blood. Don't you think I'm desperate to stop? I look in the mirror and see myself turning yellow. I know the prognosis."

"George, the only way to halt the cirrhosis is to quit drinking. If you don't, you know the consequences. I can treat you with a high protein diet, give you transfusions, but it'll do no good if you don't give up the booze."

George didn't take his doctor's advice.

ॐ

The pattern of their lives was so set that when Kristen came home from school three weeks before Thanksgiving, to see her mother looking out the large picture window that overlooked their wooded back yard, she knew something was wrong. She surveyed the room, looking for signs of booze. There were none.

Kristen was now a junior in high school. Much of her time was spent taking care of her parents. She longed for it to be the other way around.

"Mother?"

Lucy turned slowly. There was a look of despair on her face.

"Your father's in the hospital," she said softly. The doctor wants to see us. Will you drive?"

"What's the matter with him?" Kristen asked in the car.

"He's very weak and sick. They say it's his liver, cirrhosis of the liver, whatever that is."

"God, Mother, you know what that is. It's from all that drinking you both do. A blind man could see he's been sick."

"Don't talk to me that way. Your father is dying and all you can do is lecture me."

Kristen started to cry. She had held so much in for so long, the anger and frustration poured out uncontrollably.

"You're both drunks. You look like hell. You smell of booze all the time and you act like everything is fine. You disgust me. What's cirrhosis of the liver, you want to know? It's a disease that drunks get, drunks like you and Daddy."

"How dare you," cried Lucy, striking Kristen in the face with all her strength.

The vehicle swerved to the left. Kristen screamed as she turned the steering wheel sharply to the right to avoid an oncoming pick-up truck. The car left the pavement. Desperately she tried to regain control, to force the car back onto the road, before hitting an old oak tree looming straight ahead.

∽

"Mother, mother," Kristen spoke. "Oh mother, please be okay."

She heard the siren and saw an ambulance arrive.

The pain was bad. The medics were putting her mother in the ambulance. One medic drove off leaving the other to tend to Kristen.

"Is she okay?" Kristen asked. "She wasn't moving. Oh God, what have I done?"

"Stay still," the man responded.

∽

Kristen was taken to emergency. X-rays showed no broken bones. She asked all whom came to her if they knew of her mother's condition. No one seemed to have any information.

Kristen was taken to a room and sedated. When she awoke, her Uncle Jack was sitting in a chair next to her bed. He was holding her hand. A nurse was also there.

She looked around at the tidy room. It was a single. Her father had often complained about the overcrowding of the hospital. How come she was in a single?

"Uncle Jack? What are you doing here? Oh, my God! My mother. How's my mother?"

Jack Ploss was her mother's brother. They weren't close and for good reason. Jack didn't drink and didn't condone that habit in his sister or her husband. He'd tried to influence them, get them interested in his church, but they had laughed at him and told him it wasn't their thing. He believed they had lost their way and wanted to help them find eternal salvation, but eventually he stopped butting in. Jack bent over and kissed his niece.

"Kristen, I'm sorry. Your mother died instantly in the accident. She didn't suffer."

Kirsten recalled the slap. Her mother had died angry with her. She felt a terrible ache. She wanted to tell her mother she was sorry but that was forever impossible. Tears fell without a sound. My mother, my poor mother, she thought.

"Does Daddy know?"

Her uncle looked at the nurse before speaking.

"Your father died without ever knowing," her uncle said. "Oh, Kristen, this is so terrible, I don't know what to say to you,"

"No. Oh, please no. Not Daddy," the girl pleaded.

"He knew he was dying, Kristen," her uncle said. "He wrote you a letter and asked me to give it to you."

"When did he write it?" she asked as she unfolded the paper.

"Yesterday."

"He knew?"

"He was a doctor. He knew."

She looked at the writing. It was difficult to read, almost a scribble.

Dearest Kirsten

You're a wonderful daughter, deserving of a better father. I wasn't there for you, to listen, hold you, go to your plays or games. I know you stopped inviting your friends to the house because you were ashamed of me. I hated myself but I couldn't seem to stop my drinking.

Uncle Jack has promised me he will look after you and your mom. He and Aunt Jean are good people.

I didn't tell you very often how much I love you, but I do. I love you very much.

Forgive me. Daddy

She folded the letter and dried her eyes with the bed sheet.

"Aunt Jean and I wish to have you come live with us. We never were blessed with children of our own. We'd like to open our home and our hearts to you."

It was too much for Kristen to fathom all at once. "I don't know."

"You don't have to decide anything right now, I just want you to understand that we'll be there for you."

Her eyes closed.

"Sleep well, Kristen. We'll talk again in the morning. I'll be here when you wake up," her uncle told her.

∓

Kristen slowly came to love her aunt and uncle. Eventually, she allowed herself to trust and depend on them. It was a feeling she never had before. How strange for someone to say, "I'll pick you up after the dance," and then be there at the appointed time. Jean and Jack were totally reliable and it felt so good.

Kristen believed the greatest gift her aunt and uncle gave her was Jesus. They were members of the Calvert Christian Church, which ran the new Christian School. Although she had attended services on Christmas and Easter with her parents, George and Lucy had never discovered the contentment and joy of truly knowing Jesus as their Savior.

Kristen would never forget that first Sunday after she had moved in with Jack and Jean. She still mourned and missed her parents very much. They may have been unreliable drunks but she knew what to expect. Now everything was foreign to her. Her aunt and uncle seemed nice enough but they weren't her parents.

"We'd like you to go to church with us," Jack said.

"We go every Sunday. It's very important to us." Jean added.

During the service, her aunt held her hand. At first, Kristen thought how strange and considered taking her hand away. No, it might hurt her aunt's feelings.

The choir sang; the preacher led his congregation in prayer.

She looked up at him, high on the pulpit. He was tall and thin, dressed in a black suit. He held his Bible in his right hand and waved it, as if he were leading a symphony, as he spoke.

He talked of death, quoting the 23rd Psalm.

"Yea, though I walk through the valley of the shadow of death, I will fear no evil, for Thou art with me;"

He told his congregation that all who accepted Jesus would live forever in Heaven with the angels. He ended his sermon with a quotation from John:

"Whosoever believeth in Him should not perish, but have eternal life."

Kristen was mesmerized by the sermon. Her mind wandered back to her parents. Were they with Jesus? Would Jesus save two drunks who had never really accepted Him?

"What did you think?" Jean asked, as they left the church.

"It made me feel good."

Jean and Jack smiled at each other.

"We don't want to push you, but we've found great comfort in the church. We hope you'll go with us on Sundays and even attend Bible class with us," Jack said.

"I think I would like that."

"We've enrolled you in our church high school," Jean continued. "Would you mind trying it. If you don't like it you can return to public school."

"I guess so."

❧

It was Kristen's first day at The Calvert Christian School, which was part of her church and new this year. Jean worried about Kristen all day and had been watching out the window for her the past half-hour.

God works in strange ways, Jean thought. Kristen had come to them from the hospital. Had she been barren so that she would be available to give herself to her niece? The girl had suffered so much.

"How did it go today?" Aunt Jean asked.

"It was okay."

"Want some cookies and milk, or anything?"

"No, thank you. I'll go to my room. I have lots of catching up to do."

"Sure. Go ahead."

Jean knew her niece's childhood had been difficult. It would take a while for the girl to adjust.

Kristen stayed in her room until supper. Jack and Jean tried to talk with her, but she simply answered their questions without adding to the conversation. After eating, she excused herself. Jack helped Jean with the dishes.

"She's so quiet, so difficult to reach," Jean said. "I hope we didn't make a mistake enrolling her in the church school."

"It'll take time," her husband responded. "Calvert Christian will be good for her."

ဆ

It didn't happen often, and Kristen didn't want to upset her aunt and uncle with it. But it scared her. The first time was right after she moved in with them. She was in English class, paying attention, when she heard her mother speak to her.

"I'm glad everything is going so well for you, dear."

"What?" Kristen responded.

"I'm sorry," the teacher said. "Did you say something, Kristen."

Miss Ruddy was a kind woman and had been especially gentle.

The other students were looking at Kristen. She could feel the blood rushing to her head as she apologized. The voice had seemed so real.

It was to happen again, sometimes her mother; other times, her father--not often, but it always frightened her. Still she kept it to herself. Then she met Harold and the voices stopped. Or, so she thought.

CHAPTER SEVENTEEN

As a child, Harold Edwards never fit in. He longed to be liked by his contemporaries but didn't know how. His classmates laughed at his thick glasses, white socks and high-water pants. His parents just didn't know about things like corduroy Levis and Weejuns and couldn't afford them if they had.

When he was in his first year of high school, he had a crush on a girl that practically immobilized him. She was not so popular herself and maybe, just maybe, she would be interested. Still, he didn't quite know how to go about approaching her. After days of being incapacitated by fear mixed with excitement, he gathered all his courage and asked the girl to join him for a movie. She laughed at him, calling him a loser. He didn't dare risk rejection again for many years.

When Harold was seventeen, he attended a service at the Calvert Christian Church. The parishioners didn't seem to notice his too short pants or his white socks. Rather, they saw an aura in him that had not been evident to others.

He studied his Bible and came to love and believe literally in all its teachings. By the time Harold Edwards was twenty-two years old, he was a biblical scholar, teaching the Bible class at the Calvert Christian Church. His knowledge and sincerity earned him a newfound respect unusual for his young age. He became meticulous in his dress, imitating the evangelists he saw on television. His classes were always filled to overflowing with parishioners and their guests who were mesmerized by this young untrained preacher.

When he received his draft notice, Harold was prepared to do his duty but poor eyesight made him ineligible. He took a job as a florist never tiring of arranging God's handiwork in beautifully artistic bouquets. He believed he was in God's hands and Jesus would guide him on this earth and bring him to His side when his days here were finished.

೧

Jack and Jean took Kristen to the Bible class that was held in the basement of the Calvert Christian Church. She was surprised to find fifty or sixty people in attendance, each one carrying the Good Book. Kristen was familiar with the room as it also served as the auditorium for her school. Harold Edwards was at the podium.

"Please, if you'll find your seats, we can begin," he said.

There were not enough folding metal chairs set up, and the men opened extra chairs that had been stacked against the wall.

Harold Edwards spoke softly, but his voice had a commanding quality. Kristen was surprised that he wasn't much older than she. He was perhaps six feet tall, thin and dressed in a well-pressed gray flannel suit, which set him apart from the casually attired audience.

"The first and greatest commandment is to love the Lord, your God with all your heart, soul, and mind," Harold began.

From his beginning words to his last, Kristen listened enthralled.

The session ended with coffee and cakes prepared by the women's auxiliary. Conversation centered on the young man's preaching. Kristen froze as the evangelist approached them.

"Jack, Jean, it's nice to see you here this evening. We've missed you. And this must be the reason. You're Kristen, right?" Harold said.

"Yes, this is our niece," Jack responded.

"I was sorry to hear about your parents," he shook his head.

Kristen shifted her weight from one foot to the other, wondering how much he knew.

"Thank you." She wanted to tell him how much she enjoyed listening to him but was too shy. Instead, she mumbled, "I've never been much of a churchgoer," regretting her words as they tumbled out.

"Maybe that will change," the young man replied.

∿

"Jack, this is Harold. I want to ask you something."

"Yes," Jack responded into the phone, amused that the young man who spoke so eloquently each week sounded tongue-tied. He suspected the reason for the call.

"Uh, can I ask Kristen to go out with me for an evening? I would like to take her to supper or to a movie, if that's okay with you."

"That would be fine with me."

"May I speak with her? Is she home?"

"One moment. I'll get her for you."

Jack put down the phone and called for his niece.

"Who is it?" she whispered.

"It's Harold Edwards," he replied, wondering if this pleased Kristen.

She looked puzzled as she took the phone. He watched her look of bewilderment change to an ever-widening smile.

ℴ

It was Kristen's first date. As she sat beside him in the movie theater, occasionally sneaking a glance at him, she wondered what she would do if he wanted to hold her hand. It was a moot point. He never tried.

After the movie, they went to a coffee shop.

"What do you do besides teach Bible class?" she asked.

"I work for a florist."

"You do?"

"You sound surprised."

"No. Well, maybe. I never knew a florist before."

"I love flowers."

As he drove her home, Kristen edged closer to him, hoping he'd know it was all right with her if he kissed her goodnight. She'd never been kissed by a boy before and always dreamed of someone as nice as Harold being her first.

He pulled into her driveway.

"I've had a very nice evening, Kristen," he said as he got out of the car and walked over to open the door for her. Together, still without touching, they walked up the path to her front porch. When they arrived at the door, she turned to face him and brought herself as close to him as she dared.

"May I call on you again?" he asked.

"Of course. I'd like that."

"Goodnight, Kristen." He turned and left.

Her aunt and uncle were in the kitchen. She knew they were waiting to hear about her evening. How different from her own parents. How nice.

ℴ

Kristen knew Harold cared for her. Why else would he want to see her as much as he did? For the next two months, she saw him three times a week--Thursday Bible class, Saturday date, and Sunday church, and still

131

no first kiss. She cared for him, looked forward to their time together but started wondering if there wasn't something wrong with her.

෪

Kristen loved The Calvert Christian School. Her teachers and classmates were like family, hugging each other in greeting. She felt secure and nurtured not only by those at school but mostly by her Jesus.

Shortly after she began attending the Calvert Christian School, the administrator came to her classroom and told everyone to go outside. She followed her classmates, thinking it must be a fire drill until she saw everyone looking up at the roof. A young boy had his arm wrapped around the steeple. He was shouting something.

The boy threatened to jump unless the Pastor said Jesus didn't exist. Kristen became frightened. She knew the boy was Pip Marshall. She heard other kids talk about him as a sinner who didn't accept Christ as his personal savior and it made her sad.

"Come on down and I'll help you find Jesus," the Pastor said but the boy refused.

The Pastor spoke to another man and then called up to Pip. "Christ may not exist."

Pip shouted that everyone, teachers and students must say "Christ may not exist" or he would jump.

How could Kristen say this about her Savior who existed without question. As each took their turn, she slunk more to the back not knowing what she would do when it was her turn.

When there was no one else before her, she looked up at him but the words wouldn't come. She wiped a tear from her cheek before hearing herself finally respond. "Please, Pip, don't make me say it. I just recently found Jesus and it would hurt too much to betray my Savior. Please."

She looked up at him, terrified that her words would make him jump. He stared silently at her before replying. "It's okay Kristen. You don't have to say it."

An officer helped him down and as everyone filed back into the school, she noticed him being driven off.

෪

Some weeks later, much to her joy, Kristen saw Pip in church. He appeared joyful as he participated in the services. She contemplated speaking to him but for a few weeks couldn't muster the courage. Yet, she knew Jesus would want her to greet him, so after services on a bright February Sunday, she approached him. "How have you been doing, Pip?"

"I'm fine," he replied.

"I was watching you at services. I knew if you gave Jesus a chance, you would find him. I'm so glad."

"Thank you," Pip replied.

A few weeks later, Pip stopped coming to church and their paths didn't cross again for many years.

ॐ

It was a Saturday in June. Kristen had finished her junior year, and Harold suggested celebrating by going out for dinner and attending a young adult dance at the church. After the social they walked the two miles to Kristen's home. Harold would have to walk back to get his car but he said he didn't mind.

She doubted he felt any urges for her. He was attentive but showed no affection. As they strolled she put her arm through his, which seemed to please him. They arrived at her front porch and in their usual manner faced each other. Would he finally kiss her?

"Kristen, I care for you very much," he said, his eyes searching hers. "I hope you have regard for me."

"I do," she replied, smiling at his awkward formality. They were standing so close she could feel his breath on her face.

He bent over, closing the inch or two that separated their mouths. Their lips touched for a moment before he moved back.

"Kristen, I love you."

He turned and left, never giving her the opportunity to tell him his feelings were reciprocated.

ॐ

Kristen and Harold were engaged to be married the September after she graduated from high school.

"There's an opening at the shop. Why don't you apply?" he asked her.

"Would you mind if we worked together?"

"Mind? I'd love it."

Miss Dove owned the store. Although she'd been an English major in college, her fondness for flowers was like a calling, and when her father died in her sophomore year, she had abandoned her plans to write and teach in favor of taking over his florist shop. Harold had been her first and only employee until now.

Miss Dove was five-seven with short blond hair and a ready smile. Kristen was surprised by her manner of dress. She wore white short shorts, with a green tank top that read Dove's Florist Shop. The top was loose fitting, frequently exposing most of her bra-less breasts. Miss Dove was apparently oblivious to her near toplessness. Her work boots attested to the long hours she spent in the soil. Kristen couldn't help but wonder if Harold had ever noticed Miss Dove as a woman. How could he not? But knowing Harold...

"You're not afraid of getting your hands dirty are you, Kristen?"

The interview was taking place in Miss Dove's office which consisted of two folding bridge chairs and a wooden desk, cluttered with boxes, ribbons, scissors, and papers. The only thing on the desk that did not pertain to the business was a picture of a man wearing a large brimmed Stetson, sitting on a horse.

"No, Miss Dove."

"Harold says you'll be good. On the one hand, he's prejudiced when it comes to you. On the other, I trust his judgment." Miss Dove laughed heartily at her own joke. Kristen smiled. "Another problem is if I hire you, you'll go on your honeymoon together, leaving me alone."

She wasn't going to hire her.

"What the hell, you can start Monday."

℘

Kristen spent all her free time with Jean, planning the wedding. The gown was expensive. Jean and Jack insisted on paying for everything.

"Put it on for Uncle Jack," Jean said the evening they brought the wedding dress home.

"Isn't it bad luck or something?" her uncle asked.

"Don't be superstitious, dear. Put it on, honey."

"I feel bad," she told her aunt. "It cost so much money."

"Kristen, you're the child we never had. We would do anything for you. It gives us happiness. Now, for goodness sake, go try it on before I burst," she said, mock annoyance in her voice.

Kristen hugged her aunt. "Come help me."

Twenty minutes later they presented a fashion show for her uncle.

"It's breathtaking," was all he said, and Kristen knew he was right.

ॐ

Kristen and Harold were both virgins when they married. She belonged to her husband now, had promised before man and God to love, honor, and obey. It was all she wanted or ever would want. She was sure of her faith and her ultimate destiny.

They planned a weeklong honeymoon to Bermuda. Neither had ever been on a plane. Aunt Jean and Uncle Jack had given them the trip as a wedding gift. Their first night was spent at a hotel near the airport.

"Hungry?" Harold asked, after the bellhop left them alone in their room.

"No."

"You were a beautiful bride. I'm a lucky man."

Kristen knew Harold was as nervous as she was. She approached him. He put his arms around her and they kissed.

"God has favored me with a lovely wife," he said.

Kristen went to the bathroom where she changed into the pegnoir her aunt had bought. Shyly, she opened the door. Harold was in his pajamas and robe. He came to her, took her in his arms and held her close before removing his robe and leading her to the bed. Slowly his hands undressed her and gently he kissed her breasts, which he had never before touched. His kisses went lower.

"Are you okay?" he asked. "I want this to be a special night."

"I'm fine."

"You're crying. What's wrong?" Harold asked.

"Nothing's wrong, silly. It's just I love you so much. You're the kindest, gentlest man I ever knew."

He smiled as he removed his socks, got under the covers, and turned off the lamp on his night table.

"I'm glad we waited," she purred.

"It's God's commandment. He always knows best."

ॐ

Bermuda was paradise. They toured the island, indulged in too much food, and delighted in the profusion of flowers. They went to Sunday services and marveled at the power of the Lord to extend into the far reaches of each tiny hamlet.

Jean and Jack greeted them at the airport upon their return home. The newlyweds babbled about their trip.

"Miss Dove called. She wants to see you both as soon as possible," Jack said when they finally gave him a chance.

"We plan to go to work tomorrow," Harold responded.

"She knew when we'd be returning. I wonder why she called," Kristen added.

When they arrived a half-hour before opening, they were surprised to see their boss anxiously waiting. Miss Dove asked them to come into her office.

"You're not the only ones who can get married," she announced.

"You're engaged!" Kristen shouted.

A broad grin swept across Miss Dove's face. "Yes. He's a wonderful man. He's from Texas and his business is there. He wants me to join him."

Kristen felt panic as Harold verbalized her concern.

"What will you do with the shop?"

"Sell it."

"To whom?" he asked.

"You would be a logical choice."

"We don't have any money," Kristen said.

"I would finance most of it. I know you'd be successful. I don't need my money all at once, just a small down payment. See what you can do." Her happy smile never left her face.

ℬ

A trust fund!" Harold exclaimed.

"Kristen was left money when her parents died. The bank has had the money all these years. It's grown to a tidy sum. More than enough for a down payment," Jack responded.

"But why didn't you use it while I was growing up? You paid for everything, even my wedding."

"We wanted you to have the whole amount when the time was right," Aunt Jean said. "And the time is right."

ℬ

The work would have consumed them, if Kristen hadn't discovered she was pregnant.

After their son was born, Harold resisted the idea of Kristen returning to work but knew he needed her and, therefore, didn't forbid it.

For the next five years the shop took on the look of a nursery as Kristen gave birth to a second son two years after the first. When it was no longer tenable to keep the boys at the shop, Jean became their permanent baby sitter, a role she relished.

CHAPTER EIGHTEEN

"We're here," Kristen shouted as she entered her aunt's home, the boys running to their great aunt and throwing their arms around her.

"Can you stay for coffee?" Jean asked.

"Harold needs me at the shop." Seeing the disappointment on her aunt's face, she continued, "Okay, a quick cup."

Jean put the kettle on the stove.

"Nana, the cookie jar is empty," Robert said, disbelief in his voice.

"You can help me bake some tollhouse cookies after your mother leaves," Jean told the boy as she brought the cups to the table and sat down with her niece.

"How's business?"

"It's booming. Harold loves it and so do I."

Jean smiled. "I knew you'd be successful. You both are so fond of plants and flowers. I love seeing you so happy. You deserve it."

"Harold's a wonderful husband."

"We're planning to have you all here for Christmas dinner next month," Jean said, reaching over and squeezing her niece's hand.

"Why don't I do it this year?"

"You can do it when I'm too old."

"You'll never be too old," she told her aunt, giving her a peck on the cheek before kissing her boys and running out the door.

As she drove toward work and the husband she loved, Kristen was unaware that hundreds of miles away in the nation's Capital, nine judges were considering a case that would put an end to her sheltered, peaceful life.

ɛᴐ

On January 22, 1973, the Supreme Court voted that no state can prevent a woman from having an abortion.

"Oh, my God, what does this mean?" Harold asked, visibly shaken. "Life begins at conception. How can they not know that?"

"I don't know," Kristen responded. "What can we do about it?"

Harold left the shop and went to the drugstore. He returned with the local paper and the New York Times. He read everything he could find on the decision.

"Look at this," he said, handing his wife the local paper. As she read aloud, he became quiet, sullen.

> "A landmark decision was handed down by the Supreme Court today. The ruling gives women the right to abortion on demand during the first six months of pregnancy. The court agreed by a seven to two margin that as long as one person's body is the sole source of another life, that person and that person alone should decide if she wants to sustain that life or abort it. The court divided pregnancy into three parts. In the first trimester abortion is to be available to women without question, the only condition being that it must be performed by a physician. In the second trimester, the woman must be examined before an abortion. If it is decided that the abortion will not be harmful to the woman, it may be performed. It is only in the final trimester that the fetus has any rights. At that time, an abortion can only be performed to save the life of the mother. Reaction to the decision was..."

Kristen put down the paper and went to her husband. "Darling," she said, putting her arms around him. "What does it mean?"

There were tears in his eyes. He tried to talk without crying but was too filled with emotion. "They've legalized murder. They can murder innocent unborn children now. This can't be. No, this can't be. They don't understand. If they did, they wouldn't allow it to happen. Murderers!"

Kristen didn't respond. She didn't know how to console her husband, had never seen him so upset.

"I'm going home. Would you close up?" he said.

"Of course."

He tucked the newspapers under his arm and headed for the door. "You take the car and pick up the boys. I'll walk."

Slowly he hiked the three miles to his home. As he walked, an idea crystallized in his mind. There was something he could do. He knew he had the power of persuasion. He would use his skill to convince the Supreme Court to alter it's decision. Kristen and the boys still weren't home when he arrived. He took out paper and pen and sat at his kitchen table. Who did the newspaper say was the moving force for this catastrophic decision? Ah, yes, Blackmun. He was the one.

January 23, 1973
Your Honor Harry Blackmun
Supreme Court
Washington, D.C.

Dear Justice Blackmun:

Because of you, millions of innocent children will not live to see the light of day. You must not know that life begins at conception. God has commanded us to populate the earth. How can any human determine that an unborn baby may be put to death? America protects its citizens. You have chosen to ignore the unborn child's rights to life, liberty and the pursuit of happiness.

Please, I beg you for all those unable to plead their own case, let them live. Please, please, let them live.

Sincerely,

Harold Edwards

He walked to the mailbox. As he approached the park, Harold heard the sound of children playing and stopped to watch them. If Roe vs. Wade had happened a few years ago, how many of these children would be dead? Once Justice Blackmun understood, he would reverse his decision.

Kristen came home with the boys. Each ran to their father. He lowered himselff on one knee and hugged them extra hard.

"You're squeezing my guts out," Thomas laughed.

"I love you boys," Harold responded.

Kristen went to her husband and took his hand. As he rose to greet her, she knew something had happened.

"It'll be okay," he said as he held her gently next to him. "I wrote a letter to Judge Blackmun. I know now he simply doesn't understand. He can't. He and the other justices are lawmakers, not killers. They'll change their minds."

৪১

The Supreme Court didn't reverse its decision and abortion became the right of all females. Hospitals and clinics all over the country performed the operations in a safe environment. Women no longer had to go into offices of corrupt doctors or nurses who overcharged the patients and often performed the abortion in an unsafe manner.

৪১

In the wake of the decision, Harold decided to take the topic to the podium. He spoke at his church of the potential murder of millions of children.

"It is written in Jeremiah 61:4,5, 'Then the word of the Lord came unto me, saying, Before I formed thee in the belly I knew thee.' If God knew us before conception how can man abort us after conception? God has an interest in preserving the life of the unborn child that takes precedence over a woman's right to kill a baby living in her belly. The Supreme Court said that Dred Scot, a slave, was not a human. We know the Supreme Court can be wrong. But never in all our almost three-hundred-year history, has the Supreme Court committed a more grievous crime than when it legalized the murder of millions of babies who have no power to protect themselves."

The congregants gathered around Harold. They were moved by his words and wanted to help stop this 'genocide'.

"If you really want to do something, we must organize. Picket the clinic. Stop the killing. Our voices can be heard."

The following Saturday, Harold led twenty-eight followers to the clinic. They carried signs and shouted at the people entering. The next Saturday other churches joined and each ensuing weekend the number of protestors grew. After a few months, the churches organized so there were picketers every day. But it didn't stop the killing.

Harold lay in his bed, exhausted from a day of protesting, staring at the ceiling. Millions of babies were going to die, and he could do nothing to stop it.

"I'm so frustrated. We can picket, write letters, raise our voices but no one hears, no one listens..." Harold said.

Kristen nestled next to him and stroked his arm.

"What would Jesus have us do? Oh, Lord, please show me how I can do your work to save your children," he asked his God.

CHAPTER NINTEEN

Bernie Parks got married a week after receiving his orders to ship out to Vietnam. He wasn't sure how it all came about; it just kind of happened. Nancy cried when she learned he was leaving and the next thing he knew they were married. Bernie was nineteen, she was eighteen.

Why was America at war? It didn't really matter. Something about bringing freedom to an oppressed people and opposing communism.

He never questioned his orders. When he was told to search out and destroy the enemy he did it with the skill and dedication of one who had been brought up to believe that America was never wrong and God was always on her side. Decorated with a bronze medal and a purple heart, he believed he would return to Calvert a hero.

Bernie came home on May 10, 1970. One week earlier, on the Kent State Campus, the Ohio National Guard had killed four students who were protesting the United States' involvement in Cambodia.

Quickening his pace, he went up the walk to his parents' house. The white paint appeared more chipped than he remembered. He opened the door. The hall was empty. Quietly, he went to the kitchen. His mother was reaching into a cupboard, her back to him. Without a sound, he went to her, putting his hands over her eyes.

"Who's your favorite?" he whispered.

"Bernie!" she screamed, turning and embracing her son. She hugged him tightly for a long while before stepping back to inspect him, making sure he was whole.

His sister Lucille came downstairs in response to the commotion.

"Hi, kiddo," Bernie said as he threw his arms around the girl.

"Oh, Bernie, Bernie, you're safe. I'm so glad you're home. I've missed you."

He stood back, examining his baby sister. "You've grown, kiddo... you're a woman."

She laughed. "It happens."

"What's that?" he asked, looking at a button she was wearing. "Make love, not war," he read. "What's it mean?"

Lucille took the pin off, holding it in the palm of her hand out of his sight.

"It's nothing," she replied.

"Make love, not war," he repeated. "It doesn't make sense, does it?"

"Many of us thought the war was wrong. We protested."

"I don't understand. I was over there fighting and you were here protesting? Thanks a lot," he responded good- naturedly.

"Listen, if there hadn't been any war, you could have been home with Nancy getting started on your life. I did it for you."

"Cut the bullshit, Lucille," he said, his broad smile fading. "I was there for you. For freedom."

"Did you kill anyone?" she shouted with a passion that Bernie didn't expect or understand.

"I'd rather not talk about it."

"Did you kill anyone?" his sister persisted.

"Yes, I did."

"Warmonger! Killer!" she shouted.

"Lucille!" their Mother admonished.

Bernie was confused and didn't know how to respond.

"I have to find Nancy," he said. "I just want to shower...and get out of my uniform."

His sister ran to him throwing her arms around him. "I'm sorry, Bernie. I don't want to fight with you. I'm so glad you're safe and home."

"That's all right, kid."

He didn't share his Vietnam experiences with Nancy or anyone else. Bernie had killed Viet Cong who were younger than he, had seen three comrades go from life to death in a split second, had fought for his country and came home believing soldiers were always heroes.

Where was the parade he expected, the congratulations on a job well done? That day, his first day home, an anger started gnawing deep inside of Bernie that was never to go away, although he wasn't ever sure if it was directed at the protestors or at his country. All he knew was someone had done him wrong.

ॐ

Nancy had worked in a sweater factory while Bernie was away. It was full-time and not pleasing work. When her husband returned she left the plant in order to better care for him and start a family.

Bernie got a job doing road construction and settled into a life of unvarying routine. After work he came home to a few beers and supper, then watched television while eating popcorn which he washed down with another couple of beers. He was in the sack by ten.

Nancy's romantic schoolgirl dreams of an exciting life with her guy were replaced by the reality that Bernie cared more for escaping into his television and beer than he did for her. He wasn't the companion Nancy had imagined but she held her tongue. Vietnam had changed him.

He always wore a crew cut. His labor kept him strong and muscular, except for an ever-enlarging, incongruous potbelly. He almost always wore the same clothes to work, olive pants and a camouflage jacket over a white tee shirt.

&

Nancy had wanted children but when none came, she suspected Bernie was relieved. He would not consider adoption and though disappointed, she didn't pursue the matter.

More to relieve the boredom then for the money, she took a part time job in a flower shop owned by Kristen and Harold Edwards. They were a genteel couple and she was always pleased when they called her in to work.

Although Nancy and Bernie weren't religious, she became fascinated with her employers' involvement with their church.

Valentine's Day 1975 was a week away, and Kristen had asked Nancy to help sort the flowers into bouquets. The two were sitting in a garden of blossoms.

"They're so beautiful," Nancy said.

"I love the smell. Sometimes I just wish I could roll around in them," Kristen confided.

Nancy laughed. "So many different flowers. Isn't nature amazing?"

"It's God's work. And it's a miracle, like all His wonders."

Nancy nodded.

"If I'm not being too personal, do you go to church?"

"We go at Christmas and Easter."

"Harold is a lay preacher, you know. Would you like to hear him speak? He's really good. Bring Bernie."

"Maybe I'll go, but you can forget Bernie. He complains when I take him to church at Christmas."

Kristen separated the flowers into bunches and put elastic bands around each bundle. Nancy put the bouquets into large mouthed vases, sorted by price.

"That's too bad. I love going to church. Jesus keeps our family together and contented."

That evening, Nancy asked Bernie if he would join her for Bible study. He put down his bottle of beer and belched.

"Ah," he said. "That felt good."

She wondered how many times she had heard him burp and repeat those same words.

"Bernie, I'm speaking to you. Kristen asked us if we would like to join them for Bible study this Thursday. I thought it might be nice for a change."

"Can't, I'm busy." He laughed.

"What do you have to do Thursday?"

"Watch television and drink beer. Good shows on Thursdays."

Nancy looked at Bernie, slouched in his chair at the kitchen table. His work boots were unlaced and his camouflage jacket was draped over the seat next to him. His tee shirt was sweat-stained and filthy from work. There was grime under his nails, and his hands looked dirty even though she had seen him wash. She wondered if she loved him or was just used to him. He's comfortable like a pair of old slippers, she thought. But he was fixed in his ways.

"Can't you for once get off your behind and do something different?"

"Hey, most of the gals I know would give their eye teeth to have a man who stays home. The guys at work are always running. Quit your complaining."

"I'm not complaining, Honey. I'm glad you stay home. But just this once. Kristen talks about it all the time."

"Get me another beer and maybe I'll go. I'm a pushover."

&

"I never should have agreed to this," Bernie complained as he showered and dressed.

"Come on, don't give me a hard time. It's just one night."

Bernie continued his grumbling as he drove.

Harold spoke forcefully on abortion. "When they tell you that abortion is between a woman and her doctor, they're forgetting someone," he began.

A heated discussion followed. Bernie was surprised at his own emotional involvement. Damn, abortion seemed wrong to him. It was like legalized murder. But how did you fight back? At first, he was too shy to participate in the controversy.

He recalled Vietnam, the killings, memories which he had repressed since his return home. Why had he been willing to fight, risk his life? Wasn't it to protect freedom? What kind of freedom did the unborn have if they could be killed just because the woman didn't want to carry the child anymore? What had Harold called it? The rights of the unborn child...

"We're getting nowhere," a member of the congregation shouted. "We protest, we write letters, nothing happens."

"It seems you're in a war, a war that can't be fought by the victims," Bernie heard himself say. "Someone has to fight it for them. And you don't fight a war with pickets and letters. That's not the way we did it in Nam, anyway."

Nancy looked at her husband.

Bernie knew she was probably as surprised at his outburst as he was.

"You make a lot of sense," Harold responded. "But we live within the law."

"Can you afford to live within the law if the law is killing millions of unborn babies?" someone responded.

"What can we do?" another asked.

"Bomb the clinics," Bernie said. "Search and destroy."

There was a prolonged silence.

"Bomb the clinics?" Harold asked.

"If they didn't have any place to do their killing, we'd save lots of lives."

"It's dangerous," Kristen said. "We don't want to kill people. We're trying to save lives."

"The best I can figure, if you can destroy the clinics you will save lives. Bomb them late at night. No one's there," Bernie urged.

"I don't know," Harold said. "Would Jesus want that? Would we be doing His work?"

"Where would we get bombs, anyway?" a voice from the back asked.

"What's happening here?" Harold demanded. "We're a church."

"This is a war, a just war. Thousands of innocents are being murdered. It's our job to stop it," someone shouted.

An unusual excitement took hold of Bernie. It reminded him of the day in his childhood when he discovered that matches caused fire. He knew it was wrong, but, oh, that fascinating blue flame.

"Fire bomb a clinic. It'll slow them down," Bernie said, jumping up from his seat. "And I can tell you how to make them. Fill a bottle with gasoline. Stuff it with a rag. Tip the bottle until the cloth is moist. Light the rag and toss it through a window. No more clinic."

"Bernie!" Nancy exclaimed. "I don't believe you!"

"I don't believe me either," he said with a nervous laugh.

∞

That night as Kristen lay in bed, she couldn't get the image of bombing the abortion clinic out of her head. Was there no other way? Jesus would want them to save His children and God took precedence over the Law. Everything has a purpose.

Had her Savior found Bernie for them?

Part Four
Calvert

CHAPTER TWENTY

Pip and Mary Lou received offers from law firms all over the country. They turned them down in favor of opening their own office in Calvert. People were ecstatic over their decision and no one was happier than Doris Marshall. In spite of her celebrity status, she continued to live as humbly as ever.

It was a Sunday afternoon. Pip and Mary Lou were visiting Doris. She brought them iced tea and cookies.

"Mother, you don't have to clean houses anymore." They'd had this conversation many times before.

"I like cleaning houses, Pip. The ladies are my friends and treat me very well. Everyone knows I don't have to do it. Not with my famous son." She gave him a peck on the cheek. "You do your lawyering and I'll do my cleaning."

He gazed at the woman who had raised him. After Walter's departure, rather than falling apart, she became stronger. No more fear; no need to acquiesce. She could love her son unconditionally, which allowed him to flourish.

ॐ

Pip and Mary Lou stood back and surveyed the finishing touches of their new quarters. They had rented an old hardware store on the main street and renovated it into two offices with a large front area for the secretaries.

"Want to check the sign?" the painter said to them.

"Finished already?" Mary Lou asked.

The man nodded and led them outside. They looked at the gilt letters against the glass.

Marshall and Marshall
Attorneys-at-Law

Pip put his arm around Mary Lou. "Do you think we did the right thing, having a store front for an office?"

"It was cheap and it'll encourage the type of clientele we want."

Pip kissed his wife. "We did it."

"Muriel starts tomorrow," she said. "I hope we'll have some work for her."

℘

Muriel had circled the classified ad in the paper as she sat at her kitchen table drinking her morning coffee. Tim was still upstairs sleeping. She'd seen her two boys off to school.

The dread of spending another day in the apartment with her husband, at the whim of his violent temper, was terrifying and beyond her endurance. He had lost his job at the factory over five months ago and hadn't tried very hard to find anything else.

She was a big woman, at five-ten, well over two hundred pounds and both taller and heavier than her husband. Muriel had always been taller, but wondered how she allowed herself to become so damn fat!

Somewhere along the line, Tim started hitting her. At first, she thought it was her fault that if she could be a better wife he would cease. But it became impossible to please him, and she stopped trying. Constantly afraid for herself and her two boys, she knew she had to remove the three of them from his wrath.

Muriel replied to the ad without telling her husband. If she could get the job, she would have some financial independence and prepare to leave.

℘

She arrived promptly for the interview. Mr. Marshall, clad in jeans and a chambray work shirt, his sleeves rolled up, was sawing a two-by-four. He was supposed to be a millionaire. Why was he doing his own carpentry? Other craftsmen were working with him. Two women were standing in the newly constructed hallway.

"Are you here for the job?" Pip asked.

"Yes, Sir."

"My wife's running late," he said, looking around. "I'm sorry, we don't have any chairs yet."

"That's okay."

He went back to his work. Muriel watched as Mrs. Marshall led each of the two other applicants into an office. She checked her watch as they took their turns. Twenty minutes each. Two other candidates arrived as she waited. Mr. Marshall stopped his work and repeated the short conversation he had with her.

152

Muriel's heart began to race. She wanted, needed the job badly. She'd worn her best dress, had taken almost two hours to groom her massive body to its best, hating what she saw in the mirror.

Tim had punched her in the face a week earlier. He no longer seemed to worry if the bruises showed. Her cheek had been black and blue until the abrasion turned a sickly yellow. She was more embarrassed by the bruises than he was. The other candidates were applying for a job; she was trying to escape a torture chamber.

"Mrs. Krause?"

Muriel jumped at the sound of her name. "Pleased to meet you, Mrs. Marshall," she said, extending her hand.

"Follow me, please."

Mary Lou led Muriel to the new office and offered her a folding chair.

"We're waiting for our furniture to arrive." She looked down at the application. "I notice you haven't worked in four years."

"I stopped to have a family. I feel awkward tooting my own horn, but I was really very good, and I know I haven't lost my skills."

"You worked for only one firm and were there less than two years."

"I left three weeks before Roger was born."

"Have you considered returning to them?"

"I'd prefer a small office if I have a choice."

"As you know, we're just starting out. I'm not sure how much work we'll have."

Muriel did her best to impress. She wouldn't have been as bold if she hadn't felt so desperate.

As the interview was coming to an end, Mary Lou said, "We want to be advocates for causes that don't attract other lawyers, such as rights of children, violence in the home, and civil rights."

Muriel felt buoyed. Would Mrs. Marshall be telling her this if she wasn't considering her?

Mary Lou stood, indicating the interview was at an end. "I'll check your references and weigh your application. Thank you for coming in."

Muriel considered telling Mrs. Marshall how important it was to her, but thought better of it.

∽

After Muriel had graduated from high school, she'd enrolled in a secretarial course, offered at night. During the day she worked in a factory that manufactured boys' jerseys. The work was boring but she was fast with her hands, and each week received an incentive bonus for superior production.

Tim Krause was an accountant at the same plant. He worked in the office where he wore a sport jacket and bow tie, which set him apart from the factory workers. She had seen him flirt with the girls on the assembly line.

One evening as she sat in her room practicing her shorthand, he called her.

"Hello, Muriel, know who this is?"

"No, no I don't."

"It's Tim Krause... from bookkeeping."

Muriel was bewildered by the call and even more astonished when he asked her for a date. She considered saying No but Yes came out.

He arrived at her house, meticulously dressed, promptly at seven. She'd never realized before just how small he was and smiled at the thought that he might fit comfortably in her oversized handbag. He took her to dinner and a movie. At the door, he put his arms around her, as best he could, stood on his toes and kissed her goodnight.

"I had a good time," he said.

"So did I," she replied.

∞

"How did it go," whispered her girlfriend as they sat next to each other at their sewing machines.

"He's okay," Muriel replied with a giggle.

"No one's ever gone out with him twice. They say he's a jerk."

"He wasn't with me. Jeepers, I just stitched this sleeve together."

They both laughed and then fell silent. As she reached for her scissors, Muriel became reflective. Tim didn't seem so bad. But he did have a reputation. He certainly wasn't all she hoped for in a husband, but maybe she could change him. What was she thinking about! They'd only gone out once.

Five months later they were married.

∞

Tim moved into Muriel's small apartment. She liked serving him, doing his cooking and cleaning. He had a difficult job. Even when she left the factory to become a legal secretary, she continued doing all the housework. It was a woman's place.

Tim was demanding and Muriel wished he were less rigid. Maybe in time...

᠙

After six months at the law firm her boss called her into his office.

"I knew you'd do a good job," he said. "But you're exceeding our expectations. We promised you a modest raise if things worked out. I hope you won't be disappointed if instead of a modest raise, I give you a more substantial increase."

She came home that evening filled with the excitement and anticipation of surprising Tim with the news. They could look for a house and contemplate beginning a family.

Stopping at the grocery store, she arrived home a little late. "Hello, I'm home."

She walked into the kitchen, putting down her bag. Tim followed from the living room, newspaper in hand. "Where have you been? I'm starved."

"Sorry, honey. I'll start supper," she replied. "I've wonderful news."

She told him of their good fortune and kissed him, oblivious for the moment that he was not sharing her excitement.

"You'll be making more than I am."

"So what? I don't care."

"Maybe I do. How do you think that makes me feel? You like the idea, don't you?"

Her happiness was replaced by concern that Tim was feeling threatened. She didn't know how to handle it and tried to choose her words carefully. "Nothing has changed with us except we'll have more money."

"I don't think I want you working."

"Please, Tim. It's for both of us, for our future."

"Where's my supper. Or are you making too much money to do that?"

"No, Tim. I'm sorry," she replied as she returned to her groceries.

He was cool all evening. When they got to bed, she reached for him.

"I want you to suck me."

She bent over to do as he demanded. He climaxed in her mouth.

"Now swallow."

She closed her eyes and did as he commanded. Tim turned on his side and within a moment was asleep. Muriel lay on her back and stared at the ceiling. She thought about her day. How excited she had been at the size of her raise. Why couldn't Tim share her joy? Muriel had wanted to make love. Instead he forced her to take care of him while she remained unfulfilled. Turning toward him, she wondered how he could sleep so contentedly.

ℬ

They'd been married for over a year, and Muriel knew it was a terrible mistake. No matter what she did to satisfy Tim, it was never enough. He was constantly thinking up new ways to test her devotion.

Muriel had not had her period for two months and knew she was pregnant. Would it please him? Would it improve her life? She never correctly anticipated his reactions to anything.

The doctor verified her suspicion. Returning to work she wasn't her usual, efficient self as she contemplated telling her husband.

"I have some wonderful news," she told him that night as she served him his meal.

He looked up from his paper.

"They gave you another raise," he said, the sarcasm in his voice not lost on her.

"I'm pregnant," she replied, holding her breath.

"Pregnant?" There was a pause as Tim digested the information. "That's wonderful. Oh, Muriel, I'm going to be a father. I hope it's a boy." He looked at his wife and then added, "Even if it's a girl I'll be happy. You'll have to quit your job. Children come first."

"I can work until my ninth month. We'll need the money. Then I'll quit. Is that okay?" She hated asking his permission but knew it was the easiest way.

"Yes, sure."

He put his arms around her and they kissed. Maybe life will be better, she thought.

ℬ

The evening started out calmly. Roger was five months old. After dinner, Tim took him into the living room. He put the infant on the floor, turned on the television, picked the boy up and placed him on his lap as he sat down to watch the news.

Roger started to cry, and Tim reacted to the baby by mindlessly rocking him in his arms. When his son did not stop, Tim's attention went from the news to the infant.

"Shut up," he said, to no avail. "Shut up," he shouted once again.

When Muriel heard Tim yelling, she wiped her hands with the dishtowel and rushed into the living room in time to see her husband slapping the infant.

"He's only a baby," she cried.

Tim stood, putting the baby down on the chair. "Don't tell me what to do with my son," he raged.

She picked Roger up, saying nothing, bringing the baby to her bosom.

"Give me my son!" he shouted at her. "Do as I tell you."

She defied him. He punched her in the stomach and she doubled over. Falling to her knees, she managed to hold onto the baby.

"How could you?" she sobbed as he walked out of the house, slamming the door behind him.

She examined her son. No bruises. Thank God. She became aware of a pain where he'd struck her. They'd had their bad times but he never before hit her.

She carried Roger to her room, placing the crying infant on her bed before removing her dress and examining the area where the blow had landed. It was red and sensitive to her touch.

Slowly she rocked her son to sleep, holding him tightly against her. Had it been her fault? She put Roger in his crib and went to the couch where she sat, lost in her own thoughts, until Tim returned.

"Muriel," he called.

No reply.

"Muriel!"

"I'm in the living room."

He came to her. The room was dark and he kept it that way, as he joined her on the couch.

"I'm sorry, darling. I'm so sorry. It'll never happen again."

She was happy to take him in her arms, to forgive him. That night they conceived their second child.

❧

Muriel was six months pregnant. Her eating was out of control and she'd gained seventy-five pounds.

They were at the kitchen table, finishing dinner. Muriel missed her work. She loved her son but found herself constantly depressed from the tedium.

"You're as big as a house," Tim told his wife.

Roger was dropping food to the floor from his highchair.

"I'm pregnant," she replied defensively, as she picked it up.

"With how many babies?"

Muriel felt the sting from the tears on the rims of her eyes but was able to hold them back. "You little weasel," she shot back, immediately regretting her outburst.

"You think I'm a weasel?" he quietly replied, taking her arm and twisting it.

"You bastard," she cried out.

He punched her face. Covering her cheek with her hand she collapsed, more out of fear than pain. He kicked her twice. She looked up at him, uncomprehending.

"Tim, please, I'm sorry. Please, the baby." She was filled with rage but spoke as evenly as she could. Roger began to scream.

Tim took her arm and forced her back on her feet.

"Never call me a weasel."

"I'm sorry," she cried.

He released her. How had she ever allowed herself to become pregnant with a second child? He had promised never to hit her again. She must escape; she would take Roger and go to her parents. She would tell them Tim used her for a punching bag. It was so embarrassing. But where else could she turn?

God, it was so complicated. She couldn't understand her own feelings. Maybe she should stay and work it out. No, she had to escape. Maybe after the baby was born…

She took Roger to his room. Walking toward the crib, she noticed herself in the mirror. Tim was right. It was her fault. No man should have to live with such a fat pig. She would lose weight. She held Roger close to her as tears silently flowed. Tim came into the room.

"I'm sorry," he said. "I know I told you before but I promise on my life, I'll never hit you again."

"You were right, Tim. I'm a house. I'm going on a diet as soon as the baby comes."

He took his son from her and gently put the child in his crib. The boy cried and Tim responded by rubbing the infant's back until he fell asleep.

He led Muriel to the bedroom. She was exhausted. They got into bed. Tim kissed her, snuggled into her bosom and held her until they were both asleep.

ɛɔ

Muriel couldn't stop eating. During the term of the pregnancy, she gained a little under ninety pounds. Ashamed to have visitors, she put off anyone who asked. Tim stopped physically abusing her but became distant.

Severe depression set in. She considered suicide but couldn't kill her fetus or allow Roger to be brought up by that madman. Confused, she only knew how miserable she was.

ɛɔ

It was summer. Roger was four and Neil was two.

Her baby had a tantrum that morning and Tim responded by refusing to let her drive him to work. She would be without a car, and she wanted to take the children to the town pool.

"Wait. We'll be right with you," she begged.

"I can't be late," he said, stomping out.

"Please. We'll be stuck in the apartment all day."

"Serves you right."

She hated to go to the town pool, anyway. She was a freak, the fat lady in the circus, and people stared at her. It was better they stayed home. But the poor children... It was so hot.

The temperature was approaching a hundred degrees, and there was little relief from the small fan in the living room. Muriel wished they could afford an air conditioner, at least for the bedroom, but it seemed they never even had enough for the necessities.

It was two in the afternoon. Maybe a walk would cool them off. As she got the kids ready she was startled at the sound of the front door opening.

"Hello?" she hollered.

"Hello," Tim answered.

Was he bringing her the car? No, something was wrong. She went to him. His face was twisted in a scowl that immediately put Muriel on guard.

"I've been fired. Those bastards fired me. I kill myself for those sons of bitches and when things get a little soft, they give me the boot."

Muriel had been listening to him complain about his work since she had known him, aware he did as little as possible, always looking for the angle. His attitude had disturbed her, but she always held her tongue. Her job was not to set him off.

She looked at her diminutive husband who was capable of hurting her at his whim, secretly happy at the pain he was feeling, in spite of what the financial consequences would be. She had stayed with him because she was afraid to be without an income. Maybe this firing was a good thing. Could it give her the courage she needed? If only there was someone to talk to.

"Oh, Tim, I'm so sorry. They never appreciated you," she lied.

He glared at her, and she sensed the danger which was unpredictable. It had been seven months since her last beating. She could feel the tension between them and frantically searched for words to defuse him.

"You were too good for the company. They never treated you right. They didn't know a good thing when they had it."

Did he realize that she was parroting all the inane comments he always made about his work?

He smiled, a sardonic, evil smirk. "You're God damn right. I'll find another job, some place where they'll appreciate me. Where's the paper?"

She watched him look through the help-wanted ads. How long could she repress her hate, her pent-up anger?

∞

Muriel knew she was making a mistake but didn't know where else to turn. She envied her mother's trim figure and wondered how she could possibly be the offspring of this petite, well-groomed woman. Was her mother ashamed of her or was it Muriel's imagination? Was she jealous of her mother? Her feelings were deep and hard to define. She wished she could afford therapy but that was out of the question, not to mention Tim would forbid it. Damn, who was he to forbid her anything?

Muriel pulled into the driveway. The sight of the little house sitting on its small lot squeezed between its neighbors triggered a rush of memories. Her father had bought their home for fifteen hundred dollars in 1945. In a one-month period, he had been discharged from the Navy, married his high school sweetheart and became a homeowner, all without a job. He was an easy-going man who had faith in the America he had just spent three years defending. This was to be Kenneth and Pam Garceau's starter house. But the three children were more than they could afford, and although he worked hard as a shoe salesman in a retail store, he could never get out from under. Pam wanted more but knew her husband was doing the best he could and didn't attempt to push him to heights he couldn't obtain. Yet, they were a happy family, satisfied with what they had.

Muriel was their third and youngest child. Her two older brothers had doted on their baby sister as did both parents. She was always chubby with the curliest blond hair. Her skin was unusually soft and smooth with cheeks so rosy, it looked as if she were wearing rouge. She was pretty in spite of her weight.

"I'm fat, Mother."

"You're pleasingly plump," Pam always corrected.

℅

Muriel entered the house unannounced, as the front door was never locked. It was a few minutes earlier than she was expected.

There was the old piano her father had bought for her when she was eight. It was second hand then, antique now. She recalled her only lesson, which had ended abruptly when she vomited over the keys. Her teacher never returned and the piano became a gallery of family portraits. Muriel stopped to look at them. She picked up a picture of herself when she was ten and stared at this stranger with the blonde curly hair that came down in ringlets and surrounded a cherub's face. If only she could warn this little girl of the perils that lay ahead.

"Hi, Honey," her mother said, interrupting Muriel's reverie.

Carefully, she replaced the picture on the doily and turned toward her mother, noticing the appraising glance as they exchanged the perfunctory kiss.

"Want some coffee?" Pam continued. "How's your diet?"

It didn't take her mother long to slug her. Tim used his fist; her mother used her mouth. Knowing her body spoke for itself, she answered only the first question.

"Black."

She followed her mother into the kitchen, admiring her slim frame. Why couldn't she look like that? Sitting at the old kitchen table watching her mother put on the kettle, she worried about the consequences of telling about her messed up life. What was she doing here? After all, how could her mother help? Probably only make her feel worse. But she had to talk to somebody.

"Tim lost his job."

"I'm not surprised. I told you."

I told you. God, she hoped she would never use those words with her children.

"You were right. I admit it. Now that we got past that, can you not remind me again about how stupid I am? I feel bad enough."

"You don't have to get upset, dear."

"Listen, Mother, I've been here less than fifteen minutes. In that time, you reminded me that my husband's a bum and asked me how my diet is going. For Christ's sake, can't you see how my diet's going? Are you blind?"

"Do I ever say anything right? Why do you have to jump on everything I say?"

Muriel knew she was in a no-win argument. Frustration was always the only result of these confrontations. Again she considered not sharing her burden. "Oh, Mother, I'm so miserable."

Pam shifted uncomfortably in her chair. Muriel knew her mother didn't care to deal with her problems.

"It's only a job, dear. He'll find another one."

"It's not that," Muriel said in a whisper, holding back her tears with a heavy sigh. "He hits me."

"What? I don't believe it. In all the years I've been married to your father, he's never lifted a hand. He hits you? How often? The pig."

"Not often, but I'm afraid. I'm always afraid. I never know when he'll strike me or the kids."

"Why does he do that? I don't understand."

"I want to leave him, get a divorce."

"How will you live? What about the children?"

"Mother, for God's sake, he doesn't have a job. I'm not sure how we'll live if I stay."

"Make him promise never to hit you again. If he gets a job, don't leave him. The children need a father, especially boys."

"After every beating he promises never to do it again, says he's sorry, but there's always a next time."

Muriel knew she wasn't receiving the support she needed. How could this woman possibly understand? Tell him not to hit her anymore. What kind of advice was that?

"Give him one more chance. I never thought I would be defending that son of a bitch, but marriage is a sacred thing. Divorce would be bad for the children."

Muriel felt helpless. "I have to go now."

CHAPTER TWENTY-ONE

"Muriel, this is Mary Lou Marshall. I checked your recommendation. Mr. Graf told me if I don't hire you, he will. The job's yours."

Muriel's voice quivered. "You won't be sorry. Thank you. Thank you very much."

"Can you start Monday? It only gives you the weekend, if that's all right."

"Yes, yes, that will be fine."

Muriel hung up the phone and went to the living room. It was time to tell Tim. He was dozing in front of "General Hospital". Why wasn't he looking for a job? It had been five months. He was sitting in the worn easy chair, the paper draped over his lap. She sucked in her breath and went to wake him. As she gently shook him, she looked down at the paper to see if it was the help wanted section.

"Braves Beat Giants Again," she read.

"What do you want?"

"Tim, I have good news," she responded tentatively. "I found a job. Just to hold us over until you get something."

"What? Who will take care of the boys?"

God forbid you should do it, she thought. "I'll make arrangements."

"Where will you be working?"

"It's a new law firm, Marshall and Marshall."

"You don't mean that football player from high school?"

Was he excited? She relaxed, wondering if she would ever be able to anticipate his moods.

"Yes. I start Monday, if that's okay."

"How much? You're damn good, and they better not try to Jew you."

She winced. "One-seventy-five a week to start and they have a medical plan."

Tim whistled. "Not bad. Hey, maybe we could have them for dinner sometime."

"That would be nice," she replied, embarrassed by the possibility.

∞

Muriel wasn't sure what time she was to report to work. She dropped the boys off at the babysitters at seven-thirty and arrived by eight o'clock. Pip and Mary Lou were already at the office.

164

"What are you doing here so early?" Mary Lou asked. "Oh, I never told you what time to come in, did I? This is my husband, Mr. Marshall."

"You probably know your job better than we do so make yourself at home. If there's anything you need, let us know," Pip said.

℘

Within three months the office was busy beyond anything Muriel had ever imagined, but the Marshalls turned no one away.

Although she felt guilty spending so little time with her children, she was never happier than when she was at the office. Without noticing, without trying, she started to lose weight.

"Muriel, could you come in here, please?" Mary Lou asked over the intercom. "I would like you to record a conversation for me."

She grabbed her pad, sharpened her pencil and entered the office. Harry Upton sat facing Mary Lou. He was a big man, six three, weighing maybe two-hundred-and seventy pounds. Bushy flaming red hair covered both his head and face. He looked formidable.

"You know Mr. Upton," Mary Lou said, as Muriel took a seat to one side. "He's divorcing his wife. If you could take down our conversation and type it up for me, I would appreciate it. "Go ahead, Harry," Mary Lou prompted. "You were on the golf course..."

"Yes, I think it was the seventh hole. We both love our golf and were playing for a dollar a hole. We always compete... Our marriage has been rocky. Sally Mae is fifteen years younger than me. Friends told me she was after my money, told me to do a prenuptial agreement but I told them they were crazy. I guess maybe I was the one who was nuts...a blind fool.

"Anyway, Sally Mae was about to swing at the ball when she looked at me and asked, `Can I hit them?' referring to the foursome in front of us. I told her they were two-hundred-and-fifty yards from us and she couldn't reach that far on a bet. Before I finished saying it, she was swinging the club, and her ball went flying into the water."

Muriel couldn't imagine what this had to do with his divorce. She hid a smile as he continued.

"Sally Mae said, `Now look at what you made me do.' I replied, `God, honey, I was only answering your question.' She took some golf balls and threw them into the water. I just laughed. Sally Mae's a high-strung girl, and I usually get a kick out of her temper. `You think that's funny,' she screamed. `Watch this.' Then she grabbed each club and

165

one by one threw them into the pond. `Hey,' I said, `those are expensive clubs.' They were the best money can buy. She just kept flinging. It was getting embarrassing. Everyone started looking at her, thinking she flipped her lid, or something. I figured it would be over when she ran out of ammunition, but when all her clubs were gone, she hesitated for a moment, then hopped onto the golf cart. `No, Sally Mae, no,' I hollered after her as she headed down the bank for the water, jumping out just before the thing splashed into the drink."

Mr. Upton was a big wounded bear, and Muriel could feel his pain.

"Then Sally Mae looked me in the eye. `Next time, you won't talk when I'm hitting. I'm sick of you.' `Come back here,' I screamed after her, but she just kept on walking. People had gathered from the commotion. They started laughing, applauding her, not knowing why. I was real humiliated. I went to the water. All the balls and clubs had sunk. The only thing showing was the backside of the cart. The club charged me a thousand dollars in damages.

"I haven't seen Sally Mae since this happened. It was over a month ago. The police said they don't look for run away wives. I hired detectives. No luck. Then she serves me with papers. They tell me that I have to leave my house. I can't believe it. All because I tell her she won't hit some people two-hundred-and- fifty yards away."

Muriel couldn't believe it, either. This woman, Sally Mae, left because Mr. Upton spoke during her golf shot. What the hell was she still doing with Tim?

&

There had been times when Muriel missed her period without being pregnant. Whenever it happened, she would become fearful, as bringing another child into her abusive home was the last thing she wanted. In the past, her period eventually arrived and Muriel breathed a sigh of relief, each time promising herself that Tim would not force himself on her again without proper protection. But the promise was difficult to keep. Tim simply took her and any protestations could ignite his temper.

When she missed her period for a second month she knew, but where could she turn? Not her mother, certainly not Tim.

She hated to do it but Mary Lou was her best option. God, what a mess.

"Mrs. Marshall, may I see you for a few minutes on a private matter?"

"Of course, Muriel. Come into my office."

Mary Lou took her seat behind her desk and smiled as Muriel hesitated.

"Do you want to sit in the client's seat or your usual chair."

"I'm afraid I need a friend not a lawyer."

"You better not be giving your notice, Muriel. I don't know how we'd get along without you."

"It's nothing like that, Mrs. Marshall."

"Mary Lou, Muriel. When we aren't with clients, it's Mary Lou."

"Mary Lou," Muriel repeated. There was a pause as she considered how to put it, but came up with only, "I'm pregnant."

"That's wonderful," Mary Lou responded, coming around her desk to hug her secretary.

"You don't understand. I don't want the baby. I want an abortion."

"An abortion? What does... what does your husband say?"

Muriel took a deep breath. "Tim doesn't know."

"Doesn't know?" Mary Lou had returned to her seat.

Again there was a silence before Muriel spoke. "We don't have much of a marriage." She took a tissue from the desk and wiped her tears. "He can be... he can be abusive."

"Oh, Muriel, I'm so sorry. Do you want to stay with him?"

"He's a pretty good father, and he promised never to do it again."

"Do you believe him?"

"Oh, I don't know. Maybe. He's always so sorry. But I don't want the baby."

"There's the clinic. You must have read about it, the protests and all. I met a woman at a Christmas party who works there. She was very nice. We talked for a while. What was her name? Her husband was a doctor. They just moved here. We spoke about getting together but you know how it is. Reingold. Her name was Susan Reingold. She's an options counselor. Can I call her for you?"

ဆ

As Muriel approached the building, the protestors took her aback. She tried not to look but couldn't help reading the posters. "Don't Enter This House of Death." "Save the Babies." She stopped for a moment to consider what she was doing. Was it wrong? Was she killing her child? There were about six protestors and as she headed up the outside stairs, they cried out to her.

"Abortion is wrong. It's genocide," a protestor yelled.

"Please don't kill your baby," another man shouted.

Muriel entered the clinic, in tears. The receptionist came out from behind her desk and put her arm around her.

"It's okay,' she comforted. She took her to a chair. "Let me get you a cup of coffee. I just made it."

Muriel nodded as she took a tissue to her eyes.

The woman continued. "You're going to love your counselor. She's wonderful. I'll tell her you're here."

೮๑

Muriel expected Susan Reingold to be older. She followed her to a small office. Susan didn't have to ask many questions to get Muriel to reveal her situation. It was like opening a floodgate. Finally, Muriel had someone she could speak to who wouldn't be judgmental. She told of her life with Tim, her two dear boys, her mother. Almost an hour-and-a half later they got to discuss her feelings about an abortion. They spoke about adoption but Muriel didn't want Tim to know she was pregnant. He would want to keep the child.

"Is it fair not to tell your husband?" Susan asked.

"Is it fair that he beats me?"

"God, he beats you?"

They spoke of divorce. "He's a good father to the boys. No, I'm not ready." Although Susan didn't respond, Muriel knew this young woman wouldn't tolerate an abusive relationship. Why did she?

"I can recommend an abortion."

"Thank you," Muriel nearly whispered.

೮๑

Mary Lou went to the clinic with Muriel the day of the operation. Muriel couldn't believe her employer was accompanying her but Mary Lou insisted.

"I'm not letting you do this alone."

"But you can't. It's my job to help you."

"Muriel, you're not just my secretary. You're my friend."

೮๑

Muriel had no intention of telling Tim about her abortion.

"Mrs. Marshall is picking me up today," she announced.

"Why?" Tim asked.

"We have to go out of town to take a deposition."

A horn blowing interrupted the conversation.

"I have to run."

℘

Although the procedure had been easy the ramifications of having the fetus removed and discarded upset Muriel. Mary Lou held her hand during the operation and stayed with her until Susan said Muriel could go home.

"Hey, you're back early," Tim said.

"I wasn't feeling well. Terrible headache."

Muriel lay on her bed, thinking of what she had done, blaming herself and then blaming her husband. No one else would stay with this jerk. Why did she? As sleep overtook her, she heard the phone ring and wondered who it might be.

℘

Kristen arrived at the florist shop in time to relieve Harold for lunch.

"How many picketers this morning?" he asked.

"Six. That lawyer who's married to Pip Marshall came to the killing center. I couldn't believe it."

"She wouldn't get an abortion. She grew up in Calvert."

"I know her husband's a Christian. It took him a while to find Christ but he finally did. I used to see him in church every Sunday. Mrs. Marshall was with another lady. Someone on the phone committee recognized her. Said it was Mrs. Marshall's secretary. They were both going to get calls."

"Our protesting is hopeless. I don't think we've saved one life. What does God want us to do?" Harold replied.

He left for lunch, and Kristen went about preparing the orders when a familiar face entered the shop.

"May I help you?"

"I need a bunch of flowers for the dinner table," the woman responded.

"We have bouquets of sunflowers and daises. They are very nice."

"Yes, how lovely. I'll take that bunch there."

169

As Kristen took the money she realized where she had seen the customer. She felt her anger swell. How frustrating it had been to ineffectually picket day after day while the genocide continued unabated. Should she say something? What difference would it make? But she owed it to the millions of unborn babies who never saw the light of day.

"I'm one of the picketers," Kristen announced in almost a whisper.

Susan Reingold said nothing.

"How can you do it? It's wrong. It's so wrong."

Susan took her flowers and left the shop.

ॐ

"Hello," Tim said into the phone.

"Is this Mr. Krause?"

"Who's this?"

"Mr. Krause, don't let your wife do it. You can stop her."

"What are you talking about?"

"You don't know?"

"Know what?"

"Your wife is planning an abortion. She's been seen going into the killing center. You must stop her. Please."

The phone went dead. Tim returned to his newspaper but the memory of the crank call lingered. If Muriel was having an abortion, wouldn't he know? Putting the paper down, he rose from his chair and climbed the stairs to the bedroom. The door was shut. As he opened it he heard her loud breathing and went to the bed.

"Muriel," he said. "Muriel wake up."

She looked at him, not comprehending.

"Where did you say you were today?"

"We went out of town to take a deposition."

"I just had a very strange phone call. A woman said you were going to have an abortion."

"What? Well I'm not."

"Why would she say that?"

"I don't know. It was a crank call."

"Are you pregnant?"

"No Tim, I'm not pregnant. I'm not feeling very well. Please, let me rest."

"Don't lie to me, Muriel. I can tell when you're lying. Maybe I should call your big shot boss and ask her."

Muriel sat up on the bed. She wiped a tear from her eye.

"You can't call Mrs. Marshall."

"I can't? I certainly can."

She grabbed his hand as he reached for the phone. "Tim, I'm not pregnant. I had an abortion this morning." She fell back down on the bed.

"Without consulting me? It wasn't just your child."

"Oh, God, Tim, I couldn't bring another child into this house. It wouldn't be fair."

"What do you mean?"

"Tim, we can lie to the outside world but we know about... about your temper. I'm afraid for the children."

"I've never done more than spank the boys."

She started to cry. "But I'm always afraid for them. What if you beat them like you have me?"

Tim was getting angry. He didn't want to lose control, but knew he sometimes couldn't help it. It just happened. "I can't believe you had an abortion without asking me," he yelled.

"I'm sorry, Tim. Really."

"Did you tell Mrs. Marshall any of our private business, you bitch?"

"About the beatings. No Tim, I didn't."

"You better not," he shouted as he punched her in the stomach. Tim heard her gag as he left the room, slamming the door behind him.

℘

Mary Lou couldn't get Muriel out of her mind. How could she live with an abusive husband? Although Mary Lou kept little from Pip, she thought it better if he didn't know about Tim. He couldn't do anything, and it would only dredge up bad memories.

When she returned to the office, Pip looked up at her from Muriel's seat.

"Are you the new secretary?" Mary Lou asked. "I hope so. You're darn cute."

"Careful, Miss, or I'll have you up on sexual abuse charges."

She sat in the client's chair in the reception area across from her husband.

"It's impossible to work without Muriel here. How did it go?" Pip asked.

"I felt sorry for her. It wasn't an easy decision. We had to walk past the protestors shouting at us."

"Why did she want an abortion?"

"Her husband's unemployed. Things have been tough. They do an excellent job at the clinic. Remember Susan Reingold and her husband? We met them at the Schroeder's Christmas Party."

"Her husband's a doctor?"

"Hey, good memory. Well, she was the options counselor and she was wonderful. She helped Muriel with her decision.

"How was Muriel afterward?"

"She was good. Tired. I brought her home."

"When will she be back to work? I'm trying to type this brief and answer the phone. It's much easier being a lawyer."

Mary Lou slipped behind her husband's chair and kissed his neck. "Come on, let's call it a day. We're useless without Muriel anyway."

∞

Eight months after Muriel began her job, her husband was still unemployed, and he wasn't making much attempt at finding work. He moped around the house, leaving a mess for her to clean up. He never helped with dinner or the dishes. It was easier and safer to do it herself, and she never complained. No longer did she ask him about his search for a job. It was a sensitive subject, one that could trigger his temper… although he did seem calmer since the abortion.

He didn't mind her working, not for the famous Pip Marshall. Each night Tim would grill his wife about every encounter she had with Calvert's great football hero.

"I want to have them over for dinner," he repeated for the umpteenth time. "Just because you're only his secretary, doesn't mean we can't be friends. You should entertain your boss once in a while. It's smart business. Maybe they could put in a good word for me about a job. A recommendation from Pip Marshall wouldn't hurt."

Muriel shuddered. She would rather die than have the Marshals meet Tim.

"They're very busy people."

"Come on, Babe, they eat dinner, don't they?" His tone was concilia-tory and he went over to put his arms around her.

"Hey, I think you're loosing weight."

"I am," she replied.

He kissed her on the lips. She could not remember the last time he had shown affection. Sex was more like a rape, Tim always taking his pleasure, then turning his back on her and falling asleep. The only feeling she ever had was of being used.

At least there was no more chance of a pregnancy. Ms Reingold had told her that, if she wished, she could have a tubal ligation during the abortion. It seemed to be the safest way to avoid another unwanted preg-nancy.

He wants me to invite the Marshals so badly. What if it did lead to a job? He would certainly be on his best behavior that night and would surely try to please me before the big event.

They chose the Saturday night closest to Muriel's birthday.

"I'll call them, honey, and tell them it's a celebration," he said.

"Please, Tim, tell them no present. I don't want them to think I want a present."

"No problem, Babe. You won't be sorry. I know it'll lead to something good. Jesus, Pip Marshall in my house."

He danced around the room, grinning from ear to ear.

စာ

On the day of the party, Muriel and both Marshals had to work pre-paring a case that started on Monday.

"I'll take care of everything," Tim told his wife, kissing her good-bye. He was humming as she left for work. It would be the first time he had done anything in the kitchen since the early days of their marriage.

Muriel arrived home at six, only an hour before their guests were ex-pected.

"Let me help," she said. There was a recipe book on the table, and the smell of cooking in the air. Tim was dressed in a suit with a bow tie. He'd protected his clothes with one of her aprons, which almost touched the floor. The self-belt was wrapped twice around him. She had a glimpse of the man she thought she had married.

"No, I can handle it," he said.

"Where are the children?"

"Upstairs in their room."

Muriel enjoyed the normalcy of the conversation. For once, she knew he would not turn on her. It was a night off from her life of fear.

"I'll go up to see them and get ready."

"Hurry. You have less then an hour."

"Oh, Mrs. Marshall said they might be a little late. They were still in the office when I left."

"They better not be too late or they'll have burnt roast," he said with a smile.

As she climbed the stairs, her thoughts turned to her children. Neil was four, Roger six. She quickened her pace in order to spend a few extra moments with them.

God, they're my reason for living. Without them, nothing would be worth it. I wish I could afford to give up my job and be with them.

She looked at the cots, second-hand when they purchased them, metal braces now bent beyond repair. They were meant to be temporary, only until they could afford beds. She never sat on them when putting the children to bed for fear they would collapse. A small, scratched bedside table bought at a flea market separated the cots. Tim promised to refinish it but never did. Their home was filled with his uncompleted intentions.

The boys were in their pajamas. She couldn't believe it. Tim had gotten them ready for bed. They ran to their mother, Neil kissing her, Roger holding her tighter than usual.

"Mommy, oh Mommy, I'm so glad you're home," Neil said.

"I'm sorry I had to work today. I know it's Saturday but it was important."

"It's always important," Roger whispered. "How come you work and Daddy doesn't?"

"You know he's looking for a job," she replied, lifting her son up and hugging him again. Roger winced from the squeeze, startling her. As she gently put her son down on the bed, his pajama top lifted and she noticed a black and blue mark on his stomach the size of a fist. Her heart jumped. She immediately knew what had happened. That bastard, she thought. But maybe there was another explanation.

"Roger, what's that?" she asked, trying to sound casual, as she kissed the bruise.

"It's nothing. I hurt myself."

"How?" she asked, wanting desperately to believe him.

"I don't know. It just happened."

"Roger was a bad boy," Neil interjected. "Daddy had to hit him."

"It's okay, Mommy. Daddy didn't mean it. I won't be bad again."

What was the boy saying? He was protecting his father probably to prevent them from having a fight. The children had seen too many battles in their short lives.

Muriel could feel her panic grow. The light was bad in the room. Wanting to examine her son more closely, she took the small lamp from the bedside table and brought it over.

"I want to see if there are any other bruises," she said as calmly as possible, removing the boy's pajamas in one fast motion. She gasped when she saw two other welts.

Roger started to cry. "He said I shouldn't tell you. He said he would punish me again if I did. Please don't tell him you know," he whispered, wiping his tears.

She held him close as tears ran down her own cheeks. The abuse she'd taken over the years at least had served as a buffer for the boys. What was the point in anything now if she couldn't keep them from being harmed?"

"Babe, you almost ready? It's seven-thirty. They'll be here any minute," Tim hollered upstairs.

I must stay calm, she thought. They're safe for the time being. "Be right down," she responded. God, what should I do? If I don't save my sons from this monster, I'm as bad as he is. What did they call it in the office? Accessory. I'd be an accessory.

She showered and dressed as quickly as she could, not wanting him to become suspicious. When she came downstairs, Pip and Mary Lou had already arrived, and Tim was pouring the wine.

"I followed your career," he was telling Pip. "I remember you in high school, college and the pros. The law must seem pretty dull."

"It's a lot safer than being chased by three-hundred-pound tackles."

Tim laughed. Muriel had never seen him in better spirits.

"We brought you a birthday present, Muriel," Mary Lou said, handing her a small box, exquisitely wrapped.

"Oh, I'm embarrassed. I told you no gifts," Muriel said.

"We wanted to do this," Pip replied. "It gave us an opportunity to show our appreciation for the wonderful job you're doing. I don't know how we'd ever manage without you."

Muriel opened the box and lifted out a delicate gold chain. She smiled, trying to hide her inner grief.

"Oh, you shouldn't have," she said, going over and kissing each of them.

"You make me look bad," Tim said with a grin. "I guess you folks know a good thing when you see one."

"We sure do," Pip responded.

Mary Lou and Pip sat at the dining room table while Muriel and Tim brought out the food.

"Everything smells so good," Mary Lou said.

"Muriel usually does the cooking, but I don't have to tell you why I had to do it tonight. I hope everything is all right."

Muriel picked at her food. After dinner Tim came in with a candle-laden cake.

"Make a wish and blow them out," Pip said.

She closed her eyes, sucked in her breath and blew, not stopping until she had succeeded in extinguishing all the candles, as if it was vitally important that her wish come true. They all laughed.

"Wow! What did you wish?" Tim asked.

Muriel looked at him. He was so pleased at having Pip Marshall in his home. Why wasn't he suffering from guilt for the beating he had given his son? The boy was upstairs blaming himself while Tim enjoyed his guests as if he didn't have a care in the world. As she looked across the table at her husband, she suddenly knew she couldn't take any more.

"I wished you'd stop beating me and the children," she blurted out, watching Tim's smile vanish. Mary Lou and Pip looked at each other in wordless silence. Muriel drew in a deep breath and forced herself to continue before she lost her nerve. "Tim likes to use me as a punching bag. I never know when he might feel like beating me, so I'm always afraid."

"Shut up, Muriel!"

She ignored him. "Tonight I found out it wasn't only me he's been beating. Pip, I want you to look at my son."

"He misbehaved." whined Tim. "I gave him a little spanking. So what?"

"Pip, I want you to see what a little spanking looks like."

The Marshals exchanged glances as Tim's face turned crimson.

"I refuse to stay here and listen to this garbage." Tim stormed out of the house, slamming the door behind him.

Pip and Mary Lou followed their secretary upstairs to the boys' room. Neil lay motionless on his cot while Roger turned fitfully in his sleep. Muriel bent over the boy and gently kissed him. He had wet his bed.

"I'm going to change your pajamas and sheets," she whispered.

When his clothes were off, Pip and Mary Lou examined the youngster.

"That bastard," Pip exclaimed.

"I'm so sorry," Mary Lou said, taking hold of Muriel's hand and squeezing it. The three of them changed the sheets before Muriel kissed her child. Then Pip took her arm and led her into the hall.

"I hate him. I wish he were dead." Muriel started to sob. "I never want him back in the house." She wiped her eyes.

"We'll get a restraining order keeping him from the kids and you, and we'll file for a divorce at once," Mary Lou told her. "He won't know what hit him. Why don't you and the boys stay with us until Monday?"

"No. If he comes back, I'll be all right. Now that you know, he won't dare hurt us. He's a coward."

Mary Lou kissed Muriel good-bye. "You have our number. Promise you'll call if you need us."

"He won't bother you again." Pip's voice cracked.

଼

"I think I'll walk home, darling," Pip said when they were finally outside.

"It's four miles!"

"I don't trust her husband. I'm going to wait for him and make sure he behaves himself."

Mary Lou had loved Pip since she was a freshman in high school. There was nothing she didn't know about this man. Years of closeness allowed her to understand his silent pain when he had looked down at that battered boy.

Pip was a kind and gentle person, a good son to Doris and a wonderful, loving husband. His only hang up was the father whom he had not spoken to or about in fourteen years. She knew this evening must have conjured up a flood of childhood nightmares for him.

"If you insist on staying, I'm going to wait with you."

"That's not necessary."

"I'm not going to leave you alone. Get in the car." Pip moved the vehicle down the street and turned it to face the Krause's driveway.

In less than an hour, Tim pulled into his carport. They watched as he shut off the engine and slid out of the car. Pip opened his door and ran over to confront him.

"Hey, guy," Tim said. "What are you doing here? I thought you'd be long gone. I'm sorry for the way Muriel behaved. She went a little crazy."

"I saw the bruises."

"Yeah? I'm afraid I got a little carried away. Muriel and I don't always see eye to eye on disciplining the kids. I say 'spare the rod and spoil the child.'"

Pip had not heard that expression since childhood. He exploded, grabbing Tim by the front of his shirt and lifting him off the ground. Their faces were just an inch apart. Spittle flew from Pip's mouth onto Tim's face as he spoke.

"You fucking son-of-a-bitch. If you ever hit Muriel or your children again, I'll kill you. Get in your car and don't come back here again." Pip suspected Tim would do as he was told; that he would turn and walk away. But something deep inside forced him to continue. "And here's something to let you know I'm serious."

Pip smashed Tim in the face. He watched the man's eyes disappear into their sockets as he fell to the ground, unconscious. Mary Lou jumped out of the car and ran to her husband's side.

"Jesus, Pip!"

Pip looked down at Tim. "Sorry! I guess I got a little carried away," he snarled.

"Let's wait until he gets up," Mary Lou said.

Tim started to stir, then slowly got to his feet. He glared at the Marshals, then stumbled toward his car. He sat there for a while before driving off. Mary Lou breathed a sigh of relief.

"We'll have a restraining order by Monday," she said. "You're a lawyer, for God's sake, not a vigilante."

Part Five
The Crime

CHAPTER TWENTY-TWO

The life of an options counselor in a small Southern town wasn't easy. Susan's husband, Mark, was an intern at the hospital with crazy hours and intense work. She didn't want to worry him with the incidents. But they bothered her.

She was checking out groceries when the cashier looked up staring her right in the eye. "How can you kill babies?" she asked. "How can you do it?"

"What?" Susan replied, not understanding for the moment.

"How can you do it? Innocent infants."

Susan thought the woman might cry.

"I can't check you out," the woman continued. "I can't."

Susan at first became angry. She knew the cashier had to be a demonstrator. What a nut. She considered getting the manager. The woman should be fired. But then she thought of her beloved Nonnie. This woman believed as her Nonnie had.

Without responding, she packed her groceries back in the shopping cart and went to another line.

The following day Susan recognized the woman picketing outside the clinic.

ℬ

Kristen was afraid to share her revelations with Harold, or anyone for that matter. Why had Jesus selected her? Some questions just didn't have answers. At first, He visited in her sleep, and she wasn't sure it was he or just a dream. But then He chose to speak to her when she was alone at the florist shop.

"Find a way, Kristen, find a way."

She knew it was Jesus.

"I don't know how. Oh, I wish I did."

"Find a way, Kristen, find a way. Save my children."

"I want to, my Jesus."

"I know you do."

"Guide me, my Savior."

"I will, my child. You'll always be in my hands, and I'll forever protect you."

&

It was six o'clock. Mark had been on duty for twenty- two hours, and he had another fourteen to go. Susan met him for supper at the hospital cafeteria.

"You look like hell," she said, as she contemplated the assortment of unappetizing entrees.

"Thanks. Nothing like knowing I'm a sex object to my wife," Mark responded, as he put a Salisbury steak on his tray.

"I didn't say you don't look sexy. I've always been attracted to tired grumpy men."

"I have to visit a patient and then I can rest in my office. Come with me," he said when they finished eating.

She put her arm around her husband as they started down the hall.

"Dennis asked me to look in on Mr. Muther," Mark continued. "He has a bleeding ulcer. He's had two transfusions and is on a bland diet which is not to his liking."

Susan waited in the doorway while Mark visited the patient. He picked up the chart at the end of the bed. "Good evening, Mr. Muther. I'm Dr. Reingold. How are you doing?"

"I'm ready to get out," he replied. "I don't like it here."

"I don't blame you. Well, let me take a look," Mark said as he went to the side of the bed.

"I'm glad you're here instead of Goldstein. I don't like having a Jew doctor touch me."

Mark froze in his tracks. He could feel the blood rush to his head, anger engulf him. And he was bone tired.

"I don't like Jews," the patient reiterated.

Susan stared at her husband from the hallway.

"I don't like them either," Mark replied calmly. "We got your test back, Mr. Muther. I'm afraid you're going to die."

"What?"

"Your blood <u>metsofusion</u> is very low. I'm sorry, there's nothing we can do. You have about a month to live."

"This can't be true. I want another opinion. Oh my God. This can't be true. Where's Dr. Goldberg?"

"You mean Dr. Goldstein, don't you? Wait a moment. This isn't your chart. You'll be fine. My mistake."

"Mark," Susan said from the hallway, but he ignored her.

"What the hell you talking about, doc? Am I going to die or not?"

"Well yes, eventually, but for now you're fine. I just read the wrong chart."

"Jesus, doc. That's not funny."

As Mark left the room, Susan grabbed him by the arm.

"What's the matter with you, Mark? He's an ignorant man. What's your excuse?"

"I'm tired?"

"No good, try again."

"I was wrong. I'm sorry. He just pissed me off. I lost my cool."

Susan started to chuckle and leaned against her husband's chest. "I never saw that side of you before."

෨

Mark returned home at ten the next morning. Susan had left him a note.

Hi, Honey:

I hope you didn't try to scare any other patients to death. Sleep well. I may work late tonight. I'm giving a seminar on Saturday and have to prepare. Will tell you about it when I get home. Miss me. Love!

Mark put the note down and went to the refrigerator. As he ate his sandwich, he contemplated how to get back on schedule. He was always experimenting without any satisfactory results. Sleep for only four hours, and then get up at two in the afternoon might do it. Then he could try to stay awake until Susan came home.

She called at eight that evening. "Darling, I can't break away. Are you okay?"

"Yeah, sure. I understand. No problem."

"I may not be home until midnight. Wait up. I have something to tell you."

"What is it? Tell me now."

"No begging. It will have to wait."

Mark got into bed at ten-thirty. He read a medical journal, but when his eyes started closing, he switched to a mystery about a psychopathic doctor. Maybe it would help him stay awake until Susan came home. It was no use. At eleven- fifteen, he closed his eyes and was overcome by sleep.

ℰℒ

The statistics were appalling. In just one year there were over a million abortions in the United States. Kristen could think of nothing else. She became sullen and depressed. Harold worried about her.

"You can't blame yourself," he said.

"I just know Jesus is testing us. We have to do something. He's counting on us." She was afraid to share her revelations with him.

"We're doing all we can."

"Are we? I look at our precious sons and think of the innocent children being slaughtered. This is America. It isn't supposed to happen here. No, Harold, I don't think we're doing enough."

"Please, Kristen, relax."

"I want to, but I just can't."

She dwelt on the problem and its solutions. Nothing had worked. She recalled Bernie. What had he said? "Bomb the clinics. Search and destroy." When she was in the house alone, she found herself reviewing the components. A jar? A cloth? No problem. Gasoline? Harold kept a gas can on the shelf of the garage for the lawnmower.

The words to "Onward Christian Soldiers," reverberated through her brain. She was a soldier in His army, and, yes, she knew what He wanted her to do. And she could wait no longer. Too many were dying. Now she knew why Jesus had revealed himself.

The next night Kristen lay in bed until she was sure Harold was sleeping. Careful not to disturb him, she got up and listened. His breathing remained even. She crept into the bathroom where she had left her clothes. Silently she dressed, then went to the garage. She had hidden what she needed in a large storage box. She took out the gasoline can and poured the liquid into an empty quart jar that had contained tomato juice just a week ago. When the bottle was three quarters full, she stuffed a pillowcase into it, leaving half outside as a wick; soaking it with lighter fluid.

Review everything Bernie had told them. She had asked him if it was as simple as it sounded. Harold laughed at her question. "You're just the one to blow up the abortion clinic."

Won't he be proud, Kristen thought? Carefully she wiped the jar and placed it back into the storage box to keep it from tipping. She carried the box to the car and put it on the floor of the passenger side.

As she drove to the clinic, she smiled at the prospect of destroying such an evil place. How many lives would be saved because people would not have a place to do their killing? This would be only the beginning. She would travel the country blowing up abortion clinics. Harold would join her. They would do it in the early morning hours before anyone arrived. She didn't want to ever hurt people, only put those killing centers out of business.

I'll be a hero someday, saving thousands, maybe millions of babies from a hideous death.

એ

At eleven-thirty, Susan looked at all the work still on her desk. She would have to keep going if she wanted to be ready to give the seminar on Saturday. She decided to lie on the couch for a moment and rest her eyes before going back to work. As Susan turned off the lamp, she remembered she hadn't called Mark to tell him not to wait up. She was excited to share her news with her husband but it would have to wait until tomorrow.

એ

Kristen pulled into the parking area. There was one automobile in the lot, but the building was quiet and dark. She sat in her car, surveying the evil structure. She had picketed outside and pleaded with clients not to go through with the killing of their babies. It hadn't done any good. They refused to understand.

She picked up the home made bomb and held it to her bosom, fondling the cold glass in her hands as if it was one of the babies she wanted to save. There were tears in her eyes as she finally opened the car door. Twice she walked around the building, holding the bomb and a box of wooden matches. Which window should she throw it through? At first, she couldn't decide.

"Dear Jesus, help me to do Your work. Let me be Your instrument to end all abortions. Give me the strength and courage to fight for your children," she prayed.

Standing at the back of the building, the parking lot to her left, she knew she was facing the chosen window. Goose bumps covered her body. She was divinely inspired, could feel His presence. Striking a wooden match, she lit the cloth wick. It sparkled for a moment before bursting into flame. Kristen jumped at its sight, then heaved the bomb. The window shattered, a burst of flame followed.

Kristen stood mesmerized as it spread. The words to an old slave spiritual rang in her head.

> "God gave Noah the rainbow sign,
> No more water, the fire next time."

Her heart pounded as she heard her Savior reveal Himself once again. "You have done well, my child." She was truly blessed.

"Thank you, Jesus." Slowly she walked to the car. As she drove off, she heard the sound of sirens howling in the distance.

CHAPTER TWENTY-THREE

Lieutenant Kimball Dugan had served on the Calvert Police force for nineteen years and was the only detective in the department. He was slightly over six feet tall, with a weight problem he had long ago given in to. His hair was naturally curly and never required any more care than washing, though the years had severely accentuated his forehead. He never married and replaced the companionship of a wife with gourmet dining, a thorough daily reading of the New York Times, and his love for old classic films.

His passion was his work, and when he was involved in a particularly fascinating case, time and other involvements became unimportant to him. He had a good mind for solving puzzles and that was often the nature of his business.

Kimball was a man of habit, and Thursday evenings were the only time Judith, his friend of many years, slept over. On this particular Thursday, he had prepared stuffed mushroom caps followed by poached salmon accompanied with a red wine, excellent for the price. Judith had brought over a lemon meringue pie that they enjoyed with coffee as they watched The African Queen before retiring. Slowly they made love, not passionately but with a special caring. When they finished they tenderly held each other, talking until their words began to slur and they were asleep. Several hours later the phone rudely woke them. Kimball reached for the intruding instrument, knowing it had to do with police business.

Quickly he washed and dressed before leaning over the bed to kiss his friend good-bye.

"See you next Thursday," he said.

"Have a good week," she responded before going back to sleep.

&

Kristen returned home. She was proud of her deed and wanted to share her act with Harold, but wasn't sure if she should. Back in bed, the bombing hardly seemed real. Her husband still slept peacefully. If he only knew. Her heart began to pound as she relived the evening.

She thrilled at the anticipation of reading about her deed in the paper, anxious to know how those butchers would react. There was no reasoning with them. Maybe this they could understand.

She heard her Savior telling her she was as brave as the Apostles. Her thoughts became a dream. Jesus was gazing down from the heavens.

"You did well, Kristen. Look around you."

She did as she was told. A mass of babies, all shouting their thanks and repeating her name, surrounded her.

Suddenly they became adults. Her mother and father were among them.

"We're very proud of you, Kristen. God has let us into His heaven because you are our child," her mother said.

"Look, Kristen." It was her father speaking. "They are boarding up the clinics all across the land. You have made them see their evil. The murdering is over, thanks to you."

They were standing to the right side of Jesus. Her Savior spoke to her.

"You are a true Christian soldier."

"Thank you for saving my parents," she saw herself saying.

"When your work is over on earth, you'll join them."

"Oh, Jesus, my sweet Jesus, thank you."

⁊

The director of the clinic had identified the young woman. Dugan ran a check on the plates. The car belonged to the victim, Susan Reingold.

It would be his job to advise the next of kin, in this case a husband. This was never easy.

As he went to ring the Reingold's bell, the door was flung opened, momentarily startling the lieutenant. The man said something that Kimball didn't quite catch. He observed the instantaneous change on Mark's face from glad expectation.

"I thought you were my wife."

Lieutenant Dugan identified himself with the usual flash of the badge. "Why are you here? Is Susan okay? Please, what's wrong?" Mark asked.

"I'm sorry."

Dugan told Dr. Reingold all he knew.

"Not Susan. You've made a mistake. Who would want to harm Susan? She didn't have an enemy in the world. There must be some mistake." His words were spoken with a strange calmness.

"I'm afraid not. She was identified and it was her car in the parking lot. Why was she there so late at night."

"I don't know. She was giving a seminar or something..."

Dugan led Mark back inside. "Is there someone I can call to be with you?" he asked.

"Oh, God... God, no." Mark burst into tears. "It was those crazies, wasn't it? It was those bastard anti-abortionists." He smashed his fist into the wall, crumbling the plaster. "They call themselves pro-life. Killing Susan isn't pro-life." He grabbed Kimball by the arm. "Oh, God, my poor Susan. Those bastards."

℘

"Kristen, get up. You've overslept. I got the kids to school, and I have to go to work. It's quarter after eight."

She woke with a start, disappointed that her dream was ended. Remembering last night sent an exciting chill through her. Should she share it with her husband? Maybe she would wait until he heard about it on the news. She was anxious to put on the television but decided to linger until he left for work.

"I'm sorry. You should have woken me."

"I tried. You wouldn't budge at seven, so I let you sleep. Not that I had any choice. Relieve me at lunch time," he said as he kissed her good-bye.

She listened for the start of the car, went to the window and saw him drive off.

She turned on the television feeling almost giddy as she watched the Today Show, waiting for the local news.

"Sometime early this morning, a terrorist fire bombed the Calvert Counseling Center. The firemen discovered a body. The victim, identified as Susan Reingold, apparently died from burns and smokes inhalation.

"Lieutenant Kimball Dugan, spokesman for the Calvert Police Department, said the clinic reported it had received no threat before the attack and no person or group has claimed responsibility."

Kristen sat in disbelief. She saw a picture of the destroyed building and then a brief shot of Mark Reingold, leaving his house. A reporter was attempting to elicit a response from him, but he just stared, zombie-like, into the camera.

"No," Kristen spoke to the set. "No, it can't be."

She had killed a human being. She knew the victim by sight. Kristen had shouted at her to stop her evil work. Their eyes had met.

Kristen's act was the antithesis of all she believed. That car in the lot. Why hadn't she realized someone must have been in the clinic? But there were no lights on. What was she to do now?

The ringing of the phone interrupted her thought. It must be Harold. She answered mechanically, still overwhelmed by the burden of her act.

"Did you hear the news?" her husband asked.

"What news?" she lied, perhaps for the first time in their married life.

"Someone blew up the abortion center. They used a firebomb. Sounds like the one that Bernie Parks told us about. Do you think he could have done it?"

"I don't know," she stammered, not able to catch her breath.

"Are you all right?"

"Yes."

"You don't sound it."

"I'm all right. Just a headache."

"Okay. I'll see you at noontime."

Kristen sat at the kitchen table, staring into space. She didn't know what to do. She'd always been honest with Harold. Yet, could she share what she had done with him? The phone rang again causing her to look at the clock. It was twelve forty-five.

"Kristen, what's keeping you?"

"I'm sorry, Harold. I wasn't feeling well. I must have fallen asleep again. I'll be right down."

"That's okay. If you're not feeling well, stay home. I'll manage."

She returned to her problem. Maybe she should say nothing. Confessing wouldn't bring Mrs. Reingold back. She went to the garage, looking to see if there was anything that could incriminate her. Harold would never notice gasoline missing from his can. Slowly, she retraced every move. Nothing pointed to her. Nothing. She was going to try to put it out of her mind and tell no one. What was happening to her?

When the children returned from school, she ignored them. Then she heard Harold coming home. She always tried to look good for him. Running to her room, she washed her face, applied fresh make-up, took a deep breath and went to greet him.

CHAPTER TWENTY-FOUR

Lieutenant Dugan stayed with Mark until Doctor Goldstein arrived.

Though exhausted, Dugan returned to the clinic. He didn't know what he would find, but experience told him if there was any evidence, he might lose it if he wasn't quick about it.

The Lieutenant recognized the arson squad team. He spoke to the leader, Marty Shulman.

"Looks like a Molotov cocktail," Shulman said. "Broken glass, not much else."

The Lieutenant nodded. "Who are all these other folks, Marty?"

"Those two are insurance," he replied pointing. "The other three are F.B.I."

Dugan whistled. "Didn't take the Bureau long to get here. Let me know what else you find. Are you checking the glass for prints?"

"The F.B.I. boys have it," Marty answered.

Dugan went over to the agents and introduced himself.

"I'm Sol Schwartz," a short balding man spoke. He took Kimball by the arm and led him to his car. "Let's talk in private."

After they were in the vehicle, Agent Schwartz continued. "I often find we're a threat to the local constabulary and that's ridiculous. We're on the same team, want the same outcome. This is both an F.B.I. matter and a local matter. I suggest we work separately but share our findings." Schwartz took out a card. "This is my number, twenty-four hours a day. Any questions, call. We'll give you any information we find and I'm sure we can expect the same from you. Let's talk often."

Dugan had no problem with the arrangement. "You guys have the equipment. Let me know what the glass shows."

"We will."

Dugan stuffed the card in his pocket and left the car. Slowly walking around the building, he surveyed the scene, taken aback by the extent of the damage. Why did the culprit decide upon that window? He guessed it was a random choice. Any other window and Susan Reingold would probably be alive. He carefully picked up a wooden match by the ends and placed it into a plastic bag. He would give it to the F.B.I. They had a better lab.

A trailer had been set up in the parking lot. Dugan looked in. A group of people was sitting on folding chairs, talking. His intrusion ended their conversation.

"Can I be of some help?" one of them asked. "We're closed today."

The Lieutenant automatically reached into his back pocket, taking out his wallet and showing his badge. "I'm investigating this case. Can I see the person in charge?"

"The director. I'll take you to her. Catch the bastard. Susan was my friend and a damn good person."

"Why was she here last night?"

"I don't know. That was very strange."

"Was she having any problems at home?"

"Definitely not."

The Lieutenant noted how sure her response was. He had already all but ruled Mark out but it was his habit to never shut the door to any possibility. He followed the woman as she walked into a room without knocking. The director, on the phone, waved them in.

"I don't know when we'll be back in operation. The building is a mess. The F.B.I. is here."

After a pause she continued. "Yes, this trailer is a God send. How did you get a telephone hook-up so fast? Thanks again." She hung up.

"Joan, this is Sergeant... I'm sorry, what's your name?"

"Lieutenant Kimball Dugan, Ma'am."

"Sorry to keep you waiting but that was the president of my board. I'm Joan Marszalek," the director said as she stood and extended her hand.

Dugan had never seen a taller woman. She had to be six four or five, thin and small boned. He noticed she wore a wedding band and wondered about her husband's height.

"I have some questions I would like to ask."

"Of course, Lieutenant. Helping you solve this murder is a top priority to everyone here. Now, please, ask me anything you want."

They spoke about the clinic and Susan Reingold before Dugan asked, "Do you suspect anyone?"

Joan looked directly into the Lieutenant's eyes, her hands clasped on a folding bridge table.

"You know as well as I do, it was one of those kooks who protest all the time. They're probably all in on it. What do you call it, a conspiracy?"

Lieutenant Dugan was writing in his book. "Do you have any names?"

"The leader, I think his name is Harold Edwards. He's the one that gives the speeches. And there's been another one lately. I don't know his name, but he wears one of those camouflage jackets, even when the weather's warm. I've listened to him through the window. I'd question him."

"Is there any other person or group who might want to harm the clinic?"

"There are many people who think our work is evil. They believe they have some divine right to stop us. You have lots of suspects."

"Thanks for your help."

"We're all anxious to cooperate. Susan wasn't here long, but we were very fond of her. We want this nut caught."

Lieutenant Dugan went back to the station and wrote up his notes. He reviewed past police reports on the pro-life demonstrations at the clinic. Bernie Parks fit the description of the demonstrator Ms Marszalek had described. He jotted down his address. Dugan then read the report on Harold Edwards. Not much. He and his wife own a florist shop; two children no arrests. Not your typical terrorist cover but who knew.

It was five-thirty. Where had the day gone? He would see Parks at home, since he worked construction. He could catch Edwards the next day at the florist shop.

℘

"Mrs. Parks?" he asked the woman who opened the door.

"Yes."

"I'm Lieutenant Dugan," he said, showing his badge. "Is your husband in?"

"Who is it?" a voice hollered.

"It's for you, the police."

"First the F.B.I. Now the police. I'm getting mighty popular. I'll be right there."

Kimball was surprised the F.B.I. beat him to the punch. He recognized the man from the description. He was wearing his camouflage jacket.

"Let's see if I can figure out why you're here. I don't speed, so it must be the bombing. Come on in. Can I get you a beer?"

"No, thanks. On duty," Dugan replied, taken back by Park's flip, casual attitude.

"I'm not. Do you mind if I have one?"

"Be my guest."

They sat at the kitchen table. Kimball noticed two empty cans in the wastebasket. Bernie opened a fresh one and took a deep swallow followed by a satisfied burp.

"I understand you served in Viet Nam," the Lieutenant said.

"Yes."

"Did you see combat?"

"Yes."

"I was in Korea," Dugan responded, shaking his head with an understanding only those who have actually participated in combat can share. "I assume you know how to make a Molotov cocktail?"

"Is it a Russian drink?"

Dugan smiled. "You can have one more chance."

"Yeah, I know what it is. But so do a lot of other people. It doesn't mean I blew up that place."

"No, of course not."

"Listen, Lieutenant, maybe I shouldn't reveal this, but I told the whole group of them how to make a fire bomb."

"Why in God's name did you do that?"

Bernie finished his beer and fidgeted with the can before tossing it into the wastebasket and heading for the refrigerator.

"We were just talking. You know how it is. You shoot the shit. You say things. You don't really expect anyone to make one and blow some place up."

"Who was there?"

"I don't know. It was a while ago."

Dugan let the answer pass. He had a list of demonstrators from the police files.

"Do you have an alibi for last night?"

"I was here sleeping when the bomb went off."

"Can you substantiate that?"

"Listen, Lieutenant, my wife was next to me but obviously she was sleeping too. She doesn't guard the house while I sleep. This isn't Korea or Viet Nam."

$$\infty$$

Kimball arrived at the florist shop shortly before noon the next day. He approached the woman at the counter.

"I'm Lieutenant Dugan. Is Mr. Edwards here?" he said, flipping his badge.

Kimball noticed the fear that burst onto the woman's face. Her entire body started to shake and she could hardly talk.

"Are you Mrs. Edwards?"

"Yes... Yes... My husband's in the office... I'll... I'll get him."

She returned to the front of the shop with her husband.

"Can I help you?" There was an unfriendly calmness in his voice.

"I would like to ask you some questions about the bombing early yesterday morning."

"This is a business establishment, not a very good place to talk about bombings."

"It should only take a few moments. Perhaps we can go to the back room. Can you join us, Mrs. Edwards?"

"Someone has to watch the store," Harold answered for her.

"Listen. There's been a bombing. A woman was killed. You act as if you don't want to cooperate with me."

"I'm sorry about the woman but, to be honest, not about the clinic. I wish every abortion center would be bombed to smithereens. I hate them, but I assure you, we're not bombers or killers."

A customer entered the store.

"Can I help you?" Kristen stuttered as she headed toward the woman.

"Come with me," Harold said as he led the Lieutenant toward the back of the shop.

Kimball went hesitantly. He preferred to interview them together.

It was a small office with two desks that faced each other and an extra folding chair. One desk was cluttered with papers. Ribbons, scissors and flower accessories filled the other. There was a copy of The Last Supper on one wall with a family picture next to it of two boys, another couple plus Harold and Kristen.

Harold sat behind the paper-laden desk.

"Where were you last night?" Dugan asked as he sat on the folding chair.

"Kristen and I were sleeping when the bomb went off. Where do you think we were?"

"How do you know Kristen was sleeping?"

"Because we went to bed together. Why? Do you suspect her?" He laughed. "Does she look like your average every day bomber?"

The Lieutenant had to admit neither of them were your average, everyday bomber. But why had Kristen frozen when he introduced himself? Could she simply have an inordinate fear of the police?

"I'm going to meet with all the protestors. I have to assume the bomber is an anti-abortionist. You do want to see the person caught, don't you?"

Harold didn't answer the question.

"I could use your help. Point me in a direction."

"We are Christians. The Bible says 'Thou shall not kill.' The commandment is clear and we all obey God's law. No, Lieutenant, you will have to look elsewhere."

"I would like to speak to your wife now!"

"She doesn't know any more than I do."

The phone rang and Harold picked it up. He wrote something on a pad. "Yes, they will arrive by this evening."

"Maybe she can tell me something you forgot."

"I'll get her."

Kristen came to the office. She was visibly shaking. "Please relax Mrs. Edwards. This is only routine."

"It isn't every day I'm interrogated by the police."

"I wouldn't call it an interrogation. I just want you to answer a few questions. It will help me to find the killer. I'm sure you want the person brought to justice."

"I'm sorry. I've never been questioned before. The whole idea frightens me."

Her breathing was almost a gasp for air. His intuition, however, was telling him she couldn't have done it. "Has anyone in your protest group ever spoken of bombing a clinic?"

"I don't know. I can't think," she struggled to say.

Dugan decided to let her be. "Okay. Why don't we do this another time? It's not as if you might leave town. We'll talk later."

"Oh, thank you," she replied, then added, "I'm sorry, you just scared me."

&

Slowly the Lieutenant picked up the receiver, and dialed. A moment later he heard Mark's voice.

"This is Dugan. I'll be at the funeral."

"Yes," Mark replied. "That will be nice."

Dugan could tell Mark wasn't hearing him. "Listen, this is difficult for me to ask of you, not considerate, but I need your help. I'll want to speak to you at the funeral, ask you if there's anyone there you don't recognize."

"Do you think..."

"I don't know. It's possible."

℘

The church was filled with friends and family. Dugan surveyed the mourners. After the service, he watched Mark follow the casket outside before quickly walking down the side aisle and arriving at the limousine that was to carry the family to the cemetery.

"Anyone here you don't know?" he asked the grief-stricken man.

They stood together by the open door of the car. Mark scrutinized each mourner as they left the church. He pointed out a few people he didn't recognize.

"Probably friends of my in-laws."

"I'll check them out. Thanks. I'll want you to do this again at the cemetery. I'm sorry."

Mark nodded. The Lieutenant went off to speak to the people Reingold had identified. They all had a connection to Susan, friends or relatives.

Dugan watched from a distance at the cemetery. He went through the same scenario with Mark, but again no one unusual was identified.

"It's always a lot of leg-work," Dugan said. "Often it reveals nothing, but you never know. I appreciate your help under the circumstances. Anything else unusual?"

"No... Well, yes. There was a beautiful wreath without a name delivered to the church."

"No card?"

"Oh, yes, I think so but it wasn't signed. It must be back at the church." Mark's lips started to quiver as he fought back tears. "Find the maniac, Lieutenant. Please find him and hang the son-of-a-bitch. Please. Avenge Susan's death."

"We'll find him."

As if to himself he mumbled, "She hadn't told me yet."

"Told you what?"

"The autopsy showed she was pregnant. When I spoke to her that last time she said she had a surprise for me and she would tell me when she got home."

Kimball went back to the church. The wreath was still there among an abundant display of flowers and ferns. He looked it over and found the card. Printed were the words "In Sympathy," over a Cross on an angle. It was simply signed, "A Friend."

Not knowing one variety of flowers from another, he snapped off a few samples and put them in his pocket, then diagrammed the wreath in his notebook. He would check all the florists if he had to, but he knew where to start.

စာ

Harold was in the back room and Kristen was on the selling floor. She no longer received joy from the flowers and plants. She thought of her children and Harold, her aunt and uncle. How blessed she had been.

Why had the devil been able to invade her soul, use her as his instrument to kill another? When she read in the newspaper that Mrs. Reingold had been pregnant, her guilt became overwhelming. She no longer had the right to call upon her Savior. She should turn herself in but the devil was urging her not to.

"Think of your husband and children without you while you rot in prison," he spoke.

"Thou shall not kill," she responded.

"Your children, your husband." The devil laughed.

Kristen started to cry. Harold came to her from the back room.

"What's wrong?"

"I feel so bad for Mrs. Reingold and her baby."

Harold held her. As her crying subsided, he said, "Go pick up the boys. I'll be okay."

She nodded before leaving.

Less than ten minutes later, Dugan stopped by Dove's Flower Shop. The Lieutenant showed him the flowers and his sketch. "Did it come from here?"

"Yes," Harold replied.

"Do you know who sent it?"

"Of course. I did."

"Could you tell me why?"

"It was Kristen's idea. She feels so bad for the girl. Especially since her poor soul is condemned to eternal damnation. It's as if Kristen wanted to forgive her."

≈

Dugan spent the next two weeks tracking down and speaking to every protestor. Each evening, he returned to the station and reviewed his notes. He then called Sol Schwartz and they shared their findings.

"If I didn't need proof, I'd hang my hat on Bernie Parks," Schwartz said. "They all have motive but he's the only one with the expertise."

"How much expertise does it take," Dugan replied.

"He also has the balls."

"Not much to go on. A camouflage jacket and balls," Dugan responded. They both laughed. He continued. "Kristen Edwards was a nervous wreck when I spoke to her. She would never be a suspect if it weren't for her incredible anxiety. She isn't the type. Yes. Bernie Parks makes more sense."

"Could there be more than one perpetrator?" Schwartz interjected. "Could the Edwards and the Parks be in this together? Maybe the whole church was in on it. Where the hell do we go from here?"

"I'll call you tomorrow, Sol," Dugan said, yawning as he hung up the phone.

He reread his notes. Why do I keep coming back to my first meeting with Kristen? And if it is she, how do I prove it?

He reviewed the report from the F.B.I. laboratory. They had reconstructed part of the jar. It had originally contained a liquid food such as a juice. The perpetrator hadn't worn gloves or wiped the jar clean, as there were unidentifiable smudged prints. There were no prints on the match but the company was identified, Ohio Blue Tip Match Company.

Where did the bomber get the gasoline? Was it siphoned from the tank of a car or bought at a gasoline station? Not a difficult substance to obtain.

≈

Early evening, five weeks after the bombing, Lieutenant Dugan rang the bell at the Edwards' home. Kristen opened the door. He watched her closely. She appeared calm.

"Good evening, Mrs. Edwards. Can I ask you and your husband a few more questions? Just some loose ends."

"Come in," she said in nearly a whisper.

Dugan now detected a tremor in her voice. She led him to the living room. "Have a seat. I'll get Harold. He's upstairs with the boys."

The Lieutenant looked around the room as he waited. There was a cross on one wall along with pictures of the boys at various stages. Everything was in its place as if the room had just been cleaned. He picked up the Bible that sat on a small oak table next to a chair. There were bookmarks throughout the text. This was not the house of a terrorist. But after five weeks of looking under every rock, reviewing all possibilities, he knew he had to take a more aggressive look at Kristen Edwards. If she had been attached to a lie detector on their first meeting, the needle would have jumped off the chart.

His methodical mind had developed a plan.

"Lieutenant Dugan," Harold said, extending his hand as he entered the room, his wife behind him. "How's the investigation going?"

He was much calmer than he had been at their original interview.

"It's slow, not like the movies. A few more questions, if you don't mind."

"Anything we can do to help."

"Bernie Parks once told your Pro-Life group how to make a fire bomb or, as it's sometimes called, a Molotov cocktail. Were you at that meeting?"

"Yes, we were. The meeting wasn't about bombs, Lieutenant; it was about saving millions of lives, the lives of unborn babies. We had never met Bernie before. He had been in Viet Nam. There was talk about how ineffective we had been. No one responds to our pickets. He saw our frustration and told us about Molotov cocktails. Loose talk. No one took it seriously."

"Someone did," Dugan responded.

"You can't really think someone from our group did it."

"Wouldn't you?"

The Lieutenant watched Kristen carefully as he asked the next few questions.

"That's a nice lawn you have."

"Thanks," Harold replied.

"Do you care for it yourself?"

"Of course. I find it very relaxing."

"What kind of mower do you use?"

"A Toro."

"How's it powered?"

"Gasoline."

Dugan thought he saw Kristen jump as she realized where the questioning was leading. He watched as she twisted her hands, sweat appearing on her brow. Now he was sure.

"Do you keep extra gasoline on hand?"

"Listen here," Harold responded. "It doesn't take a genius to figure out where you're heading. You can't think we had anything to do with it."

"I'm sorry, but I have to look at every possibility. Do you have a gasoline can?"

"Of course."

"May I see it?"

"Sure! It's in the garage."

"Do you ever mow the lawn, Mrs. Edwards?" Dugan asked, as they walked toward the garage.

"No..." Her voice was barely audible.

"Have you ever had a reason to pick up the can?"

"No," Kristen whispered.

"If we checked for prints..."

"Oh, God," Kristen said and she fainted.

Harold went to his wife. "This has been too much for her. She's not a strong woman."

They helped her to sit up. When her eyes opened, she looked first to her husband at her side, and then at the detective looking down at her.

"You know," she said in a barely audible voice.

Dugan nodded.

"Oh God, I'm sorry. I'm so sorry."

"Kristen, for heaven's sake, what are you talking about?"

"I killed Mrs. Reingold and I killed her child. Oh, Harold, it's been so awful. I just wanted to save babies. Oh, that poor girl."

Dugan was usually delighted when the hunt was over and he had his criminal. But not this time.

"I have to bring you in," he said in a soft voice. "You can come also, Mr. Edwards." He turned back to Kristen. "You have the right to remain silent..."

Part Six
The Trial

CHAPTER TWENTY-FIVE

Muriel and Tim were divorced. Mary Lou convinced the court that Tim was a threat to his children and visits had to be supervised. At first, he made an effort to see his sons but shortly after the divorce he remarried and lost all interest in them.

For Muriel the dissolution of the marriage was better than a weight loss clinic and she looked and felt more fit than she could ever remember. The Marshals were not only generous employers but had become valued friends, on a first name basis when not in the office. The boys were heroes whenever the famous Pip Marshall attended one of their games or school functions.

When Harry Upton had first asked her out, she had gone to Mary Lou. "Any rule on dating clients?"

"We have to approve all of your dates."

"Sounds reasonable after what I put you through. How about Harry Upton?"

"Just don't throw any golf clubs into the water."

"First, I'll have to learn how to play golf."

℘

Muriel looked up from her work. Although she had never met the man, she knew who he was. He arrived fifteen minutes early for his three o'clock appointment, and it was obvious by the way he paced the floor he was nervous and impatient to see her employer.

"I'll let Mr. Marshall know you're here."

Harold Edwards did not have to wait for three o'clock. "How can I help you?" Pip asked.

"My wife's in jail. I can't believe it. She did a terrible thing."

"I've read about it."

Though not an expert on the subject of abortion, if Pip had to offer a view, it would be he didn't know when life began. He believed abortion was probably wrong, but a pregnant woman still should have the choice.

Edwards started to shake, his lips quivered and he was losing his struggle to keep from crying, as he continued. "She wishes with all her heart that it hadn't happened. But it has. We need a lawyer to help us, to tell us what to do. I know you're very busy... And I know my wife's guilty." Now he was weeping. "We've prayed for forgiveness and Jesus will hear our prayers. But our family's shattered. I don't know what to tell the children."

Harold was sincere but the reference to Jesus brought back a flood of memories to Pip. Unexpectedly, he recalled Kristen from his childhood: the girl with the unshakable faith who had looked up at him as he swung from the church steeple, those many years ago.

"I'd like to meet with your wife before I decide."

"I understand."

Pip stood and led Harold to the door. "I'll go to see her this evening."

He returned to his desk and started to work on another matter but his mind refused to leave the interview. I know Jesus will hear our prayers, Harold had said. Pip thought about his youth and the pain Jesus had caused him. Do I want to represent this woman, one of God's faithful? I've never turned down a client in need of me but...

&)

The officer accompanied Pip to the women's detention area of the jail at the police station. Kristen was the only inmate. There weren't many female criminals in Calvert. She sat on her bunk, head bowed. Her hands played with a gold cross that hung around her neck.

"Mrs. Edwards, I'm Attorney Philip Marshall. Your husband has asked me to represent you. I would like to talk to you so we can get to know each other. Then we can each decide."

Kristen didn't answer. The officer opened the door. Pip entered the cell and sat on the other bed, facing her. The heaviness of her grief was nearly tangible.

"Can you tell me what happened?" he asked in a soft voice.

"Hello, Mr. Marshall. It's been a long time."

"Yes, it has."

"You must have read about it. I blew up a building and killed that poor woman and her baby."

"I would like to try to understand what led you to do it."

She stared at him blankly, not comprehending.

"What were you thinking?"

"I thought it was the only way."

Pip didn't understand her meaning. "The only way for what?"

"To get them to see their evil."

"Yes?"

206

"That they were committing murder. I thought Jesus wanted me to do it. I did it for Him, to save His children. No one would listen. Every day thousands of babies... but I killed an innocent girl. I knew who she was. I'd seen her go to the clinic. Once she even came to my shop to buy flowers. I spoke to her, told her it was wrong. Now I've killed her and her poor innocent unborn child. They didn't deserve to die. Why was she there? If Jesus spoke to me, why was she there? I deserve to be punished."

"That's for a judge to decide." Did she really believe Jesus spoke to her or was she speaking metaphorically?

"There's only one Judge," Kristen said, her fingers never stopped tracing her cross.

"Mrs. Edwards, there's also a judgment on earth and it isn't perfect." He spoke slowly, choosing his words with care. In spite of her fanaticism, he knew he couldn't turn his back on her. "An imperfect judge and jury are going to determine how you're going to spend the remainder of your life on earth. I want to help you convince them you should live that life with your husband and your children."

"I would like that. But I don't deserve to be free. No, I should be in jail. Do you know why I did it, Mr. Marshall?"

"Can you tell me?"

"There's only one answer," she said matter of factly. "You see, Jesus would never have had me do what I did if there was an innocent victim in the building. Oh, no. I was tricked. It was my pride, and pride goes before a fall."

How foolish thinking pride's a sin, he thought as she continued.

"The devil got inside of me and convinced me he was my Jesus. He knew I would follow him if I thought he was the Lord. He told me to do it, came to me. The devil is very powerful and very evil, Mr. Marshall."

Her eyes were glazed and she spoke without looking at him.

"How did he speak to you?"

"At first, in dreams but then he came to me as I worked at the florist shop."

"I see." But of course he didn't see. "Well, let's find out what I can do about bail. If Jesus can forgive the sinner, so can man." He was a lawyer. He didn't have to believe everything he said.

℘

"Come on, I'm starved," Pip implored.

Mary Lou put down her work, shut off the light to the office, put her arm around her husband and led him to the door. "A steak and Bloody Mary should quiet you down."

They ate out almost every weeknight. Mary Lou had grown up believing she would be a housewife and mother. Somewhere along the way she got caught up in the idea of being not only Pip's wife but also his partner. She felt her biological clock ticking but wasn't sure if it mattered. They never discussed children. Their careers, at least for now, had become their life.

℘

"You're late tonight," the maitre d' said. "I was worried."

"Not enough hours in the day, Maurice," Mary Lou replied as they followed him to their table.

Pip stirred his Bloody Mary with a celery stick before taking a deep swallow. The liquid smoothly found its way down.

"Well?" his wife asked.

"I'm going to represent Kristen Edwards."

"You are? This was one case I thought you might turn down. Maybe I even hoped you would. Susan Reingold was a remarkable woman. Muriel was so indebted to her."

"But the defendant is devastated by what she did. It wasn't her intent. No, she needs me." He gulped his drink before continuing. "I think she's crazy. But she's so sincere. I'm considering a defense of insanity."

"How do you come to that?"

"At first, the woman believed Jesus wanted her to bomb that clinic. Actually believed He came to her. Then when she learned she had killed someone she claimed she was duped by the devil."

"Pip, if she's insane, then there are millions of crazy people out there. I know your feelings, and I respect them. But you can't think of every fundamentalist Christian as nuts. That isn't a viable defense."

He laughed. "I guess I'm a little prejudiced when it comes to them."

"A little?"

"But she said she spoke to God. I don't mean a dream. I mean spoke to Him."

He caught the waiter's eye and pointed to his empty glass. He needed another drink. "Maybe we can plea bargain for manslaughter. We'll see.

She's like a child and yet she blew up the clinic. If you met her, you wouldn't think it possible."

ℰℴ

Robert Lee Johnson was the assistant district attorney assigned to try the case. Pip had found him an honorable man in their past dealings.

As he drove to Robert's office, he reviewed how he could best serve his client. I'll urge Bob to accept a plea bargain of manslaughter. That shouldn't be too much of a problem, considering Kristen's past record and her obvious remorse. Would it be pushing my luck to suggest a suspended sentence? Maybe, but I bet Bob will buy one to five. Kristen would surely serve only one year or less. Maybe if the family would pay for psychiatric help, Bob would go for a suspended sentence.

Pip was immediately ushered into the D.A.'s office. Robert Lee Johnson was tall and thin and reminded Pip of Ichabod Crane. Pip was surprised to see another man there, someone he had seen before.

"I hope you don't mind," Bob said. "I've invited Lieutenant Dugan to join us. I think he'll help you to understand our position."

"No, of course not." Now he remembered. He had seen Dugan on television, trying to avoid questions about the bombing. Pip immediately plunged into his argument. "Bob, we agree on the crime, even its seriousness but you have to consider the intent and the fact that it wasn't done for material gain."

"Lieutenant, would you tell Mr. Marshall what you told me?"

Kimball cleared his throat. "Too often I spend my time tracking a criminal, only to see a soft prosecutor insult my work by plea bargaining the scum back onto the street. However, I don't feel that way in this case." He paused and looked at the two lawyers before continuing. "I interrogated Mrs. Edwards at great length, and I've told the district attorney I recommend going easy on her. She suffers great remorse, presents no threat to the community and a stiff sentence would serve no purpose. Mr. Johnson knows that is contrary to my usual position on the people I nail."

"Sounds like we shouldn't have much of a problem," Pip responded, suddenly feeling more relaxed and in control.

"Just doing my job. I'll go now if you don't need me further."

After Lieutenant Dugan left the office, Pip turned toward the prosecutor. Why was there a look of concern on the D.A.'s usually affable face?

"I had Kimball speak to you so you would fully understand our position, but I don't think you're going to be happy," Bob began.

"Why not?"

"Because Mark Reingold, the victim's husband, is putting a great deal of pressure on our office. He's insisting on first degree. I can't strike a deal for manslaughter knowing the way Dr. Reingold feels. I just can't. I believe a plea bargain must have the blessing of the victims. I would go along with second-degree murder if Dr. Reingold agreed. I would consent to a reasonable sentence, but he wants her to serve twenty to life. He keeps saying that's a better deal than Susan got. He told me that to try her for first degree murder would let everyone know you can't go around throwing bombs at buildings and killing innocent people."

"You don't have to accept the victim's position if you feel justice isn't being served," Pip responded lamely.

"You know we have to give it a lot of weight. He's extremely persistent."

"I met him at a cocktail party once. He seemed a reasonable man."

"It was the man's wife. To him, he is being reasonable. Off the record, you know it's going to be a high profile case. There are many who want to lynch her. But believe me, they're not a factor. It's Dr. Reingold."

"If she has to serve a sentence of more than a few years, she won't make it. She isn't strong enough," Pip pleaded.

"As you know, the grand jury returned an indictment of first degree murder. I'm sorry, really, but we're going to go along with it. Argue your case. The jury can convict her of a lesser-included offense. I have to consider the family of the victim."

ℰ

Pip sat in his office, emotionally beat. It would be a difficult trial. He knew in good conscience he could argue either side. His defense strategy would take considerable preparation.

Muriel interrupted his thoughts. "Your wife wants to see you."

Mary Lou had been with a client when he had returned or he would have immediately gone to her to seek counsel and comfort. With all the energy of an old man he went to her office, threw his briefcase onto one seat and collapsed on the other.

"Rough day?"

"Rough day," he responded. "Bob's charging her with murder one. I'll tell you about it at dinner. Did you want something special or just my body, because if that's what you want, I'm tired and I have a headache?"

"That's never stopped you before."

"And it won't now."

Pip watched as his wife's smile faded into seriousness.

"Helen called."

"Helen?"

"Your father's wife."

Even after all these years he felt anguish at the mere mention of his dad.

"Your father's sick. He wants to see you. Helen says it's the most important thing in his life, and I think you should consider going."

"What's wrong with him? Is he dying?"

He has Alzheimer's disease. Helen says it's pretty bad. Pip make your peace with him while you still can."

He stood and started to pace the room. "I don't know."

"Darling, Helen says she isn't sure if he would know you now. In a few months, it will definitely be too late." She put her arms around him. "If you don't go you'll regret it. He's your father."

"He was such a bastard," Pip replied. "Such a bastard."

"He's your father." There was a pleading in her voice he couldn't ignore.

"Will you come with me?" he asked.

"Of course, if you want."

"God, I have this damn trial to prepare," he said, falling back into his chair.

"He's only two hours away. We can do it this Sunday. One day."

∞

Pip usually drove but today Mary Lou had taken the keys. His stomach churned as they rode the hundred miles to Ashton.

He recalled the first time he had walked Mary Lou home. Never could he remember going from happiness to despair as quickly as when he first saw his father kissing a strange woman.

Helen answered the door. She was wearing jeans and a blue checked shirt. She was still lean and the years had been kind to her. She held out her hand to him.

"I'm so glad you've come, but I have to tell you, your father may not recognize you," Helen said as she led them to the living room.

"Does he know of his illness?" Pip asked.

"He's been told, but he doesn't always remember."

The room was small and impeccably tidy. His father was sitting in a comfortable chair watching a television commercial with apparent interest.

"Walter, Pip's here to see you," Helen said, putting her hand on his shoulder and leaning over toward him. She turned off the television.

"Why you doing that? I was watching the show." He whined like a child.

"Pip's here, darling. He's driven over from Calvert to visit with you."

Walter turned toward the couple. His mouth was open as if his nose could no longer take in air. The old man was smaller than Pip remembered him. He still had his waxed mustache, gray now. Helen must help him groom himself each day. He was meticulously dressed, as if he was ready to leave on a four-day selling trip. There was a vacant stare in his eyes. Slowly he struggled at trying to comprehend the scene, to understand what was happening, to reach for the fullest extent of his capacities.

"Pip, Pip is that you?"

"Yes, Father."

"Why have you been gone so long? You should visit more often," the old man scolded.

Pip did not reply.

"I went to so many of your games, boy. I watched you on television. I was so proud of you. I would tell people I was Pip Marshall's Daddy."

"I've not heard him so aware in a long time. You're good for him," Helen said softly, wiping the tears from her eyes.

"But then people would ask me questions about you, things I didn't know. What was it like having a famous son? I told them it was wonderful, and it was. I was proud, boy."

Pip listened to this stranger. He couldn't forget the beatings or the betrayal. No, I can never make my peace with this old man.

"I'm tired," Walter said.

"We're going to have a little dinner before you rest, dear. Pip and Mary Lou drove all the way from Calvert just to see you. Isn't that nice?"

Pip observed the love Helen had for his father. It gave him a certain comfort knowing the old man would be well cared for. And he felt a certain justice in Helen having to suffer the burden of Walter's illness.

"All the way from Calvert, to see me?" Walter was like a late night radio signal, weak, then strong, before fading once again. "Pip, I'm sorry I beat you. Sorry I broke faith with you. I was a God-fearing man. I was told God had great compassion, would forgive the sinner."

Pip was stunned both by his father's lucidity and the content of his words.

Walter continued. "I don't want His forgiveness anymore. He can be damned for all I care. But while there's still time, I need your forgiveness, boy. Please, I've loved you so long with nothing in return, nothing to show."

"I'm speechless. He hasn't been this coherent in months," Helen whispered.

Could he forgive his father? He wasn't sure. But time was running out. Feeling awkward, mildly embarrassed, he put his arms around the old man, embracing him. Their bodies had not touched for so many years.

"Oh, Father, I forgive you. I'm glad I made you proud." Could he say more? The words were on his lips. He was choking on them. "I love you, Father."

Saying it seemed to remove the hate that had haunted Pip all those years. It felt good. The burden of carrying this poison lifted.

"I want to watch my shows now," Walter said to Helen.

"You can watch them later, Dear."

"I want to watch them now."

There was anger in his voice. Helen took him to his chair and turned on the television. He immediately became engrossed in a "Mighty Mouse" cartoon. Pip went over to say good-bye. The old man's face was sunken, which exaggerated the three circles formed by his wide-open mouth and two vacant staring eyes. He was no longer with them.

Pip would visit every few weeks until the death of his father, but Walter would never again recognize his son.

∞

The two-story, red brick courthouse had been built at the turn of the century. State offices occupied the first floor. Two courtrooms filled the second.

Pip checked with the clerk. Courtroom One. He went inside. The room had stern wooden church-like pews for the public. A cheap paneling that attempted to look like wood adorned the walls. The blue tweed carpeting was worn down the center aisle and tape covered the seams that had pulled apart.

Kristen had not yet been brought to the courtroom. Harold was sitting in the front seat of the spectator section. He looked both haggard and terrified.

Pip went to him. "Judge Fredericks is fair," he whispered.

"I heard she's tough. What if she's one of those feminists? Kristen won't stand a chance."

"She won't judge Kristen on her politics."

"What if she does?" he replied as if he dared not hope. "This is all so unbelievable."

Kristen was brought in and led to the defense table. She kept her head down, not looking at anyone. Pip joined her as the bailiff called out, "All rise."

Judge Laura Fredericks came from her chambers. She was a petite woman, with brownish grey hair pulled tightly back in a bun. It was hard to tell anything else about her appearance as her robe so completely enveloped her.

"The case of Kristen Edwards," the clerk called.

"What is the charge?" the Judge asked.

"First degree murder," the prosecutor replied.

"How do you plead?"

"Not guilty, Your Honor," Pip responded.

"I don't permit bail in first degree murder cases."

"Your Honor, I believe there may be extenuating circumstances that will warrant your considering bail in this case."

"Go on, Mr. Marshall," the judge allowed.

"My client admits to the crime of setting fire to the premises at 1100 Chestnut St. that resulted in the death of Susan Reingold, but we contend it was an act of negligent homicide or, at the worst, manslaughter. She has no previous arrests, not even a parking ticket. There's no reason to believe she's a threat to the community. She has two children. Until the incident, she was a model citizen. Therefore, a reasonable bail would be appropriate."

The prosecutor rose to his feet. "Your honor, the defense admits his client blew up the clinic. He admits her felonious act caused the death of Susan Reingold, a young, vibrant woman, with most of her life in front of her. We contend the defendant did it knowing there was a reasonable chance the building was occupied and her act could cause a death. That is first degree murder and, therefore, we recommend that the severity of the crime should prohibit bail."

Pip countered. "Kristen Edwards has no previous record. She's a respected business woman who has lived here since she was a teenager. She's no threat to society." There was urgency in his voice.

"I'm sorry, Your Honor, but I can't agree," the D.A. shot back. "At the very least, she's guilty of a serious crime; at the most, it's first degree murder."

The Judge looked at both lawyers and then at Kristen. "I'm afraid I'll have to deny bail. Trial will be in four weeks. Is that acceptable to both sides?"

Pip and Bob nodded their consent.

As the courtroom started to empty, Pip looked at his client. She was sitting as she had during the entire proceeding, looking vacantly at the table. Had Kristen understood the proceedings, or what had been decided? He glanced at the gallery. Harold was crying.

For the first time, he saw Mark Reingold. The man looked more like a vagrant than a doctor--his suit disheveled, hair uncut and uncombed--and he was in need of a shave. He seemed to be glaring at the back of the defendant.

An elderly couple approached the defense table. They kissed Kristen and held her before releasing her to the custody of the patiently waiting officer.

They turned to Pip. "We're her Aunt and Uncle," Jack Ploss said.

"We've raised her since she was a teenager," Jean added. "She's a wonderful child. Please, she deserves another chance."

Pip wished he could give assurances to these woefully sad people. "I'll do everything I can."

CHAPTER TWENTY-SIX

Pip surveyed the six men and six women who would decide his client's fate. To the untrained, trial by jury appeared to be a roll of the dice, but he knew better. He had worked hard to assure a jury that wasn't prejudiced against those who believed life began at conception. He questioned perspective jurors at length, trying to ascertain each candidate's opinions and prejudices on abortion. He was allowed to excuse fifteen prospective jurors peremptorily and used them all on those he believed couldn't be at least sympathetic to Kristen's views.

One prospective juror told the court that life begins when the kids leave home and the dog dies. Pip accepted her. The decision to dismiss a prospective juror, for all his efforts to the contrary often came down to intuition.

℘

Pip had seen little change in his client over the past month. She continued to be melancholy, indifferent to her pending trial or its consequences, dwelling only on the death she had caused.

The case attracted national attention with reporters from all major media constantly fighting for a scrap of news. They plagued Pip, Harold, and even Jack and Jean Ploss for interviews. Pip had instructed them to simply respond to the hounding with the customary "no comment."

From what Pip was reading, the news people were not having much more luck with Dr. Reingold or the prosecution. This was one case where the news people were going to earn their money.

℘

"All rise for the Honorable Laura Fredericks."

The judge entered the courtroom and took her seat. The clerk read the case and announced the charge of first-degree murder.

"How do you plead?" Judge Fredericks asked.

"Not guilty, Your Honor," Pip replied.

"Are both sides ready?"

"Ready, Your Honor," Bob and Pip answered simultaneously.

Judge Fredericks turned to the jury.

216

"I want to welcome you and thank you for serving and fulfilling your patriotic duty. I have confidence in the ultimate fairness of your deliberations. You'll be asked to decide whether Mrs. Edwards is innocent or guilty of first- degree murder, second-degree murder, manslaughter or negligent homicide. You'll be able to take into consideration not only her act but also her intention. In order for Mrs. Edwards to receive a fair trial, it's imperative that you give each witness your full and undivided attention."

Pip studied the jury as the judge concluded her remarks.

"You may not discuss the case with the other jurors until you begin your deliberations, and don't discuss the trial with anyone else until the case is over. Finally, do not visit the scene of the act on your own."

She turned to the district attorney. "The prosecution may deliver its opening statement."

Robert Lee Johnson rose to his feet. "Thank you, Your Honor." As he strolled over to the jury they collectively shifted in their seats.

God, I have to stop weighing their every nuance, Pip scolded himself, knowing he probably couldn't.

"Kristen Edwards is guilty of first degree murder because she committed first degree murder," Mr. Johnson began. "She wrongfully caused the death of Susan Reingold while performing the terrorist attack of bombing a building, simply because she disagreed with the purpose of the organization that was housed within that structure. When one commits a felony knowing it could lead to a death, that is first-degree murder, plain and simple.

"A signal must go out that we have laws that must be obeyed. These laws should have protected Susan Reingold and her unborn baby. We owe it to the victim to declare firmly when the law is broken, the perpetrator must pay. If not, we can all lose our freedoms to those who believe they serve a higher purpose than the Law. Thank you."

The prosecutor went back to his seat. Pip stole a glance at his client before taking his turn. Her eyes focused on the table. As he approached the jury, he momentarily glanced at Mark Reingold. Was he planning on attending the entire proceedings? Damn.

"Madame Foreperson, members of the jury. Kristen Edwards did a terrible thing. The State doesn't have to prove it. Mrs. Edwards, with great remorse, admits she accidentally caused the death of Susan Reingold. However, the law does distinguish between first-degree murder, second-degree murder, manslaughter and negligent homicide. Sometimes it's a fine line, not black and white, as the prosecution would have you believe. If the choice was obvious, and we could all agree on which crime Mrs. Edwards was guilty, there would be no need for a trial. But that isn't the case.

"There was no malice, no intent. Yes, Kristen was negligent, yes she was reckless, but what was her motivation? She believed she was saving millions of human lives. Now, you may or may not agree that fetuses are human beings. But that's not what's at issue. What is at issue, what you must understand, is that she believes with all her being that life begins at conception."

He looked at each of the jurors in turn as he concluded. "Ladies and gentlemen of the jury, the charge against my client is murder, and if you find her guilty, she could spend the rest of her life in jail. The State will not be able to prove beyond a reasonable doubt she committed first degree or second degree or for that matter manslaughter. I know you will take your awesome responsibility seriously and will come to that conclusion."

He walked back to the defense table, put his hand on his client's shoulder and sat down. Kristen never acknowledged him.

℘

Court reconvened after lunch.

"The prosecution will present its case," the judge announced.

Pip looked around the courtroom, waiting for Bob to call his first witness.

"The State calls Bernard Parks."

He was cleaner but dressed no differently than usual, camouflage jacket and olive pants. The bailiff swore him in.

"Do you know the defendant, Kristen Edwards?"

"Yes."

"How do you know her?"

"She's a member of a church group I attend."

"Are you aware of how she obtained her knowledge about explosives?"

Bernie paused. His face flushed. "I told her."

"Could you speak up?"

"I told her."

"How did you happen to do that? Do you often tell people how to make bombs?"

"No. We were just talking. You know how it is."

"I'm afraid I don't. How did you happen to be talking about Molotov cocktails? That's what you call them, isn't it?"

"Yes. We were talking about how to get the abortion places to stop their killing." There was reluctance in his voice.

Johnson was good. It wasn't easy to get an antagonistic witness to reveal information. The prosecutor's deliberate sarcasm irritated Parks into not carefully considering his answers.

"Go on."

"They, the church group that is, were protesting but it wasn't getting them anywhere. We were talking about other ways. No one took the idea of bombing seriously. You know how it is. It was just talk."

"When did this so-called harmless talk take place?"

"I don't know."

"Think."

Bernie looked at Kristen. There was pain on his face. "Six months, maybe nine months before the... before the bombing."

"So Kristen Edwards had at least six months to plot her terrorist attack on the clinic?" Johnson looked at the jury. "Plenty of time to premeditate."

Pip was on his feet, protesting.

"I withdraw the question. Your witness."

Pip stood at the table. He knew Bernie wanted to help. He had to ask the right questions. "Do you recall the reaction of the group when you suggested bombing as a possible alternative?"

"It sounded like a good idea at first. But these are God-fearing people. By the time the meeting was over I don't think anyone believed it was the right thing to do. Or even if some did, no one took it seriously."

"Did that include Mrs. Edwards?"

The prosecutor was on his feet. "Objection. There's no way the witness can know that."

"Sustained."

"Was it your feeling that anyone left the meeting with the idea of carrying out the bombing?" The question was redundant but he wanted to emphasis it to the jurors.

"No! People were...were frustrated, but no."

"Objection," Johnson said again but too late.

"That will be all," Pip spoke.

♋

The next few days of the trial the district attorney presented witnesses that described Susan Reingold. Bob Johnson wanted to make the victim into a real person for the jury, and the witnesses spoke eloquently of their love and admiration for her. Pip had no questions for any of them.

♋

"The State calls Joan Marszalek," Johnson announced.

Pip watched the jury stare at this unusually tall woman as she took the stand and was sworn in.

"What do you do?" the prosecutor asked.

"I'm the Executive Director of the Calvert Counseling Center."

"What is the function of the center?"

"We work with pregnant women who believe they don't want to go to term for one reason or another."

"Do all your clients end up having abortions?"

"Absolutely not."

"Could you explain?"

"Forty percent of our clients decide to give their baby up for adoption, or keep the infant. It's our job to help them reach whatever decision they perceive as best for them."

"It seems like a highly personal decision."

"It is."

"Does your agency perform abortions?"

"Yes."

"What happens if a client can't decide? Do you ever decide for them?"

"No. We may help them organize their thoughts, but the decision must always be theirs."

"What did Susan Reingold do at the clinic?"

"She was an options counselor."

"Did she believe in abortion as an alternative?"

"She believed women had the right to choose. When I hired Susan she told me abortion would always be wrong for her. It was a personal matter. But it was also her conviction other women had the right to do what they wanted with their bodies."

220

"Did you know she was pregnant?"

"Yes. She told me the afternoon before she died. She couldn't wait to tell her husband but I guess she never got the chance."

"Was she good at her job?"

"She was excellent. Susan was one of the least judgmental people I have ever met. That's what made her such a good counselor."

"I have no further questions."

"Mr. Marshall, you may cross-examine," the judge spoke.

Pip stood at the defense table, not approaching the witness.

"I have just three questions for my cross examination," he said. "What are your hours?'

"Hours?"

"Yes! The hours you are opened."

"Seven to four-thirty, eight to twelve on Saturdays"

"How often does anyone stay over night at the clinic?"

"Never."

"Why was Susan Reingold there?"

"She was working late. She must have fallen asleep. To the best of my knowledge, it wasn't her intention to be there."

"No further questions."

As Joan was taking her seat Johnson announced: "The State calls Mark Reingold."

Pip knew the judge would allow the witness as a way to determine the degree of guilt. Reingold was sworn in and introduced to the jury.

"How long had you been married?"

"Almost three years. It would have lasted forever."

"How did you learn your wife was pregnant?"

"She called me the night she was killed. She said she had some news for me, would tell me when she got home. I asked her to tell me what it was but she refused. Said I would have to wait. She never got to tell me. I learned from the autopsy report. I later found out she had seen her gynecologist that afternoon."

"Did your wife ever express concern for her well-being working as an options counselor?"

"I was more worried than she. Those nuts were out there every day shouting and taunting her. But she said the Law protected her. She was wrong about that." Mark's lower lip began to quiver. "The murder of my wife is more than I can handle. I'm devastated. They say they protect the unborn." He pointed a finger at Kristen. "Well, you killed my baby."

Pip was on his feet to object when Johnson announced, "I have no further questions. The prosecution rests."

Kristen started to cry. Her body shook. Mr. Johnson turned and looked at her.

"We'll take a recess. May I see counsel in chambers?" Judge Fredericks announced.

As Pip headed for the Judge's chambers, he saw Harold go to his wife. No one stopped him as he put his arms around her.

"I'm guilty. I killed her, and I deserve to be punished," Pip heard his client say as he was about to enter the judge's office. Glancing at the jury, he wondered if they had heard this unfortunate outburst. They were all staring at Kristen.

&

"This is a most difficult trial," Laura Fredericks began. "If it's to be fair, your client must not influence the jury with her tears. If she does that again, she'll not be able to remain in the courtroom. Do you understand?"

"Yes, Your Honor," Pip replied.

"Can you make Mrs. Edwards understand?"

"I'll try. I think so."

"I'll announce a recess for today. That will give you the weekend."

&

Pip sat with Kristen in the visiting area of the jail. It was a barren, windowless room, furnished only with a large rectangular table and four straight-backed wooden chairs.

"Please. You can't cry out. The judge won't allow it," he pleaded with her.

"I'm sorry," she said in a barely audible voice. "I deserve to be punished. That poor woman and poor Dr. Reingold. All because of me. I want to be found guilty of murder. Tell them that. It's what I want."

Pip knew his client had a right to plead guilty if she desired. If he couldn't change her mind he'd withdraw from the case.

"If I'm to defend you, I can't let you do that. You have a husband and two boys who need you."

"Oh, I miss my boys. I just can't stand it. I'm so confused." Her hand played nervously with the cross around her neck, her eyes avoiding his.

Memories of Pip's childhood flashed into his mind. He knew what he had to say. God, I'm such a hypocrite, he thought. "Kristen, you know Jesus has forgiven you. He forgives all sinners who believe in Him and are repentant. Now you must forgive yourself. Do it for your boys and your husband and do it for your Savior."

"I'm so miserable. I miss my family. I hate being locked up," Kristen cried. "But every time I think of Mrs. Reingold and her baby, I detest myself and want to be punished. Why did she have to be there and why, oh, why did she have to be pregnant?"

"You must forgive yourself as Jesus has forgiven you."

"I'll try. I want to go home. Oh, God..."

Pip had to get out of there, away from her. "I'll see you Monday."

೮ಾ

A few minutes before six, an exhausted Pip returned to the office. Muriel was putting on her coat and chatting animatedly with Mary Lou.

"Pip, look at Muriel's ring," his wife exclaimed.

The secretary held up her hand, revealing a massive, pear shaped diamond.

Pip just didn't have the energy to display the enthusiasm he would have felt under different circumstances. "It's beautiful," he responded, struggling to show excitement. "You and Harry?"

"Of course, me and Harry."

As if that was the signal, the door flung opened and Harry entered. A wide grin encompassed by his full red beard expressed his happiness. He kissed Muriel, oblivious to the laughing.

"Come on, Honey, let's escape before these slave drivers make you work all weekend," he said putting one arm around her while pointing to Pip's bulging briefcase.

Like the hurricane he was, he rushed his fiancée from the office.

"She's a kid in a candy store. It's good seeing her so happy but I hope we don't lose her. She won't need the money anymore," May Lou said. "How was court today?"

She watched her husband collapse into a chair, then walked up behind him and began massaging his temples,

"You can never tell. Kristen wants us to lose the case more than Bob does. It's bizarre. I try to convince her to defend herself. If she'll cooperate, I think we have a fair chance but I need her help. If only she didn't act so damn guilty. The jury can see it. God, she just stares at the table. Today she started crying... right in the courtroom."

"That could help. Get the sympathy of the jury."

"I can't tell. All I know is if she does it again, the judge is going to remove her and that certainly won't help."

"What's your strategy?"

"I'm not sure. I might call only one witness, her husband. I think he could be the key. I don't know. It's such a screwy case. I really could have used Muriel this weekend. Why did you have to become a lawyer? Why couldn't you have been something useful, like a secretary?"

She picked up a pillow from the couch and threw it at him.

෨

It was a weekend of thinking and evaluating options. Each path had its opportunities and pitfalls. Bob had concentrated on the victim. Pip had to convince the jury that, yes, Susan's death was a terrible senseless tragedy, one that was frustratingly irreversible, but it was done without malice by someone who reasonably believed the building had to be empty at that hour. His client deserved a second chance.

෨

Pip had Harold come to his office early Saturday morning. "I'm going to put you on the stand. You'll be my entire defense."

"I thought I couldn't testify," Harold responded.

"The prosecution can't call you but I can. Once I do however, the D.A. has the right to cross-examine. You'll help show the jury her intentions were only to save lives, never to take them."

Harold paused as if he needed a moment to choose his words. "I love my wife. However, these past weeks have been difficult not only on me but especially on the children."

"What are you saying?"

"She's so different. I don't recognize her. You have to understand... how unbelievable... I mean when she confessed, I still didn't believe... Kristen wouldn't... Jesus doesn't teach us to..."

"She believed she was saving lives," Pip urged.

"I also have felt the same desperation. I don't know." There was a pause before he continued. "I wouldn't blow up a clinic. What was she thinking? It's not just what she's done. It's what she's become."

"She's going through a very difficult time."

"But I don't recognize her. I must be honest with you. I think she's possessed. The Kristen I know could never commit such an act. Never. How do I explain her actions to the children?"

"My God, man, she needs your help, your support," Pip responded, giving no clue to his revulsion. Kristen was having a breakdown, and Harold believed she was possessed. Pip knew there was no way to reason with this man. He knew it only too well. However, his testimony was still the key.

"The jury must understand she believed she was saving lives and it's up to you to convince them."

Harold nodded. Pip went over the questions he and the prosecutor would ask.

℘

"All rise."

Pip continued to try to read the jurors' minds. Were they paying attention? What did their facial expressions indicate? It was a futile exercise but one that obsessed him.

"Be seated," the clerk announced after the judge had taken her place.

"The defense may present its case," the judge said.

"We call Harold Edwards," Pip responded.

Kristen looked up. She watched as her husband approached the stand. Her eyes still looked glazed, as if she wasn't aware of her surroundings or comprehended what was happening. Pip put his hand on her shoulder before heading toward the witness. The bailiff swore Harold in.

"Your name?" Pip began.

"Harold Edwards."

"What's your relationship to the defendant?"

Harold looked at Kristen before answering. "She's my wife."

"What were your feelings when you learned what she had done?" Pip asked.

"I couldn't believe it."

"Why?"

"We're florists. We have two children. We value life. We attend church. We believe we're on this earth to do God's work and live by His word."

"If Kristen believes the way you say she does, how could she blow up a building?" Pip cast a glance at the jurors. He wondered about their response to his descriptive choice of words.

"She reads about the millions of babies who are aborted each year, who literally never get a chance to see the light of day. She sees these children as if they were her own. She... we feel the weight of their deaths. More children have died at the hands of the abortionists than all the victims of Buchenwald. We know life begins at conception. How would you feel if, how can I put it, if these were three-month old babies...? That's how we feel each time we hear of an abortion. We're overwhelmed with sadness and despair. I guess the mass killings were too much for her to bear." His lips quivered as he tried to hold back his tears. It was impossible and involuntarily, he started to cry. "All those poor babies."

"Is that any reason to break the law?"

"Should good Germans have broken the laws in 1938 or should they have stood by while six million Jews were killed?"

"Then you condone what your wife has done?"

"What?"

"You don't believe she committed a wrongful act?".

"Killing Mrs. Reingold was wrong, terribly wrong and Kristen would do anything if she could change that. But how could she know someone would be in the building so late at night. She thought she was saving lives not taking them."

Mr. Johnson was on his feet. "Objection. Mr. Edwards can't speak for his wife."

"Sustained."

"No further questions. Your witness."

Pip sat down next to his client. She never moved, had an almost lifeless look. Did she know where she was, what was happening?

Robert Lee Johnson stood tall as he slowly approached Harold. Even though he would have been happy to settle for the reduced charge if the victim's husband would have allowed it, he was a professional and was representing the victim and the community to the best of his ability.

"When did you learn your wife was the person who bombed the clinic?"

"The day she was arrested."

"She kept it from you all that time? Why did she do that? If she was proud of her actions why didn't she share them with you?"

"I think she planned to until she discovered what happened."

"What do you mean?"

"The woman."

"The murder of Mrs. Reingold and her baby?"

Harold nodded.

"Please state your answer."

"Yes, the death of Mrs. Reingold," he replied in a barely audible voice.

"You said quite eloquently that a fetus has a right to life. Did Susan Reingold and her unborn baby have a right to life?"

Pip was on his feet. "I object, Your Honor."

"Sustained."

"I have no further questions," Mr. Johnson said.

"You may stand down," the judge directed the witness. Pip turned to his client. Her hands hid her face.

"The defense rests," he said.

"Court will stand in recess until ten o'clock tomorrow morning."

∞

"What happened to you?" Mary Lou asked as Pip entered her office. His hair was disheveled, his clothes rumpled. "You look like you've been through a meat grinder."

"I look the way I feel," he replied.

"Reporters have been calling from all over the country." Mary Lou told him.

"They're swarming over the courthouse. Kristen's overwhelmed by it all. I have to constantly convince her not to plead guilty to first-degree murder. Tomorrow's the summation. I'll be stuck in the office most of the night."

"Want me to help?"

"You've got your own cases," he answered.

"Hey, we're partners. We'll grab a bite, then work."

Impulsively, he stood and took her in his arms. She had been his rock since high school and still was all he wanted. He cupped her face in his hands and they kissed. He stood back and looked at her trim body. She wore a fitted, gray tweed two-piece suit accented with a white, bowed silk blouse. Her shoes had low heels that brought her almost to his height. Her auburn hair was evenly clipped in a soft pageboy. He led her to the couch.

Later she said, "Most lawyers don't get to do this with their law partners."

"I guess this means we won't have time for supper," he replied.

"I think we made the right choice. Let's get to work."

CHAPTER TWENTY-SEVEN

Pip walked through a crowd of reporters, whose shouting questions mingled together into an unintelligible, garbled noise. "I'm sorry, but any response to your questions wouldn't be in my client's best interest," was his only response.

The courtroom was packed. Pip had been the center of attention many times from high school to Super Bowl. Others had depended on him before, and the stakes always seemed high. But, ultimately, football was only a game to him. His responsibility to Kristen Edwards was greater than all that had gone before.

"How are you doing?" he asked his client as he sat down at the defense table.

"I'm guilty. I did it."

"Kristen, that's for God and the jury to decide."

He squeezed her hand hoping it would give her strength. Her self-recriminations left him weary, and he felt dishonest every time he used God to make a point.

The courtroom rose as the bailiff announced the arrival of Judge Laura Fredericks. She took her seat at the bench and surveyed the packed courtroom while touching the bun at the back of her tightly pulled, graying hair. She then wielded her gavel twice. Whispers could still be heard.

Judge Fredericks spoke to the gallery. "This trial seems to have caught national attention. That is the right of the people in a free society. However, our only interest is in a fair trial for the defendant. I, therefore, must warn you, if there is any disturbance from the spectators, I'll be forced to clear the courtroom. Is that understood? Mr. Marshall, we'll hear your summation now."

Pip stood at the sound of his name. He briefly glanced at his legal pad resting on the defense table. Mary Lou had helped him write his closing argument and had listened to him deliver it, at first with notes and then without them. They hadn't worked that intensely since all night study sessions at Michigan. He didn't get to bed until two that morning and was up before six. Yet he wasn't tired.

Pip approached the jury, these twelve people whose minds he had been attempting to influence for the past two weeks. "The question isn't when does life begin. It makes no difference whether you believe in a woman's right to choose or life begins at conception. The question you must answer is what would you do, if you believed as Kristen Edwards does.

"What would you do if the law of the land said that until a child left home and could choose for himself, he may be put to death by the parents, if they decide they don't want him or her? Perhaps you find the analogy to be ludicrous. No one in his right mind advocates that position. Considering the parallel will help you to understand how Mrs. Edwards views abortion.

"The question, it seems to me, is not what she did. We all know the unfortunate answer to that. No, you must dig deeper, into her intent.

"What was her intent? Why did I tell you about parents having the right to kill children up to the time they left home? Because Kristen Edwards feels no differently toward the unborn fetus than you would toward a seven-year-old child, or a twenty-five year old, or one who is eighty. To her life truly begins at conception. You don't have to believe a fetus is a human life. What I ask of you is to understand that Mrs. Edwards believes it. She believes it with all her being. And she mourns the death of these unborn babies as you might suffer over the slaughter of innocent seven year olds in your community.

"To Kristen Edwards, millions of humans are legally being put to death every year. You heard her husband compare it to a concentration camp in Nazi Germany. Kristen could no longer remain a bystander to what she sees as genocide. She had to become a resister to this mass murder.

"Was her motive to destroy someone else's property? The answer is no. Did she hope her act would lead to material gain? Again, no.

"Her act did cause the death of another human being, and she has suffered great remorse because of it. But she committed the act at three in the morning. She chose that time because she believed the building would be empty. You heard the director of the clinic tell you at no time, to her recollection, had the building ever been occupied at that hour."

Pip drew himself close to the jury. He made eye contact with each of them as he concluded.

"Yes, ladies and gentleman of the jury. Kristen Edwards committed a terrible act, an act she wishes with all her heart she could undo. But her intent was to save millions of lives, never to take one. I believe you will find the charge of first, even second-degree murder or manslaughter, not pertinent in this case and return Mrs. Edwards to her husband and children, where she belongs. Thank you."

He returned to the defense table. Kristen was watching him. For the first time since the trial began, there was a spark of life in her face. Pip hoped his summation convinced not only the jury but Kristen as well that she deserved to be forgiven.

Judge Fredericks glanced over to the courthouse clock. It was approaching the noon hour. "I don't want to interrupt your closing statement, Mr. Johnson. Why don't we recess for lunch?"

Pip's job was done. There was nothing else he could do but watch. Suddenly he felt exhausted and hungry. As the bailiff came for Kristen, he stood and stretched his weary body before heading for the hot dog vendor outside the courthouse. He even chatted with the reporters as he contemplated rewarding himself with a third loaded dog.

"Mr. Marshall," Kristen's uncle Jack Ploss called to him. "Can we have a word with you?"

The Plosses had been to every session of the trial. Pip led them away from the reporters who followed.

"Is it possible to have a private conversation?" Pip asked of them. The news people let them be.

"We pray every night that our niece will return to us as whole as she was," Jack said. "She's such a good person."

"We just want you to know," Jean went on, "whatever the jury decides, we feel you've done a wonderful job. We just need you to know that." Her lips quivered.

"Thank you. That's important to me," Pip said.

They seemed frail and frightened. He tried to say something to bolster their broken spirits. "We can only hope the jury will see her real goodness and give her another chance."

"You've done all you can," Jean responded, giving him a peck on the cheek. "We just wish you to know how grateful we are."

֍

The hot dogs and Coke were doing their work and Pip controlled a belch, as Robert Lee Johnson was called upon by Judge Fredericks to deliver his summation. All trial lawyers are actors, Pip thought, as he watched Bob approach the jury. The prosecutor reached into his vest pocket, took out a gold pocket watch, glanced at the time and put it back.

"There's no need for me to be lengthy," the prosecutor said as he established eye contact with each member of the jury in turn. "You're intelligent people and you've heard all the facts in this case.

"There's a lot we all agree on. Kristen Edwards did make a Molotov cocktail. She drove to the Calvert Counseling Center, walked up to a window, lit the wick and hurled the bomb, shattering the pane. The fireball fell down on Susan Reingold, innocently asleep on the couch, and consumed her and her unborn baby in smoke and flame, causing their deaths.

"Is this murder? The law clearly thinks it is. If a death occurs due to a felony, and the felon reasonably knows that death could occur, it's murder in the first degree."

Bob looked at Kristen for a long moment before turning back to the jury.

"Defense counsel spoke eloquently of intent. What was in Kristen Edwards' mind when she caused the death of Susan Reingold? We know she understood the difference between right and wrong." Mr. Johnson spoke slowly, deliberately as he continued. "Therefore, it's reasonable to conclude that when she made the bomb, went to the building and blew it up, it was her intent to knowingly break the law, and she certainly knew there was a possibility, even though I grant you it was remote, that she could cause someone's death. These facts are not arguable, and that constitutes first-degree murder.

"You heard Joan Marszalek testify that never to her knowledge had anyone been in the clinic at three in the morning before that fateful night. However, Kristen Edwards had no way of knowing that. As far as she knew, someone may have slept there every night. It simply made no difference to her."

Pip glanced at the jury. If it wasn't the summation, he would be on his feet objecting.

"I'm going to ask you to consider two questions. First, if you find her innocent, what guarantee do you have she won't bomb again? Secondly, if you find her innocent, what message will you be sending to the public? Will others attempt to take the law into their own hands because they know there's no punishment in our state for murder?

"You must send the message loud and clear by finding Kristen Edwards guilty of murder in the first degree. Let it be known that killing another human being can't go unpunished. Those who disagree with a law, can change it through our democratic process, not by blowing some-one up."

Pip heard a muffled weeping and turned toward the sound. It was Kristen's Aunt Jean. The judge used her gavel, sending Jean into uncon-trollable sobs as she rushed from the courtroom.

Mr. Johnson continued. "You may feel sorry for Kristen Edwards. I know I do. And that's what makes your job so darn hard. Because to do your duty, you must not put Kristen Edwards back into society. It would be the wrong message. It wouldn't be fair to the people and it certainly wouldn't be fair to Susan Reingold."

He looked at Kristen then back at the jury. "Thank you."

Judge Laura Fredericks waited for Bob to take his seat. The courtroom filled with conversation. She again used her gavel to reestablish quiet.

"Members of the jury, before you retire to deliberate and reach a find-ing, I want to say a few words.

"The facts in this case have never been at issue. You know Mrs. Ed-wards did indeed commit the act. And yet you do have some weighty decisions to ponder. You must decide if the defendant is guilty of first-degree murder. Was it premeditated? The answer is obviously no. How-ever, did she know she was committing a felony? That is the real question. Remember, Mrs. Edwards, to be convicted of first-degree murder had to have been aware she was committing a felony. It's your job to determine if she was aware or not. Secondly, the law tells us the possibility of death must be reasonably foreseeable. It's again up to you to decide if it was or wasn't.

"If you find her innocent of murder in the first degree, you must then consider murder in the second degree. Second degree carries a much less severe penalty, although the defendant would still have to serve from eight to twenty-five years in prison. If you believe she's guilty of murder but there are mitigating circumstances, or you believe such a harsh sentence would serve no purpose, then you should find her guilty of second degree murder."

Judge Fredericks looked over the top of her half-framed reading glass-es trying to communicate to the jury in simple non-legalese. "If you find her innocent of second degree murder, you must consider the option of manslaughter. Crimes of passion can be considered in this category. If you believe she was so emotionally involved with the issue that she could not control her behavior, then manslaughter is appropriate.

"If Mrs. Edwards fits none of these charges, you must consider negligent homicide." Judge Fredericks spoke more slowly and deliberately, as if that would help make her words easier to understand. "A person acts negligently if she fails to become aware of substantial and unjustified risk and the act causes the death of another. The risk must be of such a nature and degree that her failure to become aware of it constitutes a gross deviation from the conduct a reasonable person would observe in this situation.

"What makes an act one thing rather than another? The act is the same. Kristen Edwards has thrown a bomb, and Susan Reingold is dead because of it. The defendant's actions have caused a death.

"The facts fit the definition of first degree murder, second degree murder, manslaughter, and negligent homicide. You, the jury, have to decide what to call it based on your belief as to the mental state of the defendant. Why can't I tell you which choice is the proper one? Because, based on the evidence, it becomes a question of judgment, not of fact, and the defendant has chosen to put that responsibility in your hands.

"During your deliberations, if you have any questions of law, write them down and give them to the bailiff. I'll share the question and my answer with both counsels and then send my reply to you. You have a grave responsibility. I trust you will not take it lightly."

As the jury filed out, Harold came to the defense table and took his wife's hand. She looked up at him and smiled weakly. He bent over and kissed her.

"I wish they would allow me to stay with you," he said. "I'll be with the boys. They send their love. We miss you, darling. We need you at home. Jesus will answer our prayers. We have to have faith in the Lord. He's forgiven you and I know He delivered Mr. Marshall to us."

Harold turned to Pip. "I'll be at home. Call when the jury comes back. I'm only ten minutes away."

Pip nodded. Harold kissed Kristen lightly on the lips and turned to leave.

"We have to go," the bailiff said in a gentle voice. Kristen automatically put out her hands to be cuffed.

It was Wednesday afternoon. Pip had a lot of catching up to do at the office, and there was no telling how long the jury would be out. They had many questions and alternatives to consider. Pip had never been so nervous about anything in his pressure packed past.

That night he couldn't sleep and when he tried to work or read his mind refused to concentrate. Time crawled and there was nothing he could do to accelerate it.

He arrived at his office early Thursday morning and stared at the clutter. Where to begin? He picked up one folder, put it down and picked up another. He sifted blankly through his mail. No use. He comprehended nothing. He checked his watch: ten forty-five. He went out for lunch, dawdled with a cup of soup, paid the check, and walked to the jail. Screw the work. He wanted to visit his client, make sure she was okay.

Kristen was kept in a cell at the police station across the street from the courthouse. Pip was escorted to her. She was sitting on a wooden chair at a small table, staring, always staring.

"Hello, Kristen."

She gave him a half smile.

"May I stay with you a while?"

She nodded, and he sat on a stool facing her.

The police station had been built in 1901, and the years had taken their toll. The cell area was gloomy in its dank darkness. There was no air conditioning and the hot stale air was nearly unbearable. This had been her home since her arrest. Even state prison would be an improvement.

"I'm forgiven," Kristen said in a soft voice. He wasn't sure he had heard her correctly.

"What?"

"Jesus has forgiven me, and that's all that matters. I have prayed, and He has heard me."

Pip nodded.

"Oh, Mr. Marshall, I don't want to go to prison. I want to be with my children to bring them up and be their mother again."

"It's in the hands of the jury. I have real hope for you. I wish I could promise..."

"I know I did wrong. I'm so sorry. Poor Mrs. Reingold. Oh God."

"Mr. Marshall?"

Pip turned to the voice that had called his name. It was the man who had brought him to the cell. Was the jury back?

"Mrs. Marshall's here to see you."

"How did she know where to find me?" he asked of no one as he followed the guard out of the lock-up area.

"How are you doing?" she asked.

"Okay."

She took his hand. "It's your father. Helen called. Walter died this morning. If you want, she'll delay the funeral until after the verdict's reached. She hopes you'll be there."

"I'll be there."

"I'm sorry, darling," she said, reaching up to kiss him. "I'll call Helen."

"His timing always was lousy," Pip said, a smile crossing his lips. "I'm going back to Kristen."

"How's she doing?"

"She'll never survive prison."

"Here you are." It was the bailiff. He was a rotund man, and his shortness of breath indicated he had been tracking Pip for a while. "Mr. Marshall, the jury's reached a verdict. Court will resume in thirty...fifteen minutes."

Pip checked his watch. It was twenty after five. The jury had been out a little over twenty-four hours. What did it mean? Stop trying to figure everything out, he scolded himself. He put his hands in his pockets to hide their sudden shaking.

"Would you call Harold Edwards?" he asked the bailiff. "He'll be at home."

℘

Mary Lou accompanied her husband to the courtroom. They worked their way through the reporters and spectators to the defense table. Kristen looked up at them, her face ghost white, mouth open, but incapable of speech. As Pip took his seat, he reached over and squeezed his client's icy cold hand. "It'll be all right," he said, trying to sound convincing aware of his own fear and powerlessness.

Harold Edwards and Mark Reingold were both in the first row on opposite sides of the aisle. Mark was talking to a reporter. Harold stared straight ahead.

"All rise," came the booming voice of the bailiff. The courtroom fell silent as everyone rose to their feet. The door behind the bench opened and Judge Fredericks entered. After she took her place, the bailiff instructed the courtroom to be seated.

"Bring in the jury," the judge ordered.

They somberly filed to their seats. Pip tried to read their minds one last time.

"Madame Foreperson, has the jury reached a verdict?" the clerk asked.

"We have."

"What say you, Madame Foreperson? As to the charge of first degree murder, does the jury find the defendant guilty or not guilty?"

"In the charge of first degree murder, we find the defendant not guilty."

Pip crossed his fingers.

"What say you, Madame Foreperson? As to the charge of second degree murder does the jury find the defendant guilty or not guilty?"

"In the charge of second degree murder, we find the defendant not guilty."

"What say you, Madame Foreperson? As to the charge of manslaughter, does the jury find the defendant guilty or not guilty?"

"In the charge of manslaughter we find the defendant not guilty."

The worst was over. Pip looked at his client, knowing she had not comprehended the meaning of the verdicts so far.

"What say you, Madame Foreperson? As to the charge of negligent homicide, does the jury find the defendant guilty or not guilty?"

"In the charge of negligent homicide we find the defendant guilty."

"Guilty? So find the jury, Madame Foreperson?"

"Yes."

The clerk turned from the foreperson and now addressed the entire jury.

"So find you all, ladies and gentlemen of the jury?"

A unanimous yes filled the courtroom. Johnson was on his feet. "Your Honor, I move to poll the jury," he requested

"Motion granted," Judge Fredericks responded matter of factly.

The clerk began. "How say you, juror number two." As the twelfth juror agreed with the others, the courtroom filled with chatter.

Pip embraced his client. "The worst is over," he whispered. "The judge will be fair."

"Do I have to go to prison, Mr. Marshall?" she asked.

"Possibly, but at most you'd be free after only a few years. You'll still have your life in front of you." The judge gaveled the courtroom back to order. "There will be a hearing on sentencing in ten days. Because I believe the defendant is not a threat to society and is not likely to fail to appear, I'll release her on her own recognizance for that period. I want to thank the jury for a job well done. You're excused. Court adjourned."

The press rushed toward the defense table. Kristen turned to Pip. "Does that mean...?"

"You may go home. There will be a hearing in ten days for sentencing. The probation department will recommend a sentence to the judge."

"I can go home? Thank God. I can't believe it. Oh, thank God, it's over. I'll be all right, Mr. Marshall. Even if I have to go to jail, I'll be all right."

Harold rushed to her side. They held each other, oblivious to the crowd around.

"Come, Kristen, I'll take you home now," he said. The children are waiting."

As they turned to leave Mark Reingold confronted them. Pip, talking to reporters, saw what was happening from the corner of his eye. He tried to get through the crowd to his client before Mark spoke, but couldn't.

"Mrs. Edwards, you believe in the Bible?" Mark asked.

Kristen was flustered by the confrontation.

"Yes, of course I do."

"Genesis 21:24 `an eye for an eye, a tooth for a tooth,'" Mark said. There were tears in his eyes, and his face expressed his anguish. "Even if you go to jail, you'll be free in a few years, but my Susan's gone forever."

"Oh, Dr. Reingold, I'm so sorry," she said but he had already left the courtroom.

CHAPTER TWENTY-EIGHT

"There aren't many people here." Pip said. "I guess my father didn't have lots of friends."

"He's been dead almost a week. People have probably already paid their respects," Mary Lou answered.

They were sitting in St. Elizabeth's, in Ashton. It was a cavernous wooden structure. The sun filtered through the stained glass windows, causing a rainbow of colors to wash through the nearly empty sanctuary.

"I can't believe Walter Marshall is being buried in the Catholic Church. He taught me that to believe in the Pope was blasphemy and a direct route to Hell. All Catholics were condemned to the perils of Hell. No exceptions to that rule."

Mary Lou smiled and took his hand. "People change."

There were less than twenty mourners in the church. Pip stared at the wooden casket that housed the remains of the man whom he had loathed and forgiven but, to the best of his recollection, had never really loved.

Walter had spent his life worrying about his immortal soul, convinced of the existence of Heaven and Hell. Well, Father, is there a Heaven and Hell... and where are you residing?

The priest stood majestically at the pulpit, reading the prayers that would help bring his father to the right side of God. Pip's eyes fixed on the casket, his mind recalling the Walter Marshall of his youth. Spare the rod and spoil the child. Was Walter the reason he hadn't wanted to bring children into the world? Maybe it wasn't too late. He squeezed Mary Lou's hand. The priest began his eulogy.

"Walter Marshall has been a member of our church for almost twenty years."

Was that possible? He knew so little about his father. A Catholic for almost twenty years?

"He sang in the choir, attended Mass and was a loving husband and father."

A loving father?

"He was editor of the church bulletin and chairman of the ritual committee. He loved his God."

That much was true.

"And those who knew him, know Walter Marshall is home at last."

Pip and Mary Lou followed the casket out of the church.

"Come back to the apartment after the funeral," Helen whispered.

"We have to get home," Pip responded.

"Please."

There was a smell of death in Helen's home, medicine, blended with human waste. She kissed them both. They followed her into the living room.

"I'm going to miss Walter very much. It's important to me for you to know I loved your father and how worthy he was of my love. We were very close, as close as I hope you two are. But Pip, there was a great void in his life, an emptiness I couldn't fill. It was the unreturned love he had for you. Don't get me wrong, he only blamed himself..." There was a pause as she seemed to recollect something, her face communicating a sad reminiscence. "But he longed for your forgiveness. He wanted me to give you something. I have it in the other room. I'll be right back."

Pip was uncomfortable. He wanted to hate this woman who had destroyed his childhood family. But she seemed to be a kind and gentle soul.

For the first time, Pip realized a simple truth. His father's leaving had immeasurably improved his own life and probably even his mother's. Helen returned, struggling under the weight of a large carton, which she barely managed to carry to the couch before dropping it between her two visitors. Carefully, she opened the box, as if its contents were sacred, and took out five thick scrapbooks, which she placed on the floor. The volumes were numbered, each cover a different color. Mary Lou and Pip joined Helen on the carpet. For the next three hours, they turned the pages of Pip's life from the gridiron of Calvert, to Michigan, and on to the pros. Each article was carefully cut and pasted with a date next to it. The last entries concerned his defense of Kristen Edwards.

"Dad was sick. How could he have been aware of the trial?" Pip asked. Dad! How strange the word felt on his lips.

"I had to feed him, take him to the bathroom, change his pants, clean him. For almost all of the time, he couldn't get a sentence straight. But every day, he asked me if there was anything about you in the paper. We always got the Calvert Monitor. He would watch me clip and paste. It was his most happy time.

"Up to his death, he would spend hours every day turning the pages, looking at the pictures and staring at the words. If you didn't know better, you'd think he was reading.

"'Someday when I'm gone,' he would say time and again, 'you give these books to the boy. Then he'll forgive me. I'll see him from heaven.' I'm not sure he made it to heaven but I do know he loved you."

෩

Harold had whisked Kristen from the courtroom and into their car.

"It's over for now, darling. Let's go home."

Even if she went to jail, she knew she'd survive. Jesus had truly died for her sins. Her joy at the verdict, however, had been offset by her confrontation with Mark Reingold, whose forgiveness she would never have.

Harold kissed his wife before starting the engine. "I'm not used to being free, even if it's only for ten days," Kristen said.

"We'll all go to church tonight to give thanks."

Robert and Thomas didn't know Kristen was coming home. When they saw their mother, they both let out wails of joy and ran to her, crushing her with their embraces.

"How I've missed you both and your hugs," she responded. Slowly she walked from room to room, reacquainting herself with her surroundings. Her family followed as if she were the Pied Piper.

"It feels so good to be home, home with my family."

All three hugged her simultaneously.

"Now do you know what I want to do?" she announced.

"No," Harold said.

"What, Mommy?" Robert asked.

"I want to go into my kitchen and cook my family supper."

After dinner they went to church. The parishioners had quickly arranged the service. The prayers of the congregation were full of joy and thanksgiving for the return of their beloved Kristen.

Kristen got the children ready for bed. Telling them she might have to leave again would be the worst part. No need to do that before sentence was passed. She stayed with the boys until they were asleep, then sat for a while watching their even breathing, before kissing them each on the cheek. She crept from the room, quietly closing the door behind her.

Harold was waiting. He put his arm around her waist and led her to their bedroom. They undressed. It was a cool evening and Kristen put on her pink flannel gown. She looked at Harold in his red pajamas.

"We wouldn't make a very pretty flower arrangement," she observed.

In bed, she snuggled against her husband. How she had missed the warmth of his body. He stroked her arm as they talked until her words became a slur and she was asleep.

"Do you believe in the Bible?"

It was Mark Reingold.

"Yes, of course I believe in the Bible. It's the word of God," she heard herself reply.

"'An eye for an eye, a tooth for a tooth,' that's what the Bible says."

"Mark."

She turned to see Mr. Marshall.

"Mark, Jesus tells us to turn the other cheek. He has forgiven Kristen. The jury has had their say, now you must forgive her." He was still her advocate.

"I'll never forgive her." Mark turned to Kristen, glaring at her. "You killed my wife. You killed my unborn baby. 'An eye for an eye, a tooth for a tooth.'"

"Mark, turn the other cheek. Forgive my child." Now Jesus was speaking to Dr. Reingold on her behalf. There was a sadness in His eyes, a pleading. Her parents were to the Savior's right. Kristen looked from them back to Dr. Reingold.

Mark spoke to Jesus. "It was your Father who told us 'an eye for an eye, a tooth for a tooth.' Do you not heed the words of your own Father, God of the universe?" Then Dr. Reingold turned and looked at Kristen, his eyes piercing her own, finding their way deep inside her soul. "Jesus has spoken on your behalf. He has asked me to turn the other cheek. Could you turn the other cheek if I had killed your husband and children; if I had removed all joy, all reason for being from your life? I think not. Listen to the Father of Jesus. 'An eye for an eye, a tooth for a tooth.'"

Jesus spoke to Mark with an awesome sadness. "If you cannot forgive my child then I must take her home with me."

Kristen found herself suddenly awake. Harold slept peacefully at her side. She kissed him gently. He purred his pleasure at having her home with him. She stood and surveyed her surroundings with tears in her eyes, then walked to the boys' room. She kissed each child before turning to leave. At the doorway, she looked toward them one more time.

"I love you, my children."

She drove to the abortion clinic, parked the car and walked around the building. All was still.

"Oh, Jesus, why can't they understand? How can the killing go on? I'm sorry. I know I did wrong. Forgive me, Lord."

She returned to her car and drove to the florist shop, parking in the rear. Clouds hid the stars and moon. Her tears further blurred her vision. She walked to the receiving door, found the key, and fumbled for the lock. Once inside, she was greeted by the familiar soothing smell of fresh cut flowers and lush green houseplants.

She walked through the office to the front of the store.

Kristen had been surprised when Harold had first showed her the twenty-two pistol. "Why do we need that? It's dangerous," she'd said.

"I'm sure we'll never use it but just in case." he had responded.

She took the gun from under the register and held it in her hand. Unexpectedly her Savior revealed himself to her. "I forgive you, my child. Come home now."

"Thank you, Jesus," Kristen replied. Putting the pistol on the counter, she designed a floral arrangement of roses, baby's breath and greens, took a card and wrote a note. She addressed the envelope to Mark Reingold and placed it in the vase.

Kristen picked up the gun. The metal was cold. As she put the weapon to her temple she cried her last words to the empty room. "Satan, I'm rid of you now and with my Jesus forever."

એ

It wasn't until nine the next morning that Harold Edwards found Kristen. Lieutenant Dugan was with him. They had been looking for her for two hours.

She was on the floor, the gun by her right side. Kimball picked up her wrist, feeling for a pulse he knew wasn't there.

Harold fell on his knees beside his wife. "Why, Kristen? Why now? You had everything to live for." He sobbed hysterically as he answered his own question. "The struggle was too great." He kissed her hand. "Oh, I love you so very much."

Kimball noticed the envelope addressed to Reingold in the vase. He read the contents before handing it to Harold.

"I thought it might be a suicide note."

Harold looked at it. His hand began to tremble. "It is," he replied. "Damn him. Damn him to Hell."

The note read, "An eye for an eye, a tooth for a tooth."

EPILOGUE

As We Forgive Those Who Trespass Against Us

Mark had walked from the dinginess of the courthouse into a glorious sun filled day. The brightness hurt his eyes and at the same time brought home the realization that even on sun-shining days his life was an empty void.

He returned to his apartment. Why was Susan dead while Kristen walked free as she awaited sentencing? Why? Negligent homicide, a slap on the wrist. It wasn't fair. He walked from room to memory-laden room. His hand gently rubbed the smooth walnut bureau they had bought from an antique dealer. He thought it was a piece of junk until Susan lovingly refinished it. He stared at a picture she had taken of him the day they went fishing, his face all scrunched up in a response to her request for him to smile. The apartment was so damn quiet, not like the silence when he had been there alone, knowing she would return. No, this quiet was filled with an empty loneliness.

The household chores had been a joy they shared together. Now clothing was scattered throughout; old food rotted where it was left. The bed, never made, smelled of unwashed sheets. He had stopped functioning when she died.

Aimlessly, he wandered through his museum-apartment. In the bathroom he stared at Susan's toothbrush which, after all these months, still lay on the sink where she had placed it, not knowing she would never be back to use it.

His anger boiled as he conjured up a vision of Mrs. Edwards reunited with her husband and children. How could they not put that lunatic in jail forever? How?

Mark picked up a lipstick Susan had casually left by the bathroom sink on her last day. He turned the bottom of the container, watching the deep red lipstick rise, before putting it down. Gently, he touched her robe, then placed his nose to the soft velour trying to smell her presence. Looking up, he saw his reflection in the mirror. In an effort to eliminate his being, he smashed his fist at the image, shattering the glass. He laughed a sick, sad laugh as he wondered if that would mean seven years bad luck. The smile turned to tears.

Ignoring his cut hand, he screamed cries of anguish as he began to destroy the apartment, smashing furniture, walls, everything. When there was nothing else to ruin he fell to the floor, and like a child, cried himself to sleep.

℘

After Mark read about Kristen's death in the newspaper, he began to have a recurring dream, one that would haunt him for the next several months.

"Susan, oh my darling, you're alive," he would shout, his joy overwhelming. "You're not dead." He went to put his arms around her, hold her once more. She stepped back.

"Mark, I loved you."

The past tense startled him. "Don't you love me anymore?" There was terror in his heart as he asked the question.

"How can I? You're not the man I knew. After I died I went looking for you. I found your body but your soul was missing. You knew. You knew."

He didn't understand. "What do you mean, I knew? What did I know?"

"You knew I wouldn't want revenge. You knew I would forgive her. Mark, where are you? Where's the man who couldn't pass a street person without helping? I want my Mark back. Find him for me so I can rest."

Mark would sit up in bed, the dream startling him back to reality. He missed Susan dreadfully, and the dream spoke a truth that now haunted him. She would have hated to see him like this.

℘

After Kristen's death Harold became incapable of productive work. His faith was shaken. Why had his Lord not saved his wife? She only wanted to do His work.

He tried to raise his sons and tend to business but his sadness overwhelmed him. Dove's Flower Shop had a reputation for beautiful floral arrangements at fair prices but he was no longer able to produce those extraordinary bouquets. When he totally forgot a wedding, the story got around and quickly led to the demise of Dove's Flower Shop.

Pip represented Harold when he was forced to liquidate. He explained to his client that bankruptcy would eliminate all obligations, but Harold

245

would not hear of it. He took a job as a manager of a flower department in a grocery store and continued to pay his creditors each month out of his wages.

છ

Muriel knocked on Pip's door before poking in her head.

"You won't believe this. Dr. Reingold called. He wants an appointment with you. I told him I would have to check."

"What could he want?"

"Probably to sue a patient for 'mal-illness.' He's not the nicest man."

"A lawyer's curiosity. Set up the appointment."

A few minutes before ten, the next day, Mark Reingold was ushered into the office of Philip Marshall. This vindictive man's presence in his office incensed Pip. And, yet, if it had been Mary Lou...

Dr. Reingold appeared uncomfortable, playing nervously with his hands. His suit was rumpled and ill fitting.

"What can I do for you?"

"This is not easy for me," Mark began. He was mumbling and Pip had trouble hearing him. "After Susan died, not much else mattered. The only thing that made sense was revenge."

"I know," Pip could not help saying.

"I was furious when you got Mrs. Edwards off with negligent homicide. At most, she would serve a few short years before she would be free to be with her children and family while I had nothing. Where was the justice? Then I read about her death. This should have pleased me but it didn't. A short time ago I received a letter."

He placed a paper on Pip's desk.

Dr. Reingold:

Kristen left a note that simply said, "an eye for an eye, a tooth for a tooth." She wanted to pay for what she had done.

I can now understand your rage. When I saw my Kristen, dead because of you, I loathed you. My two dear boys had lost their mother and I, my life.

Kristen has been gone a year and although you probably have no need for my forgiveness, I want you to know
I do forgive you.

Sincerely yours,

Harold Edwards

Pip passed the letter back and waited for Mark to continue, still wondering what was the point of their meeting.

"Susan was a wonderful person. The one thing I always knew but
never would admit to myself, never allowed myself to dwell on, was how
Susan would have wanted me to treat Mrs. Edwards."

His mumbling became worse and Pip strained to understand what he
was saying.

"I would have been a great disappointment to my wife. Harold Edwards' letter has made me realize..."

He suddenly stopped mumbling.

"I want to make it up to Susan and then maybe I can get on with
my life. I'm not a rich man. My practice hasn't grown much since Susan
was... since she died. Maybe now I can get back on track, become the
doctor I wanted to be.

"I need your help. I want to contribute as much of my income to the
Edwards' family, for as long as it takes, to get them back on their feet, get
the boys educated if they want. My only condition is that Mr. Edwards
never know the source and that we can somehow get him to accept the
money so that he doesn't feel it's charity. I have the feeling he's a proud
man."

∞

"I have a client who needs an investment," Pip said.

"An investment?" Harold responded.

"I suggested you. He's from out of town, and I've been given author-
ity to represent him. Would you be interested in another florist shop?"

"God works in strange ways," Harold replied.

හ

Pip was alone in his office. He was suddenly exhausted. Harold's response whirled through his head. God works in strange ways. He thought of the blindfolded lady holding the scales of justice. On one side was all the good caused in the name of God; on the other, all the evil. He wondered if the scales ever balanced.

The End

Laura Jane Silverman

About the Author

Donald Silverman is a writer who shares his time between New Hampshire and Florida. He's the patriarch of a writing family. Daughter Susan wrote Jewish Family and Life, a Guide to Parenting. Daughter Laura has penned short stories and comedy routines while daughter Jodyne has written the book, Dump Em. Sarah has written the screen play, Jesus Is Magic plus many comedy routines. Donald has written 3 novels. The Event was a finalist in the Ernest Hemingway First Novel Contest.

Also by Donald Silverman, *THE ENEMY IS ME* and *THE EVENT*. His e-mail address is donaldjan@mac.com.

Printed in the United States
204200BV00001B/385-435/P

9 781434 367853